STAND FOR THE DEAD

STAND FOR THE DEAD

DAVE CASE

THORNDIKE PRESS
A part of Gale, a Cengage Company

Copyright © 2024 by Dave Case.
Thorndike Press, a part of Gale, a Cengage Company.

ALL RIGHTS RESERVED
This novel is a work of fiction. Names, characters, places, and incidents are either the product of the author's imagination, or, if real, used fictitiously.
The publisher bears no responsibility for the quality of information provided through author or third-party Web sites and does not have any control over, nor assume any responsibility for, information contained in these sites. Providing these sites should not be construed as an endorsement or approval by the publisher of these organizations or of the positions they may take on various issues.
Thorndike Press® Large Print Hardcover Western.
The text of this Large Print edition is unabridged.
Set in 16 pt. Plantin.

LIBRARY OF CONGRESS CIP DATA ON FILE.
CATALOGUING IN PUBLICATION FOR THIS BOOK
IS AVAILABLE FROM THE LIBRARY OF CONGRESS.

ISBN-13: 979-8-88579-944-7 (hardcover alk. paper)

Published in 2024 by arrangement with Dave Case.

Print Number: 1   Print Year: 2024
Printed in Mexico

I dedicate this to both my mother and father, Peggy and Les Case.
I miss you both.

"Life every man holds dear: but the brave man holds honor far more precious-dear than life."

— William Shakespeare,
Troilus and Cressida

Chapter 1
Oh brother,
what have you done

The smell of death rode on the wind. John Altar crested the hilltop and brought his horse to a stop. He'd smelled it a ways off, but the breeze had all but stilled some time ago. The stink remained. He whistled low and the dog that had been his companion for a while, some kind of wolf half-breed, sat on its haunches close on his left. The fat gray clouds overhead threatened rain, and no wind stirred the thick expectant air, which was hot.

As he stared down the slope, he cut a hunk of tobacco from his plug, sliding it off the blade directly into his mouth. The leaf was hard and dry. It had been wrapped in a cloth in his saddlebag for a time. Spit washed over the scrap and the bitter flavor crept into his senses.

Below, at the bottom of the slope, a series of double tracks had been worn into the earth by scores of wagons over the years.

Upon that trail were the remains of some homesteaders who had been on their way to what they'd hoped to be a better life. Nothing moved down there, except the black flutter of buzzards' wings as they fought over bloated corpses. He couldn't tell how many settlers there had been, and by the butchery, he figured more scavengers than just the buzzards had visited this site.

Being that it was going on late summer, this seemed kind of late in the season for pioneers to be this far down the trail. Unless of course, they were Mormons. They wouldn't be going all the way to Oregon or California.

Still don't see many Mormons moving west this time of year, Altar thought, but there were always those late to the party. Seemed like most who'd wanted to migrate had already done so, no matter how austere the conditions might be.

He had to wonder if he was going to find Bobby down there. He'd been dogging his younger brother, and the collection of dirty, low-down, no-account Johnny Rebs Bobby had taken up with, for weeks. Could those ne'er-do-wells be responsible for the carnage down below?

Could Bobby?

Or his brother might be among the dead.

Only one way to find out, he thought.

Altar steered his horse forward, despite the animal's reticence to approach the field of death. He reached out and patted the horse's neck in reassurance.

"Easy, boy. I'm not liking this any more than you do, but we got to go down there."

The inevitable dread of what he might find weighed as heavily on him as an anvil around his neck.

He yanked his blue handkerchief from his back pocket. Unfolding it, he rubbed the cloth on the horse's sweaty flesh and got it good and wet. The lather smelled strong, but it probably wouldn't help much gauging from the putrid odor lingering in the air from this distance.

He gave the chaw a grind with his molars to break it apart and moistened the results with spit. Then he spat some of the ground tobacco and juice onto the blue fabric and roughed it in hard. He fastened the cloth in place around his head, bandit style. He was hopeful, as the mixture of animal and tobacco odors made him wrinkle his nose, that the powerful smell would somehow mask the overwhelming stench of the charnel house below. But as he made his way closer, he knew it wasn't going to be much help.

The only sound was the buzzing of insects, the swish of his horse's tail, and the not-so-distant rumble of thunder.

A storm must be coming.

He looked at the dog. "Stay."

The dog settled onto its belly and laid its head on crossed forelegs, ears ever alert.

Altar drew his Henry repeating rifle and laid it across his lap as his horse started forward with the slightest nudge from his knees. Nothing was moving on the horizon, no dust clouds. He wove his horse all the way down the incline through the scrub, all the while watching everywhere, alert for any movement or sound out of place.

Safe at the bottom of the slope, Altar studied the gruesome scene. The settlers had apparently taken no defensive posture, no circled wagons, no firearms strewn about, though those could've been stolen to be sure. Not much of value remained after a massacre. The area was a wide-open expanse. They sure should have been able to see the attack coming. Why hadn't they at least circled their wagons?

But his gut spoke to him, and he suspected he knew what had happened here. God knows he'd seen its like in the war. *Looks like they got bushwhacked.*

Bobby, what have you done?

As he neared, the reek grew worse, and he could practically taste it. Lots of distended green-blue bottle flies buzzed nearby.

He dismounted at the end of the carnage and looped his reins around a broken fragment of wagon wheel jutting from a groove in the dirt. The horse snorted and bucked at the pervasive odor of nearby death. Altar patted the animal once more and scanned the horizon again.

Nothing yet, besides the approaching clouds every bit as bloated as the feasting flies. His ever-alert dog was still quiet up on the ridge.

The clouds, and the flashes of lightning, were the only things that looked threatening. He pulled his slicker from his saddle and unrolled it. The heat was stifling, but he put it on anyway.

Prairie schooners, mostly covered, had been overturned, their canvas torn, and the cargo, what wasn't worth taking, was strewn across the trail. Oxen had been killed; and in a couple of instances, steaks had been cut from their flesh. There was even a dead dog. A horse or two had been killed, which was unusual, but he suspected most of the quality animals had been stolen.

A smattering of rough arrows, fletched with feathers he didn't immediately recognize, were prominent on some of the dead animals. Men lay dead, too, the tops of their blond heads shorn to the bone, and their soft bellies torn open.

He came across an old woman's body. She lay on her back with her skirts up around her head. She'd also been scalped, and her lady parts had apparently been mauled, probably by some wild critter. They were only doing what any hungry critter would do, and he couldn't really fault them for that. Might as well get mad at the clouds for raining.

But it wasn't no animal that hiked her skirt up like that, Altar thought. *That was done by a two-legged kind of varmint.*

A baby lay under her. It was dead too, but from what he couldn't tell.

These were among the worst killings he'd ever seen, but he couldn't really hold no ill will with the animals.

A fat raindrop splattered on the back of his hand, and then another. It wasn't until the moisture brought his mind round back to the present that he realized he was gripping his Henry so hard his scarred knuckles were white. The skies unleashed a torrent of rain as he stood and stared at the butchery that lay before him. Even the cold rain didn't divert his attention from the slaughter.

He reckoned no amount of water would wipe away the stain of this massacre from the earth. At least nothing short of the forty-days and forty-nights rain that his mama read to him and Bobby about from the Bible. He stowed his rifle back in its saddle boot and covered the Henry with his blanket, even though some blue sky was already visible over the hills to the west. He turned back to the trail and set his teeth. He had a grisly task ahead of him.

Oh, Bobby, he thought, *were you a part of this? Am I gonna find you?*

Would it be better if his brother were among the dead, rather than having participated in this slaughter?

Perhaps so.

But on to the task — time to bury the dead.

He hadn't stopped for anything but water until the sun was about set, then he cobbled together a fire halfway to the top of the rise, upwind from the dead. The material for burying them all had been almost conveniently close thanks to the nearby rocky expanse, but any appetite he'd worked up was long gone. He settled for some pan coffee and hardtack soaked some in the dark liquid.

All of the dead looked to be pilgrims. At least none had been his brother, nor had any of the others appeared to be the ne'er-do-wells he'd heard Bobby was now running with. While that was a relief, it also made him ask what the hell had happened to his brother. The boy he once knew would never have participated in anything like this. What had happened to him in the war?

The war.

The damn war . . . So many lives ruined.

Altar had served with the Union, and Bobby had gone with the South.

The brutal conflict between the states had divided his family and how many others?

He fished the oilcloth-wrapped locket from his saddlebag. He cradled the bundle in his hand for a long moment, and then opened it. The orange-red flames flickered in the reflection on the small metal oval. He thumbed it open and gazed at the shadowed picture within, not really seeing her likeness as much as some remembrance, though those had faded, like the picture, to near nothing.

How many times had he opened this same locket in the field?

When he fought in Missouri or out west,

after some battle or skirmish, when his thoughts were dark with death and dying, he'd found comfort by opening it. At one time, memories of her had driven some of the horror from his mind. Though the time apparently had driven memories of him from her mind as well. She'd married someone else while he was away fighting.

Married some farmer with a hundred head of dairy cattle or some such. Why couldn't those images fade with time, as was the case with his memory of his love?

That thought brought him back around to the massacre. He hadn't found anything that led him to believe the wagon train had been herding any livestock, other than a few oxen. That was strange. Most of the wagon trains he'd known had at least a hundred head of cattle or sheep with them.

He replaced the locket in his saddlebag and went to sleep with his freshly oiled rifle next him and his revolver tucked partially under the saddle upon which he laid his head.

The wind shifted in the night, and he awoke with the death stench heavy in his nose and mouth. He rose and hiked up to the top of the hill. The sun's rays were breaking over the hilltops in the east, but the bottom of the slope was still obscured in darkness.

A shadow for the dead, he thought. *Just as well.*

The dog loped up to him and sat, its tongue lolling out. Altar stood there and let the rays reach him, warming him against the chills of the past night. When he turned to go back to his makeshift camp, he gazed again at the ruins below, now basked in radiant sunlight.

The way he read the signs, these homesteaders had died with their killers most likely hiding among them. And not like they were overrun by Indians or butchered by marauding men on horseback. Even though scavengers had been at the bodies, they hadn't done enough harm to make it look any different than it was. It didn't seem as if these people had time to even panic, let alone run, just die.

And what about the smattering of random arrows?

Indians?

Some of the folks had been scalped, but the arrows in some of the animals hadn't been what killed them. The feathered shafts weren't driven in deep. It was more like they were stabbed in by hand, not shot from a bow. No, this hadn't been the work of Indians, although measures had been taken to make it look that way. All the tracks of the living he'd found had been wearing boots, nary a moccasin among them. And the horses that had ridden off were all shod. He'd never known an Indian to ride a shoed horse.

Altar knew what had really happened. And he had a real good idea of who was responsible. It made him sick to his stomach. He reckoned these pilgrims had been killed by the men he'd been tracking, and they'd tried to make it look like savages had done it.

The men he'd been trailing . . . The men his brother had joined up with after being released from the prisoner of war camp in Chicago. Up until now, he'd only thought of them as outlaws, stealing and the like, not murderers. The tactics were like what he'd seen the guerrillas in Missouri use during the war, infiltrate and destroy from within.

As he stared at the debris a while longer, the way the wagons had been overturned seemed more suited to men doing it deliberately as opposed to panicked animals. The battleground didn't look like any Indian attack he'd seen in his years in the army. But it sure did look like how the Confederate guerrillas had burned some communities to the ground in and around Missouri. And the people killed.

"These folks got bushwhacked," he said aloud. The dog looked up at him. Altar nodded as if the animal understood.

"A damn shame," he said. "But there's something eviler if men make it look like someone else done it, getting people all riled up at the wrong folks." He started down the incline, back to his fire and bedroll.

"If we hadn't of happened along, Dog," he said, "whenever this here got discovered the Indians would've been blamed. And people would've been happy to believe it."

He shook his head as he kicked dirt onto the coals.

"Talking to a damn dog, guess I been on my own too long." He grinned. "But it ain't like them homesteaders been talking much."

He looked in the direction the tracks led off. It didn't seem right that no one was doing nothing about these people.

Hell, once he left here, would anyone even know?

Altar sighed and placed the blanket and saddle onto his horse's back. The nagging question remained in his gut like solid stone.

Had Bobby been a part of this?

When Altar had begun this journey, he'd

just been looking to bring his brother back home to their farm in Missouri while their mother was still alive. But now, he didn't know what to think. The little brother he knew before the war would never have been involved in anything like this, but the war did strange things to people. Still, he didn't want to think it had turned Bobby into the kind of man that could do what he'd seen these last two days.

He took his hat off and wiped his brow with his shirtsleeve and looked at the dog.

"Mama always said I looked for trouble, even when it wasn't none of mine to begin with." He mounted his horse. "I know it would kill her, for certain, if she thought Bobby was involved in some way. So would his hanging for it."

A grim smile suddenly overtook him as he twisted in his saddle and looked back at the site of the carnage.

There I go talking to that mutt again, he thought.

But as he rode away, his mother's reproachful voice kept echoing in his mind: *Go find your brother, John. Bring him back to me before I die.*

I'll do my best, Mama, he thought.

Altar pulled his reins over and set off after

the tracks of the killers, including his little brother.

Chapter 2
Back on the Trail,
now awash in blood

There hadn't been any effort to conceal the trail left behind. Altar counted fourteen horses, all shod, and the wagon that had been there since day one. It seemed to his eye that a couple of the horses were without riders, which would make the count twelve men. But the tracks he'd been following for close to a week now had indicated thirteen riders. How many were riding on the wagon? Had someone been hurt enough to not be on horseback?

Where had he lost one? Or had he? Or lost two? He couldn't say that he saw any tracks veer off. Had a couple of them ridden off from the wagon train? It was a big camp. He might've missed one or two riders.

The attackers had joined the wagon train a couple of days before the massacre. Had some been killed? All of the dead looked like sodbusters to his eye. So, he discounted that any of the outlaws had died. At least at the wagon train.

He hadn't found any young women among the bodies and he wondered if they'd been spared, though he couldn't be certain. Those bushwhackers wouldn't want them telling any tales. Unless they were keeping them bound in the wagon. What fate awaited them, should any have been kept alive, was unpleasant to think about.

He'd read all the signs, much of it having to do with the dead. Maybe, in their own way, the homesteaders had talked to him.

Or maybe he needed to spend some time with live people for a spell.

At the end of the first day, he and Dog had made camp a ways off the trail of the killers. It looked like a couple of the cowboys had gone off on foot on their own, and Altar figured they were hunting for game. He followed their trail for about a hundred yards before he stopped under a tree not far from a stream and made camp.

Better not to be right up on their tracks, he thought.

He built a small fire and made some coffee, such as he could with what little grounds he had left. His jerky was tough and chewy. Dog was on his own to forage.

Altar threw dirt on the embers as soon as he was done heating his coffee.

That night the stars were out and bright, and not a sound was audible above the insects and the occasional lonely howl of a wolf or coyote. He pulled the locket out and stared at the faded image of Fannie Wyatt. But he thought, *she's not a Wyatt any longer, she's a Vogel these days.* That was the name of her husband.

The locket didn't hold any relief this night, and he closed it.

He lay back and stared at the lights in the sky.

Was his mama looking at these very stars, he wondered?

Was his brother, Bobby?

Or his sisters?

Or Fannie and her sodbuster husband?

The speculation grew tiresome, but one question still burned in his mind:

What had Bobby done?

Why would he be mixed up with a gang of no-goods like this bunch?

It didn't even seem possible to Altar. But he knew plenty of men who had been changed by the war, no matter which side you fought for.

The next morning, Altar awoke with the sun edging the horizon. Dog was lying on the other side of the dead fire. His head rose when Altar stood.

"Hey, boy," Altar said, stepping away to relieve himself.

He broke his fast with more jerky and a hunk of particularly unyielding hardtack. When Altar threw a piece of the hard biscuit toward Dog, the half-breed mutt let it hit the ground and watched it roll. Then he sniffed it, turned, and ran off looking for his own breakfast.

As Dog made his way back, he stopped and sniffed something. While Altar saddled his mount, the dog howled, maybe another hundred yards away, more or less on the course the two bushwhacker cowboys had been walking. Altar finished saddling his horse and then rode over to see what the nosy critter had found.

Dog was on his haunches close to the charred remains of another fire. It looked about as old as the fire at the killers' original camp.

Curious. Altar dismounted for a better look.

He crouched next to the dead campfire, but something didn't look quite right. He grabbed a stick and poked around in the ashes. It had been a rather substantial fire, he thought. A faint, repulsive odor wafted up as he stirred the blackened remnants.

The smell was unpleasantly familiar, and he had a good idea what it was. He kept probing and came across what appeared to be a strip of leather on the edge of the charcoal. When he flipped it over, he saw what remained of some blond human hair.

Before Altar stood, he took in the boot tracks left by the two cowboys who'd made the fire. They were about average in size and didn't have the depth of a fat man. But one of the heels was chipped and had left a track that was easy to recognize. The track was familiar to him. He'd been watching Chipped Heel for a time now, ever since he'd gotten on this group's trail.

They'd burned the scalps. They couldn't let anybody see them with those grisly trophies. It wasn't proper for a white man to be hauling around the scalps of other white folks. Maybe if they were expecting the army to pay them for Indian scalps, but that wasn't what these men had in mind. They wanted people to believe the Indians had taken the settlers' scalps. Scalps that for the most part were blond, and he'd never seen a blond Indian.

Later that day, Altar saw a cloud of dust up on the horizon that he figured was kicked up by some riders. Being all alone, he didn't want to get caught in the open if they were hostile, especially if he wasn't on the high ground. Seemed unlikely, but what if it was the bushwhackers coming back?

Looking around, he figured there were a couple of places he could hole up and see what could be seen before the riders learned of his presence. Altar chose a stand of trees. He rode up and around them to where a little meadow opened in the middle of the thicket of aspen and pine. He tethered his horse to a branch, took his rifle from the saddle boot, and found a shady spot to watch. Once in the shade of the trees, he pushed his hat back so it was suspended from the cord around his neck and then ran his sleeve along his forehead.

Altar worked the lever of his rifle to chamber a cartridge and rested the Henry, barrel up, against a birch tree. He thumbed the leather loop off his revolver's hammer. It wasn't that he was looking for a fight, but he didn't have a habit of running either.

Dog lay in the meadow, rolling on his back and wiggling like he had an itch.

A man on horseback came over the hill. The man had his hat pulled low, and long hair hung to his shoulders. He wore a vest over his shirt, with his sleeves rolled up. He looked like he had a gun rig on, and some kind of rifle slung on his horse.

The man stopped and surveyed the land in front of him, probably looking for threats of danger. After a quick glance behind him, he pushed forward and looked at the ground as if he were following signs. The man was approaching where Altar had peeled off when he stopped. His head moved like his eyes were following Altar's horse tracks.

The hair on the back of Altar's neck stood on end. He'd been discovered, but he'd reckoned for that possibility. The man below probably recognized that a single rider had been by. And pretty recently at that. After the man looked around, he turned his horse just as a group of riders came over the hill.

They spurred their mounts to a trot and closed with the man in short order. He must be their scout, waiting for them. Altar counted a dozen altogether and all of them bore some kind of firearm, though many had their revolvers tucked into their waistbands, and long guns hanging by rope cords.

Not good odds for a gunfight, he thought. Were the men pressed civilians or destitute outlaws?

A flash of silver on one of the men's shirts caught his attention. The rider was a tall lean man. Was he a lawman? It sure did look like a star of some kind.

Could this be some kind of posse? How could they already know of the murdered homesteaders? Altar knew he'd read the signs right. He was on the trail of those responsible for all that killing. No one had escaped and ridden off. Altar hadn't seen any trace of that.

But what if his brother was involved in the killing? Altar couldn't stand to see him hang.

The big man with the star pinned to his shirt seemed to be giving the orders. Two men split off and rode up along the trail left by Altar's horse.

When they got closer, Altar could see that one of the riders looked like a farm boy, not much more than seventeen, with overalls, plow boots, and a scattergun in one hand. The other rider had on a jacket that flapped open, revealing what might've been a star on his shirt. This fellow looked more like a lawman, with a gun rig tied down on his leg and a set of leg irons fixed across his horse's withers that jangled when it moved.

The lawman was following Altar's tracks, careful to stay away from them.

Maybe they were just going to see what was on top of the rise. But they'd see he'd turned off into the trees.

Well, shit, Altar thought. Maybe he hadn't thought this thing through as much as he should have.

The two riders passed out of his sight and Altar figured he had a couple of minutes at the most. He grabbed his rifle and clucked at Dog before blending into the trees. The jangling of the shackles stopped a few moments later. Altar heard what he took to be whispers, then the creaking of saddle leather made him think one of the riders had dismounted.

After a minute a deep voice called out.

"C'mon out of them trees with your hands where I can see them."

Altar didn't say anything but pushed to where he could see the riders.

The farm boy was still mounted, and the other rider was standing in front of their own horses, not far from Altar's mount.

Some thirty feet from the man, Dog stood, his teeth bared. A low growl emanated from deep within his throat.

"I know you're in there somewhere," the man said. "C'mon out, don't make me shoot this dog a' yours."

"I wouldn't do that, mister." Altar stepped out from the trees. He was yards from where the man was facing. Altar leveled his rifle at the speaker. "I wouldn't take kindly to anyone shooting my dog."

The man turned his head to look at Altar.

"I'm the law," the man said. "You shouldn't be pointing that gun at me."

"I'll point at anyone threatening me and mine," Altar said. "Dog. Down."

Dog lowered his head, still snarling, but sank until his belly was on the ground.

"How do I know you're the law?" Altar asked.

The lawman eased his jacket aside, showing a small silver star.

The farm boy, who was wearing a floppy field hat and was clean-shaven, was even younger than Altar thought, maybe not even fifteen. He sat still, watching the scene play out from the corner of his eye, as if he was afraid of attracting any attention.

The lawman shifted to face Altar but kept his hands clear of his pistol's handle. He was older, had to be in his late thirties, if not early forties, with a thick droopy mustache under his dusty cattleman's hat. "You wanna tell me what you're doing hiding in them trees?"

"Just me and my dog on the trail." Altar lowered the hammer of his rifle. "Couldn't be certain who you were, given what I rode up on a ways back."

"What was it you rode up on?" the lawman asked.

"Homesteaders," Altar said. "Got themselves killed."

"Heard some about that," the lawman said. "Like you to tell the marshal about what you seen."

Chapter 3
While the trail grows cold

Altar rode back down with the two of them to where the knot of men waited. What was he going to do if his brother was involved with this gang of murdering outlaws? To keep Bobby from hanging was the only answer he could figure. But how was he supposed to do that?

He heard the farm boy lean closer to the lawman and say, "He sure did get the drop on you, Uncle Shep."

The lawman didn't respond other than to turn his head and stare at the boy. The kid quickly looked away.

"Marshal," Shep said once they'd gotten to the knot of riders. "This fella said he came across them settlers."

The big man cantered his horse through the group of men and took his hat off, wiping his face with a gloved hand before running it through the graying hair atop his head. The palm of his leather glove came away wet. He was tall and lanky, and he also had a bushy mustache.

"My name's Gulliford and I'm marshal around this territory. And who might you be?" He clamped his hat back on his head.

"John Altar."

"Where you from?" Gulliford asked.

"Missouri." Altar shifted his weight in the saddle, trying to get comfortable.

"You're a long way from Missouri."

"Ain't that the truth." Altar noticed that Dog had settled himself about halfway down from the stand of trees.

"What're you doing out this way?"

Altar rested his hands on his saddle's pommel. "Been looking for my brother before I came across those people."

"Looking for your brother?" Gulliford asked.

"That's right."

"What's his name?"

"Robert," Altar said. "Might go by Bob, Bobby."

"Don't you know?" Gulliford asked.

"Ain't seen him since the war."

"Well, John Altar," Gulliford said. "What is it you saw exactly?"

"I come across a band of settlers who'd managed to get themselves killed."

"Managed to —" The marshal tilted his

hat back a smidge with his gloved finger. "Indians?" he asked.

"Someone sure went to a hell of a lot of trouble to make it look like Indians done it," Altar said. "But I don't think so."

"We heard it was Indians for sure," Gulliford said. "What makes you say different?"

"Where'd you hear that from?"

"You'd be best to remember, I'm the one asking the questions around here." The marshal frowned. "What makes you say it wasn't Indians?"

Altar thought a moment before he answered. "I seen regular folks killed by Indians before. This don't seem like it."

"And how you know that?"

"I rode with the First Missouri," Altar said. "I've scouted and fought Indians plenty."

"I been told them dirty heathens raped the women," Gulliford said, "and took scalps."

"I can't speak to no rape." Altar thought of the old woman with her skirts up around her head. "And there wasn't too many women except old ones and real young ones. But someone took scalps, that's plain enough."

"Smith!" the marshal said.

"Here," the lead rider spoke up from the

other side of the group.

"Get on over here!" Gulliford said.

The lead rider peeled away and rode around the outside of the men, coming to a stop in front of the marshal and across from Altar. Smith was over twenty by a couple of years and wore a flat-crowned hat pulled low over long blond hair badly in need of a wash. Even through the shadow cast by his hat's brim, Altar could see a knife scar that ran the length of his left cheek. Smith wore a plaid shirt with sleeves rolled up and a vest with sweat stains, and had his striped trousers tucked into his boots.

"Thought you said those homesteaders got slaughtered by Indians?" Gulliford asked.

"They was," Smith said. "I'm as sure as if I'd seen it with my own eyes."

"How come this Altar fella says different?"

Smith shrugged but stared at Altar like he was a ghost.

Why's he looking at me like that? Altar wondered.

Gulliford stared at Smith. "Tell me again how you knowed it was Indians."

"Like I told you before," Smith said. "Some of them folks had been scalped. And I seen arrows shot in them animals. And all the womenfolk, those that was there, had been raped. We know them damn redskins do that. Wouldn't no white man do that."

"All sorts of men rape women, let me tell you." Gulliford shook his head and looked to Altar.

"Them arrows weren't shot outta no bow," Altar said. "They wasn't in very deep, like someone stuck 'em in by hand."

Smith spat. "Everybody knows them scouts like this fella is kissin' cousins to Injuns." He yanked on his horse's reins to lift the animal's head. He spat again and used a sleeve to wipe a brown stain from his chin. "And he ain't likely to squeal on his people."

"If he's part Indian, sure would explain how he snuck up on Uncle Shep like he done," the farm boy said.

"Shut up, both of you." The marshal looked back at Altar. "What else?"

"Didn't see any moccasin signs." Altar reached down and patted his horse's neck. "There wasn't any broken weapons, no arrowheads. And all their horses were shod."

Gulliford leaned back in his saddle, then sat forward.

"Missing women don't mean a thing one way or another, but we're going to take a look-see," Gulliford said. "Why don't you show me where they're at." It wasn't a question. The marshal looked sideways at Smith, who was shaking his head.

"I been tracking the killers," Altar said knowing he couldn't afford to lose any more time if he was going to find the men responsible for the massacre and maybe his brother. "And hell, looks like you cut their trail yourself."

Gulliford's eyes narrowed. "What do you mean?"

"Only one set of tracks went off from that wagon train," Altar said. "And I'm on 'em."

"You're telling me that you're trailing a band of killers who wiped out a whole wagon train," Gulliford said. "All by your lonesome."

"Was the case 'til y'all came along," Altar said.

"And you're telling me you didn't see any sign of a war party or nothing like that?"

Altar shook his head. "Nope. Except for my tracks, you're not gonna see anything but that group leaving, like I told you."

"Weather's been mixed," Gulliford said. "Mighta wiped out any Indian tracks."

"Wasn't none to get wiped out," Altar said. "While I was there it rained some, but not enough to make that killing disappear. I walked all up and down that place collecting the dead; I'm sure I stepped on a lotta sign myself. But there wasn't no Indian sign as sure as I'm sitting in front of y'all."

"I want to see," Gulliford said. "We got some conflicting explanations and I want to see with my own eyes."

Altar shifted his weight in the saddle. "Awful lot of hungry critters around them parts, afraid I buried the dead best I could. Don't think you're going to see an awful lot besides turned-over prairie schooners."

"Best I take a look," Gulliford said. "I am the duly elected marshal."

"And you'll be wasting your duly elected time, you ask me," Altar said. "I'd just as soon stay on their trail. I don't want to lose no days backtracking."

"My man Smith, here." Gulliford pointed at the lead rider. "He said he come across those very same settlers that you did, but he says Indians done it." Gulliford nodded toward Altar. "And now I got you saying they didn't. Who am I to believe?"

"Believe who you like, Mister Gulliford," Altar said. "But I'm hunting those men down that killed them people, and they ain't back thataway."

"Let him go, Marshal." Smith's eyes shifted to Altar. "Can't help us none if he can't even tell Indians killed them folks. You'll see."

"That's just it," Gulliford said. "How do I

40

know you're any better, Smith? I don't know you, and you just come into town spouting off about this massacre. And all you got to show for it is an arrow you say you pulled out of an ox."

"Sure is a good sight more than this sidewinder has showed you," Smith said.

"Let me ask you this, Marshal," Altar said. "You ever known any Indian to have blond hair, or to burn the scalps they took?"

"Can't say that I have," Gulliford said. "Why?"

"That first night after they left the wagon train, two cowboys walked off some from the other folks and made another fire where they burned up the scalps. Blond scalps."

"How do you know that?" Gulliford asked.

"Found the fire where they done it," Altar said. "No Indian woulda done that. And whoever started that fire was wearing boots. I never seen an Indian wearing cowboy boots."

"You make a compelling argument, Altar." Gulliford settled back in his saddle. "But I still gotta see for myself. And you're going along. That can happen one of two ways and it's all up to you."

"You saying you're gonna arrest me?" Altar asked. "If I don't come along voluntary like."

"Can't say I like to hear it put like that," Gulliford said. "But that's the short of it."

Altar sat still on his horse for a moment, then shook his head. "You're making a big mistake. You're giving them murdering bastards an extra couple days' head start."

"Well," Gulliford said. "We'd best get a-going, then."

The marshal was true to his word, and they rode hard and didn't camp until neither Altar nor Smith could see the tracks clearly.

Smith avoided Altar as best he could, but the next morning, once they were back on the trail, Altar got him peeled off by himself.

"How was it you came along them homesteaders?" Altar asked.

Smith didn't answer but tried to go around Altar's horse with his own. Altar reached out and grabbed Smith's arm, pulling the foul-smelling man closer.

"I asked you a question."

Smith tried to yank his arm away, but Altar's grip was strong.

"I'm used to people answering my questions." Altar gave Smith a jerk. "I didn't see no lone rider tracks except my own. So, I'm wondering how it was you came across them folks."

Smith tried to tug his arm away two more times and failed.

Finally, Altar let go.

Smith spurred his horse. "Shows what you know," he said from a safe distance away. "I came in the same way I left, leading some horses I gathered up."

"Why didn't you do anything for the dead?"

Smith spit. "What am I gonna do? Critters gotta eat, too."

Later that night, Altar saw to his horse and petted Dog some. Just before they kicked the fire out, he sat next to Gulliford.

"Just what did Smith tell you?" Altar asked. "I'm curious."

Gulliford was wrapped up in his own effort to scrape out the bowl of his pipe with a small folding knife. "He told the farrier in town that he had some horses to sell." Gulliford put the knife away, apparently satisfied with his efforts.

"Guess Smith got to telling how he came across the animals?"

Gulliford pulled a pouch of tobacco from his saddlebag. "The farrier told Shepard, my deputy over there." He pointed at Shepard with his pipe's stem. "And Shep told me. When we spoke to Smith, he seemed a little reluctant to tell us the specifics, but we eventually got him talking."

"He tell you how it was that he come upon them?" Altar opened his canteen and drank.

"Yeah." Gulliford packed his pipe with tobacco. "Said he was their guide."

Altar struggled to swallow. "Guide?!" He coughed. "How is it he ain't dead, then?"

"Said he'd seen some Indian signs earlier and was out trying to figure what they should do." Gulliford struck a match and puffed on his pipe, holding the flame to the tobacco. He exhaled smoke that had a sweet scent. "When he returned, they were all dead." With each word, smoke escaped his mouth in puffs. He leaned back and drew deeply on the pipe.

Altar capped his canteen.

"I don't like him," Altar said. "Smith's as slippery as a greased hog."

Gulliford looked at Altar from the corner of his eye.

"I suspect he'd say the same of you."

Chapter 4
The bullywooger

Midafternoon the next day they came across the stone cairn Altar had built a ways from the scene of the massacre. It was low on the edges, about four feet high, and grew as it reached the center of the rectangle structure. It was twenty feet across and a little longer than six feet deep. The stones, as tightly packed as he could manage, did nothing to contain the fetid reek of decaying flesh. The broken, overturned prairie schooners and putrefied livestock carcasses lay beyond the final resting place of those nameless Mormons.

They paused atop the hill. Gulliford took his hat off, as did Shepard. Everyone followed suit, including Altar. Smith looked around before being the last to bare his head.

"Well, I'll be goddamned," Gulliford said.

Altar nosed his horse next to the marshal. Gulliford looked over at him.

"Hard to really picture in your head till you see it," Gulliford said. "Goddamn shame."

"Over there's where I come upon them." Altar pointed across the wagons and up the hill on the other side. "Suspect you can still see my and Dog's tracks some if you were to take a look." He pointed toward another part of the same slope. "That's where I camped, kept my fire below the crest."

"Gotta hand it to you, Altar," Gulliford said. "That was a hell of a lotta work you done to cover up those people."

"Ain't right letting the critters have them," Altar said. "Can't say I'd want to be eaten when I depart this Earth."

"My first impression," Gulliford said. "Wouldn't matter none to me. But the more I think on it, I wouldn't want to be eaten neither."

The group rode down to the broken wagon train. Gulliford was careful to approach from a direction that was clear of any previous tracks. He called a halt when they got close.

"Shep," Gulliford called out.

"Yep." The deputy rode forward.

"Altar," Gulliford said. "I want you to take Shep and show him what you seen. What's left of it, anyways."

Shepard sneered, not having said so much as a word to Altar since the incident at the meadow.

"I thought we came so's you could see?" Altar asked, dismounting. There was nowhere to tie his horse, so he handed his reins to the marshal. Gulliford took them.

"I see right enough," Gulliford said. "Go on."

Smith cantered up. "Want me to go, Marshal?"

"Nope," Gulliford said. "You can wait like the rest of us."

Smith pulled his horse aside and let the animal take a few steps away from the group. "Don't see what the fuss is all about. It's just like I told you."

"Who was the captain?" Shepard looked at Smith. "And which wagon was his?"

"Can't say for sure with them all broke up like they are," Smith said. "Don't see how it'd matter none, no ways."

"They didn't have any livestock?" Shepard asked.

"Nope, just what got killed and the couple of horses I saved."

Shepard swung off his horse. Altar walked ahead of Shepard as they picked their way through the broken prairie schooners. They stopped at a half-eaten ox. Two arrows lay next to the carcass. Altar turned to Shepard, while pointing at the fletched shafts.

"What's wrong with them arrows?" Altar asked.

Shepard shrugged.

"Like I told the marshal," Altar said, "they were only stuck in the body, by hand."

Shepard nodded.

"See anything else?" Altar asked.

Shepard lowered himself to his haunches and studied the scene before him, but he didn't say anything.

"They wouldn't have brought that animal down, not even if they'd been shot out of a rifle, much less a bow," Altar said.

"That's what I'm thinking. They ain't got the right placement," Shepard said. "Suppose some could say the Indians were just pissed and took it out on the animals, but that don't sound right to me. For savages to be cruel to an animal, there has to be a purpose."

"Agreed."

Shepard stood. "What we got ourselves here is a first class bullywooger."

Altar glanced at the deputy. "Can't say as I know what a 'bullywooger' is, but I suspect I'd agree if I did."

Altar and Shepard each chose a wagon and went through the discarded items lying about. Even though he was unsure as to what exactly he was looking for, Altar kept searching, thinking he'd know when he found whatever it was.

His searching of one prairie schooner after another brought him to the end of the wagon train. He stood looking down the path the pioneers had traversed.

Altar had surmised that the outlaws joined the homesteaders in the days before the massacre and had already searched the subsequent campsites. But now he found himself wishing he'd circled the outside of those camps to see if anyone had just ridden off on their own. Was it worth it to go back? The homesteaders' last camp had been almost a day's ride from here, and sunset wasn't far off. He'd have to let it go for another day at least, if it was even worth it to backtrack some more.

Altar started back toward Gulliford. Something crunched under his boot. It was an apple that had rolled out of a bushel basket from one of the overturned wagons. He reached down and picked up the now deep-red overripe fruit, before tossing it aside. He walked over and took his reins from the marshal.

Shepard walked up, holding a book in his hands. Sheafs of paper jutted out from the binding. He stopped in front of Marshal Gulliford.

"Seems I found the captain's Book of Doctrine and Covenants, and there's extra papers. They was Mormons for certain, just like Smith said." Shepard handed the book up to the marshal. "Figured you'd want to take a look-see."

"Sure enough." Gulliford twisted around in his saddle. "Let's find some shade and get off these horses for a spell."

Altar stood off to one side, still in the sun, and thought about how much time he was losing as he watched the marshal.

Gulliford, sitting on the ground, his back against the trunk of a cottonwood tree, looked through the papers real close. When he finally raised his head, he cast about until he saw Shepard.

"Shep," Gulliford said. "Put these in my saddlebag."

"They shed any light?" The deputy took the proffered book and papers.

Gulliford stood. "Can't say these do much of anything except to provide us with a list of names."

Shepard nodded slightly and went off to the marshal's horse.

Smith, sitting on a log, spat in the dust at

his feet and stood, muttering. All Altar could make out was "Mormons." Then Smith looked toward Gulliford. "You find any money in there with my name on it, Marshal?"

Gulliford stared at Smith for a moment before answering.

"Can't say I did." Gulliford brushed at the dust on his butt. "Why would there be any money for you?"

"They owed me twenty-five dollars," Smith said. "Only paid me half when we pushed off from Independence. Mormons is a cheap lot."

"Seems you already been overpaid." Altar stepped into his stirrup. He swung himself up onto his horse. "Guide's supposed to keep people alive as well as get them where they're going, regardless how they practice their religion."

Smith squinted at Altar but spoke to the marshal. "Guess I'm gonna move on, then. I done what I set out to do."

"What's that?" Gulliford asked.

"Why," Smith said, "led you all here's what I said I'd do, and I done it. Nothing more for me here."

"Don't you want to see justice done?" the marshal asked.

"Army will more than like catch up to

those murdering Injuns before we could. Ain't nothing in it for me."

"Well," Gulliford said. "If it's all the same to you, I'd just as soon you come back to town with us. You can ride out from there once we get to the bottom of this."

"Well, it ain't all the same to me," Smith said, "and I'll just ride outta here, thank you very much."

Gulliford shook his head. "It's like I told Altar. You can come with us all peaceful like, or I can have Shepard truss you up some and you can ride your horse back to Spring Creek belly down on that saddle of yours."

"Huh? What in the hell for?"

"This matter's still under investigation," the marshal said. "That goes for you too, Altar."

Altar had figured as much.

Smith spat and looked from the marshal to Shepard, then finally to Altar, where his stare lingered. He spit a tobacco fleck off his tongue before raising his hands.

"Have it your way, Marshal," Smith said.

"Think I will." Gulliford winked at Smith. "Let's move on before the sun goes down."

They made camp by a stream, under some tall oaks. Gulliford, apparently fancying himself a cook, started the dinner fire and left setting the watches to Shepard. The deputy picked a couple of men that Altar suspected weren't actual lawmen, but deputized townsfolk.

Altar was left with nothing to do except care for his horse and play with Dog. It was after dark before Gulliford served up some lean steaks taken from a small deer killed by one of the outriders. He fixed some beans and biscuits, too.

Altar sat back from the fire and shared some of his venison with Dog. The animal wasn't alarmed as the farm boy walked up.

"Can I sit with you for a spell?" the young man asked.

"Suit yourself." Altar motioned to the empty space around him with a hunk of meat spiked on the tines of his camp fork.

The boy sat and made himself comfortable, then commenced to eating like he hadn't been fed all day. He ate with his fingers, scooping beans off his plate directly into his mouth, using a hunk of biscuit like a broom.

Altar set his plate in front of Dog and let the beast lick it clean. He was still licking the tin when the boy finished and looked up.

Altar laughed. "You gonna take a breath now that you shoveled all that chow down your gullet?"

The boy wiped his mouth and chin with his sleeve, then belched.

"It sure was good." He glanced toward the fire where Gulliford was scraping the last of the beans from a pot into Shepard's bowl. "Darn, ain't gonna be no seconds."

"Don't seem to be any with this crowd," Altar said. "Go get you a drink. That water's good and cold. It'll fill whatever hole you got left."

"That water come from them mountains, I expect." The boy put his plate in front of Dog. The animal sniffed it, then began licking, but stopped after a couple passes of his tongue.

The boy laughed. "Sorry, guess I didn't leave ya much." He looked at Altar. "He got a name?"

"I expect he does," Altar said, "but he hasn't shared it with me."

"Didn't you name him when you got him?"

"We come together kind of strange like." Altar leaned back against his saddle. "Didn't really take the time to think of no name. Plus." Altar nodded at the dog. "He wasn't a pup when we started riding together."

"What do you call him?"

"Dog."

"That ain't a name," the boy said. "That's just what he is."

"What do people call you when they don't know your name?" Altar asked. "They call you 'boy,' right?"

"I guess, but my name's Conner."

"Okay, Conner," Altar said. "Most people call me Altar. First name's John. When Dog shares his real name with me, I'll be sure to tell you."

"Can I pet him?"

"Well," Altar said. "It'd probably be best you ask him. Watch yourself, though, he's still a mite bit hungry. Best to let him smell you first."

Conner watched Dog, but his hands remained in his lap. Then he hesitantly reached out and let Dog smell the back of his hand.

Dog sniffed the hand, then canted his head to let Conner scratch his ears.

"He's so big," Conner said. "He looks an awful lot like a wolf."

Altar nodded. "I reckon he does."

"I heard you tell the marshal that you was in the war."

Altar watched the boy but didn't answer.

"What was it you done in the war?" Conner crossed his legs and leaned forward.

Altar didn't answer, just pulled his hat

over his eyes and scooched lower to rest his head against the worn leather.

"From that saddle you got," Conner said. "You must've been with the cavalry. That there's a genuine McClellan saddle, I bet it got the army stamp on it somewhere. So, was you in the cavalry?"

Altar snugged his hat lower as if that would shut the kid up.

"You fight Johnny Reb some?"

Altar's mind flashed back to a field of the dead and the dying, many of the same age as this kid. He fought to keep those memories sealed in a deep, dark place where they couldn't break out unbidden. He thought of the locket, but it would just keep this kid yapping, and it hadn't held much magic of late. Not since that letter had caught up to him.

If this kid only knew what really constituted fighting a war, he wouldn't sound so goddamned eager, Altar thought. Maybe if the politicians had to fight in a war they declared, there'd be a lot less war.

"You fight Indians too?"

Altar ground his teeth. Sure, he'd fought Indians, but it wasn't something he talked about, and not with some snot-nosed sodbuster to be sure. This boy wasn't going anywhere unless he was encouraged to move on, and Altar suspected anything short of a thump on his noggin wouldn't suffice.

"What was it like tracking down Indians?"

Conner paused for a moment, but Altar knew better than to be hopeful.

"Was it like what we're doing now?"

Altar felt his chest tighten and knew he was close to shutting the kid up. All he wanted to do was close his eyes. Finally, he pushed his hat brim up enough so he could see the boy.

"You're right, it was just like this, Conner."

The boy nodded.

"Figured."

Altar lowered the brim again.

"I heard you tell the marshal you was from Missouri, ain't that right?"

Altar held his breath in his chest and counted, thinking of how his mama had always warned him about his temper.

"Smith told me he was from Missouri too," Conner said. "And he told me he fought in the war just like you."

Altar waited; the kid had his attention now. Smith was a Missourian? From his accent, Altar wasn't so sure, but he was unpleasant, and Altar didn't like him.

"But he says he was a raider, I guess that's a kind of cavalry too, right?"

A raider? Quantrill? Altar chewed his lip. Could Smith be one of the outlaws?

"He says he raided towns and stuff," Conner barely paused for breath, "smoking out enemies and the like."

Altar pushed his hat off his face. He wasn't going to sleep anytime soon.

"Says he killed plenty of people. He's talking about soldiers, right? I guess he could be talking about Indians, but he didn't say Indians exactly, you think he might've killed Indians too?"

Altar sat up. If Smith was one of the outlaws, why would he lead the posse back here?

"He ain't real friendly like, keeps this big knife handy, like he might have to cut something or someone all of a sudden . . ."

And what were the other outlaws doing now? Altar asked himself.

"Can't say I like the man," Conner said. "I see the way he treats his horse, he's downright mean, for no reason. He's steady setting that bit hard."

Altar wondered if Smith knew anything about Bobby.

"I don't know why that poor beast ain't throwed him by now." Conner continued to pet Dog's massive head.

Altar had figured the outlaws for Missouri

raiders. He'd fought enough of them to recognize their tactics. And that would certainly explain how they killed all the settlers and why the settlers hadn't seen it coming. Infiltrate them posing as friendly guides, or fellow travelers, striking when the poor bastards least expected it. Though he didn't see the outlaws doing it if they had nothing to gain. The dead stock hadn't seemed of particular quality, and the wagons were old and cobbled together. Nary a soul wore any good boots, and those pious Mormons looked woefully poor.

"Guess he done beat all the spirit out of that horse," Conner said. "Damn shame too, that's a right fine animal. Sure, you gotta be firm and all, but he's just mean for the sake of being mean. I seen it."

Altar continued to ignore the boy. What if, Altar thought as he got to his feet, what if Smith's leading the posse on a goose chase was only to smoke all of the men from out of whatever town the posse had come from? It would leave the town defenseless. Seemed like a plan devised by some of the raiders Smith claimed to have ridden with, like the bushwhackers Altar had hunted back in Missouri and Kansas. Altar didn't figure Smith for a Jayhawker, that was for sure.

"Where ya fixing on going?" Conner asked. "Thought you was going to sleep."

What was Smith's reward? Probably was why he tried to ride off earlier — he wanted to go meet his gang and get his cut.

Altar looked down at Conner. "Where's Smith?"

Chapter 5
Suit yourself

Altar strode across the camp. It was well past time to get some answers. Everyone was separated, laying out their bedrolls, getting ready to bed down. The light was mostly gone, and no other fires had been permitted by the marshal. As he navigated by starlight, Altar was thinking maybe Smith had skedaddled when he finally saw the last man carrying his saddle away from where the horses had been picketed.

It was too dark to make out the individual horses, but Altar would lay good money on Smith's being nearby, at the end of the line, closest to where he was about to bed down. Perhaps that was because Smith was a loner. Most guides were, including Altar himself. Or it could be because the man was such an ass that no one wanted to be around him. Or, more likely, Smith planned on slithering out in the middle of the night like the snake Altar suspected he was.

Altar waited for Smith to drop his rig. It hit the ground with a thud and tinkle of harness brass. Smith leaned his rifle against a tree, and then hefted the saddlebags off his shoulder and laid them down beside the saddle. He straightened and stretched, his arms up high, then swinging out wide.

Smith yawned, then squatted down and fished in his saddlebag for something. Whatever he brought out fit in his fist. Altar watched Smith lift whatever it was to his mouth. Then he heard the distinct crunch of an apple as Smith bit into it.

Where'd he get an apple out here?

Altar hadn't seen anyone else with one. They hadn't ridden by any apple trees. He remembered seeing a couple of bushel baskets, mostly empty, in the wagons. The ground had been littered with crushed fruit and he'd stepped on the one earlier.

But Smith hadn't gone near the wagon train today, he thought.

"What ya got there, Smith?" Altar asked as he stepped closer to the supposed guide.

Smith spun and crouched, his long knife in his hand, the apple gripped in his mouth.

"Whoa, it's only me," Altar said. "What's got you so skittish?"

"Don't be coming up behind me," Smith said after he'd taken the fruit from his mouth, knife still in hand. "Would hate to kill you by accident."

"Be a damn shame," Altar said. "But that'd be assuming you could."

Smith blew out a breath and a quiet curse before taking another bite from the apple. He sheathed his big knife as he chewed. The blade had the battered look of a weapon that had seen plenty of use, along with the dullness of neglect, though Altar saw that the edge had a glistening sheen from being honed. The weapon might be old and dirty, but he'd guess it was as sharp as any stropped razor.

He couldn't help but wonder which came first, Smith's knife or the scar running down the side of his face. Was one the result of the other or were they unrelated?

"Where'd you get that apple?" Altar asked.

Smith smirked and took a quick series of bites until nothing was left of the fruit except its core, which he heaved into the darkness.

"Last one," Smith said. "Now, get."

"I asked you a question."

Smith turned on his heel and threw his fist up in an arcing swing at Altar.

Altar blocked it and with his open palm slapped Smith on the side of the head. The blow sent Smith's hat flying off. The strength of the clout knocked the man sideways, dazed.

Altar stepped into him and drove a fist into the man's gut, doubling him over, and followed up by slamming his knee into Smith's face, throwing the other man backward, over his saddle and onto the ground.

Smith was laid out, bleeding from his nose, mouth, and even his ear.

Altar stepped over and knelt, grabbed a handful of Smith's greasy hair, and pulled his head up.

"Go ahead, "Altar said. "Go for your knife, or better yet, that revolver. Give me a reason to kill you, you double-crossing son of a bitch."

Smith tried to spit, but the frothy, blood-streaked spittle ran down his chin.

"I don't know what part you played in them settlers dying." Altar shook Smith's head. "But I'm gonna find out. And when I do, I'll string you up my own self if I have to."

"I don't . . ." Smith tried to spit again but only blew a blood bubble that popped, sprinkling his face in crimson speckles. "I don't know nothing what you're talking about."

"Save your horseshit for someone else," Altar said. "I'm not buying it."

"I was their guide." Smith coughed. "I was trying to save them."

"Who'd you ride with in the war?" Altar asked.

Smith stopped coughing and stared at him, his eyes filled with malevolence.

"The war? What you wanna know that for?" Smith spat gore from his mouth that landed on his chest.

"I ain't going to ask you again." Altar increased the pressure on Smith's hair. "Better tell me 'fore I scalp you with my bare hands."

Smith grimaced, showing his bloodied teeth. "You son of a bitch!"

Altar twisted his fist. "Who'd you ride with?"

"Quantri—"

Gulliford grabbed Altar's shoulder and pulled. "What the hell's going on here!"

Altar rocked back, then wrenched free.

"Let go of him," Gulliford said. "Or I'll have Shep hog-tie you and you can finish the ride draped over your horse."

Altar let go of Smith's hair.

Smith went for his knife.

Altar drew his revolver and clocked Smith on the side of the face with a dull thud. Smith's head fell back again, his hand on his knife hilt.

"This man was in on the killing of all those people back yonder," Altar said.

Smith shook his head. Blood dripped from his open mouth. "He's crazy, Marshal," Smith slurred, and spat a tooth into the dirt.

Gulliford straightened and put his hands on his hips.

Altar spoke clearly without looking at Gulliford, keeping an eye on Smith.

"I think Smith's one of the men responsible for all those people being killed. He was about to tell me he rode with the Confederate guerrillas in Missouri, they did things like what we seen."

Gulliford shook his head.

"I'm not so sure the two of you ain't in cahoots." Gulliford looked to Shepard, who was standing on the other side of Altar and Smith. "If either of these two commence to fighting again, put 'em in leg irons."

"You're making a mistake," Altar said. "I suspect we're gonna find your town's been ransacked by this outlaw's gang. He led you away so they could go there and take whatever they wanted."

Smith's laugh was ragged, probably from the blood in the back of his throat. "You tell some tall tales, mister."

"We'll see," Altar said and stood. He looked at Gulliford. "Marshal, I'd hog-tie this bastard if'n I was you."

Gulliford looked over at Shepard, who spit tobacco juice on the ground between his feet. It was the deputy who finally spoke. "Makes a lot of sense, Marshal."

Gulliford shook his head. "He ain't a-going nowheres, no need to tie him up none."

Altar patted his palms together as if he was rubbing all traces of Smith from them. Then he pushed past the growing crowd of cowhands.

"Suit yourself."

Chapter 6
News from Spring Creek

Altar awoke, startled from sleep by Dog's growl. His hand came out from under his saddle blanket holding his revolver, with his finger on the trigger. But nothing threatened him, though Dog's attention was focused on some point in the darkness that he couldn't see. He threw off the blanket, setting his gun down, and reached for his boots. Once he'd pulled them on, he stood and looked around.

It was dark, but there seemed to be people moving on the other side of camp. Seemed the horses were roused up, too. Altar strapped his holster rig around his waist; he'd slept in his long johns and jeans. Forgoing his shirt, he stuffed his Remington 1861 .44 where it belonged. He thought about slipping the leather thong around the hammer but left it off as he started for the commotion.

He found Gulliford and Shepard and a

second deputy, whose name he didn't know, standing around a figure on his knees. The men were in their long johns too, while the new figure was dressed for riding, including a handkerchief around his neck and a hat that had been thrown on the ground.

The figure spoke between gulps from a canteen. The stranger was slight, and younger than Conner from the looks of it.

"The other night, they come outta nowhere," the youth said. "Rode in and shot Cobb straightaway, gunned him down in front of the marshal's office like it wasn't nothing."

Shepard took a deep breath, then looked at Gulliford, who just stared at the kneeling youth as if he couldn't believe what he was hearing.

"They kill him?" Gulliford asked.

"Sure enough did," the kid said. "Best I know. His body was still laying there when I rode out. He ain't moved a twitch."

"Where was Harmon?" Gulliford asked.

"I don't rightly know," the boy said. "Ain't seen him at all."

"What'd they do after they shot Ol' Cobb?" Shepard asked.

"Well, most of them rode up to the tavern." The boy drank some more. "A couple went over to the stables." The boy gulped down more water, as much drooled down his chin as made it to his belly.

"All right." Shepard took the canteen away from him. "Can you finish telling us what happened?" The deputy waved the canteen toward the stream, sloshing the water within. "Whole crick of water just a-waiting for you to drink it dry if you've a mind to. What'd them boys do next?"

"I heard tell they met up with a man who'd been in the tavern."

"Who?" Gulliford asked.

"Don't rightly know," the kid said. "Heard he was a stranger, had only been in town for a day or so."

"OK, then what?" Shepard asked.

"Guess some of them went and woke up the bank owner. 'Cause they drug him back and made him open the bank. Then they cleaned out the vault."

The kid stood; his legs were shaky.

"They commenced to shooting up the tavern, and drinking." The kid paused. "They done something awful to a bunch of the women and girls they'd rounded up."

Shepard swore, while Gulliford shook his head.

"Don't say you weren't warned." Altar turned from the group. "I'm going to get Smith."

"Hold fast there, partner," Shepard said, his revolver pointed at Altar. "Like the marshal said, we ain't sure who's side you're on."

Altar stopped and turned, his hand out from his gun handle. He was like to kick himself for not seeing that Shepard was armed.

Mistakes like that can get you killed, he thought.

"That's the second time you've pointed a gun at me, Shep," Altar said. "Can't say I like it none."

Gulliford reached out and put his palm on Shepard's revolver, pushing the barrel down.

"I don't trust him much, but I think we can count him more friend than not at this point," Gulliford said. "And he's got a good idea. Let's roust Smith and see what he's got to say."

They followed Altar as he strode over to place he'd found Smith. The man wasn't there, and neither were any of his traps.

"Damn, looks like he lit out," Altar said.

"Which one's his horse?" Shepard started for the picket line of animals.

"Dean," Gulliford said to a deputy. "Fetch us a lantern and see that it's fired up."

"Will do, Marshal." Dean turned and

walked off, calling for a lantern.

Altar took off following the trail where he'd seen Smith carrying his saddle. As he got close to the picket line, he heard a sob. He found Conner sitting with his back against the tree to which the end of the line was affixed. Conner held his arms tight across his stomach. A crimson flow of liquid seeped through his fingers.

Horses snorted and pulled against the rope.

They smell blood, Altar thought.

He knelt next to Conner. When he went to tug the kid's arms away from his stomach, Conner shook his head violently.

"No," Conner said. "If I move my arms, my guts'll fall out."

Altar gently moved the boy away from the tree trunk and laid him down on the ground. "Let me see."

"Why'd he cut me like he done?" Conner said. "I ain't gonna get to see my mama or sister again, am I?" He sobbed.

Altar stopped when he heard the boy's croak. He knew Conner wasn't long for this Earth.

"Let's not get ahead of ourselves just yet, Conner. Who cut you?"

As if he had to ask.

"Smith," Conner said between sobs. "That

low-down no-account slit my belly open when I asked him where he was fixin' to go."

Altar pried Conner's arms away an inch until he could see the dark, coiled wetness that lay underneath. He let go of the kid's arms.

Shepard and Gulliford came up behind him.

"Conner's hurt bad," Altar said.

"Smith?" Shepard asked.

"Yep," Altar said. "Conner, where'd Smith go?"

Conner was shaking now.

"Sit me up," he said with a croak. "Can't breathe." His voice was a gargled whisper.

Altar lifted the boy up. He screamed and a stream of hotness washed over Altar's forearm. It took Conner a couple of seconds to calm down.

"You know where Smith went after he cut you?" Altar asked.

"Saddled . . . his . . . horse . . . rode off's . . . all I . . . know."

Conner gulped air.

"Promise . . . me," he said with a gasp, his eyes wide. "Tell . . . my . . . mama . . . sister . . . I love . . . 'em." The boy's body shook and his eyes rolled up into his head.

"I will," Altar said, watching Conner's last

breath get strangled in his throat. Gently, he laid the boy back down.

"Son of a bitch," Altar said in a low growl. He found Conner's hat lying nearby and put it over the boy's face. Then Altar slowly rose to his feet.

He looked at Gulliford and Shepard.

"S'pect you boys might wanna put some pants on before we ride after Smith."

"Can't do that." Gulliford shook his head. "But we are going to have to get dressed sure enough."

"What do you mean, 'can't'?" Altar asked. "You saying you ain't gonna ride after this murdering son of a bitch?"

Gulliford turned and walked past Dean, who had arrived with a lit lantern.

"I'm the duly elected marshal of Spring Creek," Gulliford said. "After what we just heard, I reckon my place is back there just now."

Altar shook his head and looked at Shepard for a long moment.

"You got some rope?" Altar asked.

"What for?"

"Gotta tie Conner up, keep his insides where God meant them to be."

"Dean," Shepard said. "You heard the man." Dean followed after Gulliford.

Shepard squatted next to Conner and

74

lifted the boy's hat.

"Goddamned shame," Shepard said. "Gonna be hard on his mama and his sister." The deputy lowered the hat back over Conner's face and sniffed, then rubbed his eyes with a large hand. "I've known him his whole life."

Altar knew the best chance of finding his brother lay in trailing Smith. By the time the posse got back to town, the outlaws would be long gone. But he suspected Smith knew where they were going. And that was where Altar was headed.

"Seemed like a good boy," Altar said.

Shepard stood. "He is, was." The deputy rubbed his sleeve across his cheeks. "His mama's my sister, and it's gonna kill that woman something fierce."

"The marshal really headed back to town?"

"I suspect so," Shepard said. "Being the duly elected official and all."

"That don't sit well with me," Altar said.

"Can't say it do with me neither." Shepard looked over his shoulder, back where Gulliford had disappeared. "How long 'til there's enough light to follow that murdering bastard?"

Altar looked at the sky. The barest hint of a pinkish sliver colored the eastern horizon.

"I reckon an hour, maybe two if the tracks are faint," Altar said.

Shepard nodded. "Once we get Conner fixed up, I'll go get dressed."

Dean came back with a coil of rope in one hand and the lantern in the other.

Altar smelled the cookfire as he washed his hands and forearms in the stream. The water was ice cold and the bloodstains stubborn. He figured if he could get his hands on some of Smith's clothes, he could see if Dog could track the man. Smith had most likely taken everything with him. But it would be worth a look where the man had spread out his bedroll all the same. Maybe Dog could pick up a spore just from the ground where Smith had lain.

Did he want Shepard along? It was just one man, but the deputy might not be interested in talking to Smith. He might just kill him. If it wasn't for Altar's need to question Smith about his brother, he'd kill him outright himself. At this time, though, Smith was his best chance to find Bobby. He got ready; if Shepard was quick enough, he could ride along.

That is, Altar thought, *until he gets in the way.*

Chapter 7
Like a turd on an offering plate

Not an hour later, with the dawn's deep gray tones, Altar cinched his saddle tight on his mount. He threw his saddlebags over the horse's withers, picked his Henry off the ground, and slid it into the boot attached to the saddle.

He looked about one last time for Dog. He'd hoped to see if the animal could catch a scent of Smith from where the man had been sleeping. If Dog could sniff something out, he didn't need the sun. It would be a spell before he could discern tracks.

Gulliford strode over, half dressed in pants held up by suspenders over the long johns, his pipe lighted and trailing smoke behind him.

"And just where do you think you're going?" Gulliford asked.

Altar leaned with his forearms against his mount.

"After Smith."

"I said we're heading back to Spring Creek." Gulliford drew on his pipe and let out a cloud of sweet, scented smoke. "Smith'll have to wait."

"I reckon you didn't tell Smith," Altar said.

"Don't matter none," Gulliford said. "We're headed back to town."

"Go right ahead, Marshal." Altar gave a wavelike salute. "But I'm going after the man who gutted that kid over yonder. Me and Smith gonna have us a reckoning."

Altar felt a weight against his leg and knew Dog was back. He couldn't help but smile as he reached down and scratched between the animal's ears.

"C'mon, Dog." Altar walked past Gulliford, leading Dog to where Smith had camped.

The marshal followed, yapping about one thing or another, about how he was duly elected and in charge. Altar ignored him.

Altar got down on his haunches and patted the ground where he wanted Dog to concentrate his efforts. The big canine came over and sniffed around in widening circles. Finally, with a yelp, the animal bounded off.

"Got him," Altar said.

He went back to his horse, Gulliford following. Altar could hear Dog's barking getting farther off. He slipped his horse's reins from around the line and saw Shepard leading his mount past the other end of the picket. Dean trailed behind him on foot.

Shepard was dressed, ready to ride.

"There you are," Gulliford said to Shepard. "I want you to put Altar in irons until he sees that going back to town is the most prudent course of action."

Altar checked his saddle's tightness and shook his head. "I wouldn't try that if I was you."

Shepard looked from Altar to Gulliford. "Can't do that, Marshal."

Gulliford stammered, smoke leaking from his mouth and nose.

Shepard pulled something out of his vest pocket. He looked at it before handing it to Gulliford.

"I know you're duly elected and all," Shepard said. "But that boy over there is my kin. And I'll be damned if I'm going to turn my back and let his killer just ride away."

"That's not what we're doing at all." Gulliford held his pipe in one hand and Shepard's star in the other. "We're going back to assess the damage to our homes. We'll organize and get after the men who did this.

Smith among them. I promise you."

"All due respect," Shepard said. "But I ain't looking my sis in the eye and telling her I let her little boy's murderer ride away like he done."

Gulliford frowned, looking like he'd been slapped.

"C'mon, Shep," Altar said, climbing onto his mount. He kneed his horse forward. "Before Dog runs off to where we can't hear him."

"Sorry, Marshal." Shepard climbed up on his big horse. "We been together a long time, but that's my blood that man spilt and I'm going to see to it Smith pays in kind."

Altar snapped his horse's reins, and they rode off after Dog.

They caught up to Dog and rode in silence for most of the morning. Finally, Shepard spoke as they made ready to water the horses at a creek where they'd stopped. The animal didn't pay them any attention as his head was down, lapping the cold water as if he hadn't had anything to drink since last night.

"Thought he'd be veering north by now," Shepard said.

Altar took his saddle off his horse and placed it down next to where his mount pulled at the thick grass.

"Why's that?" he asked.

"With the town being up north and all, thought he'd be making tracks headed thataway." Shepard pulled his saddle off his horse and set it down.

"I'm guessing the town's old news for him." Altar put his hat on top of the saddle.

"Where's he headed, then?"

Altar went to the creek and squatted down. He palmed water to his lips and swished his mouth out, spitting the grime away, then drank. He gulped many handfuls, then soaked his handkerchief in the water, wringing it out and soaking it some more. The creek was shallow, but he was able to get most of his hair wet, shaking the excess off like Dog. He stood, tying the handkerchief around his neck.

"Don't say much, do you?" Shepard asked as he filled his canteen.

"Nope."

"You got any ideas as to where Smith's headed?" Shepard tapped the canteen's cork in place and checked it by holding it upside down.

"I figure he's meeting up with his compadres," Altar said.

"Be a good guess, I reckon." Shepard dropped his canteen by his saddle. "How many you figure them for?"

Altar shrugged his shoulders. "Probably a dozen or so would be my guess, give or take."

Shepard nodded as if he agreed.

"You think that son of a bitch knows we're dogging him?"

"Sure," Altar said. "But I suspect he thinks the whole damn posse's after his scrawny ass. He doesn't know about that kid riding into camp."

" 'Bout right." Shepard nodded again. "Guess we better keep our wits about us, then. Desperate men are dangerous."

Yep, Altar thought. *They are.*

There was still sunlight, though the sun was sinking in the west. They weren't ready to stop, but Altar sat on his horse and stared.

Dog was circling, his nose to the ground. He'd lost the scent at the water's edge. Not that they'd needed his help after there was enough light for Altar to make out the tracks. But it was good to know he and Shep were on the right path.

Altar took in a deep breath. Something about the ground in front of him gave him pause. It was only a matter of time before Smith would try to lose them and Altar had expected it before now. The man had to know someone was on his trail. He'd be a fool not to.

Shepard nudged his horse closer, and Altar held up his hand before the man could speak.

In front of them lay a confluence of a river and a couple of tributaries. The river appeared rather shallow. The two streams were several hundred yards apart feeding into the larger flow. Smith's tracks led down the bank into the water, but even from where he sat, Altar could see Smith hadn't come out on the other side, not at least where it was clear.

Altar dismounted and walked to the side of the river. He studied the direction of the tracks as they entered the water.

He went back to his horse and took his boots off. He stood and undid his holster rig, looping it over his shoulder. He stuffed his boots under his saddlebags and waved Shepard over. When Shepard drew near, Altar handed him the reins.

"Stay on the bank and follow me." Altar turned toward the muddy bank.

He waded into the water, staring at the river's bottom for any sign of how the horse had turned, because it had changed direction some kind of way. When he got to the middle of the flow, the bottom was obscured. He pushed through toward the other side, where the water rose to mid-thigh and would've reached his holstered gun had he not taken it off.

"Didn't he just go straight across?" Shepard asked.

Altar didn't look up from his inspection of the muddy bank.

"Nope."

"What you think he done?"

Altar continued his scan, turning upriver.

"Just about every varmint I've ever tracked, including men," Altar said, "always try and double back to lose their trackers."

"And you done a fair share of tracking, have you?"

"I have," Altar said, thinking of the different men and Indians he'd learned from and worked with in the war and in the struggles with the red men in the plains.

His gut was telling him to look for Smith to try a double back here, but as he pondered it, a double back wouldn't make sense.

Had Smith used the one creek that would constitute going back the way he came, it would have led the outlaw into the open, right past Shepard and Altar, and close enough to make it a bad idea. And Smith must be thinking the whole posse was after him, not just two men, which would make him have to account for outriders.

Altar moved upriver some more. There was no sign in the mud or the river bottom that Altar believed told of Smith's passing, so he pushed farther.

"See anything?"

Altar ignored the former deputy's question and continued to scour the river.

Just before he was about to give up and climb out of the water, he saw another creek emptying into the river. This one was on the same side as Shepard, but farther upstream.

Altar waded back across, his feet growing numb from the cold, and stared at the shallow delta-like flat where the tributary joined the river. He looked up and down and his heart sank. There were no impressions.

Where the hell had Smith gone?

Then he saw a plug of chewing tobacco in the mud, kind of like a turd lying on an offering plate. It looked pretty damn fresh, too.

Altar smiled and whistled.

Shepard led Altar's horse to the water's edge, and Dog followed. By the time Altar climbed back on his horse, some of the feeling had returned to his now-booted feet.

"So," Shepard said. "You're saying Smith

went into the river only to keep going the same way we was going already?"

"Yep," Altar said.

Where Smith and his horse had climbed out of the creek bed, more than a mile upstream from the river, Altar got Dog to reacquire the scent. After a little nosing around, Dog bounded off, following along the tracks Altar could still see. Smith had stayed in the direction he'd been going all day.

Altar grudgingly gave the son of a bitch credit; he had wanted them to believe he was doubling back. If it hadn't been for that plug, he probably would've gotten away. Altar explained this to Shepard.

"That's a right nifty trick." Shepard nodded toward Dog.

"Yep," Altar said. "Now we can push past sundown."

"You figure we've cut his lead some?"

"Can't say for sure. He cleared that river faster than we did, but I reckon we've closed the distance some since we set out. Tracks are still fresh, that's for sure."

"You thinking he's fixin' to bed down?" Shepard asked.

"Maybe," Altar said. "Kind of depends on if he knows where he's going or not."

Shepard turned in his saddle and cocked

his head to the side like a curious dog.

"You figure he does?"

"If he knows where he's a-going, he don't need the sun," Altar said. "But if he's looking for a landmark or something, he needs to be able to see, so he'll knock off 'til he can see again. Either way, be alert."

"Since there's only the two of us," Shepard said, "maybe he won't recognize us 'til we're close enough to shoot him."

Altar laughed. "Don't be staking your life on that kind of thinking."

"Reckon you're right, on that account." Shepard laughed too, but his eyes didn't stray from scouring the countryside ahead.

They kept riding into the evening, and even as night descended on the landscape, casting dark shadows. Altar knew they'd better stop soon; if they didn't, they could walk right into an ambush. And with only the two of them, they couldn't afford any casualties.

Finally, he stopped them halfway up a ridge. He held his finger to his mouth. Shepard nodded, apparently knowing to be quiet.

Now, Altar thought, all he had to do was to teach Dog that lesson.

There was no cooking scent in the air. Smith hadn't lighted a fire, at least not close enough for Altar to detect it.

After letting the mounts drink some at a brook, he and Shepard took their saddles and gear from the horses and tied them to a tree with enough grass to keep them happy. Any conversation they needed to have was done in sotto voce. Dog had run off to hunt.

Altar ate a hunk of jerky and part of a biscuit.

Damn thing's god-awful hard, he thought, chewing as much of the dry biscuit as he could stomach. Maybe he'd have more later.

He tapped Shepard on the shoulder. When the man looked at him, Altar bent down to whisper. "I'm headed to the ridgeline to take a look-see. Keep the horses company for a while."

Shepard nodded and took a corked bottle from his saddlebag. He held it up so Altar could see the dark liquid within. Even in the shade of the night, Altar saw the grin underneath Shepard's busy mustache.

The thought of the liquor warming his gut felt good to Altar. "Save me a nudge or two," he said.

"Maybe." Shepard set the bottle next to his leg before he went back to digging in his saddlebag. "Maybe not."

Altar grinned, but then thought, *I better keep my head out of the bottle. It wouldn't do no good to crawl back in there.* At least, not until he'd brought Bobby back where he belonged. Home.

Chapter 8
Bet you'd like to know

Altar made his way up the slope, being as quiet as he could. He maneuvered through scrub pine and trees; the grass was thick and tall, but dry. He didn't really expect to see anything, especially since there wasn't any scent of smoke in the air. But, he told himself, they were upwind, which would've made it unlikely he'd smell anything even if Smith had been cooking. With the wind blowing like it was, it also meant that he and Shepard wouldn't be lighting any fires.

When he was just below the ridgetop, he slowed and kept going. There weren't many clouds, but the stars were bright. He could see a far piece but didn't detect anything. They would have to get up and follow the tracks just like he had already planned. He watched the shade-cloaked landscape until he was sure there wasn't anything to see.

He made his way back to camp, where he found Shepard leaning against his saddle, the bottle next to his leg. He was eating something. There was no sign of Dog. Altar was being so quiet, he got right up to Shepard before the man looked toward him.

"Goddamn," Shepard said in a whisper. "You're 'bout as noisy as a ghost."

The deputy reached down and took a canning jar off the ground. He twisted the top off and held it out to Altar.

"Want some marmalade?" Shepard put the lid down and wiped his knife on his pants leg. "Makes them biscuits almost tolerable."

Altar took the jar and sniffed. The scent of oranges was strong, and the brown sugar too.

"Thanks." Altar took the knife and went to his saddlebag. He pulled the other half of his earlier biscuit from his sack. He spread the marmalade across the top and cleaned the blade like Shepard had done. He took a bite and returned the blade to the former deputy. He held up the biscuit as he chewed and whispered, "Good."

Altar finished the biscuit and sat across from Shepard, their ankles even.

Shepard uncorked the liquor bottle and took a short pull. He wiped the top with his sleeve and handed it to Altar, who took the offered bottle and held it up to Shepard as if in a toast before taking his own short swallow. It was whiskey and burned just right.

Shepard reached around to the saddle horn, where he'd looped his gun rig, and pulled his Navy Colt from its holster. He rubbed the revolver down with an oiled cloth. Without looking up from what he was doing, Shepard spoke in a low voice.

"Been wishing I'd a' listened to you 'bout hog-tying that no-account."

Altar nodded. "What's done is done. Leave it go."

Shepard nodded as he ran the cloth up and down the seven-and-a-half-inch barrel of his Colt. "I'm gonna have to answer to my baby sister. Conner was her only boy."

Altar took another slug from the whiskey bottle and let the searing heat warm him from the inside out.

"Girl's had a bad run," Shepard said. "Lost her man a while back on account of Indians."

"Can't say I've known many women who haven't had a bad run of it," Altar said, leaning back. "Frontier's a hard life."

"Her man was about as hardheaded as any mule," Shepard said. "Rest of the farmers came in when we heard the savages had come south raiding by us. At least he let

Elizabeth and the children come by my wife and me."

"They burn his place down?"

"Sure enough, part of the barn's all that's standing last I was out that way. They chopped him up something fierce, too. Left him in pieces just out of reach of the fire."

Shepard holstered his Colt and took the whiskey bottle. "You know much about the Lakota and their ilk?"

"I know they're a fierce and proud people. Very capable warriors."

"That's one way of saying it, I suppose." Shepard scooched lower and leaned his head back against the saddle. "I prefer to call them what they are, murdering, thieving heathens."

"Give them their due." Altar laid back as well. He put his hat over his face, his Remington revolver on his lap. "Never good to underestimate your opponent."

"You learn that in the army?"

"Yep." Altar closed his eyes.

"Heard you tell the marshal you was with the First Missouri?"

"Among others." Altar figured Conner got his inquisitiveness honestly. It ran in the family. "Good night."

"You don't think we should set a watch?"

"No need. We got Dog."

And even as he felt the pull of slumber, Altar said, "And I'm a light sleeper."

"I bet you are at that."

Altar was up before the sun, and Dog was nowhere to be seen, out hunting probably. The wind had shifted, and he still couldn't smell any scent of a cooking fire. He retrieved his spyglass from his saddlebag and stopped for a second when his hand nudged the oilcloth-wrapped locket.

Suddenly, he found himself wishing he'd taken it with him last night up to the ridge, might could've spent some time contemplating it and his life, he thought, what it had become. Maybe what it could've been had he asked Fannie to marry him. Would that have changed Bobby's life, as well as his own? Had he acted on the feelings in his heart as opposed to the ones in his head and gut, maybe death wouldn't be his constant companion.

Altar shook his head and took off for the ridgeline. By the time he was at the top, the sun was breaking the horizon behind him.

He scurried over to a set of boulders and sat facing the direction Smith had taken, and waited. The large rocks behind him would prevent his silhouette from giving him away, and when he leaned back against the stone, the cold seeped through to chill him. As soon as there was enough light, he opened the glass and scanned the landscape, looking for any sign of the outlaw.

Altar watched the sunlight slowly expose the rolling countryside in a wave of radiance. He looked for any kind of water, thinking the outlaw would want to get something to drink for himself and his horse. Altar started where the sun burned away the darkness and his eye lingered in places where he'd think to make camp himself.

Motion returned his attention to a stream and a thicket of trees he'd already examined. There it was again, a flash of something whitish. Then Smith, naked and paste-white except for his lower face and hands, sauntered from under the trees and waded into the stream. He splashed about for a minute, cupping handfuls of water under his arms and crotch before he ran from the water as if he were cold.

Altar shook his head. No wonder the man stank, he didn't use any soap.

The country between him and Smith was dotted with clusters of trees and scrub pine. After a few minutes, Altar snapped his spyglass closed and started back down the slope to get Shepard.

He found the horses saddled, and a biscuit and a hunk of jerky wrapped in a handkerchief where he'd normally sit.

Shepard came from around a tree, buttoning his pants.

"Check your saddle," Shepard said. "That horse a' yours don't like nobody else fixing him up."

Altar smiled. "He's particular, all right." He checked the cinch and had to snug it up some. Knowing where Smith was meant he and Shepard could talk without worrying about discovery. "Smith's a couple of miles ahead of us. We might be able to catch him before he heads out."

"Let's go kill that son of a bitch."

Altar mounted and reined his horse around.

"Need to talk to him before we get to killing him."

Shepard stepped into his saddle. "Why's that?"

Looking around for Dog, Altar started for the top of the ridge in an indirect line more suitable for horses. He knew he couldn't tell this former deputy that he was looking for his brother who was riding with these outlaws. Dog was still nowhere to be seen.

"Why's that?" Shepard urged his horse to follow.

"Because," Altar said, "Smith knows where his compadres are at."

"Hadn't thought of that. All I'm fixin' on is killing him."

"You think the marshal's gonna find them outlaws laying about town?"

"Reckon not," Shepard said. "But we can track 'em sure enough."

"Maybe," Altar said. "But you're not taking into account these men are seasoned guerrillas and —"

"What in tarnation you call them?"

"Guerrillas," Altar said. "Irregulars, local people fighting for the other side, like the bushwhackers in Missouri fighting for the Rebs or the Red Legs fighting for the Union."

"You learn that in the army too?"

"Yep," Altar said.

"You learned a whole bunch," Shepard said. "You ever have time for fighting?"

Altar rode in silence as his horse negotiated some rocks. There was something about Shepard he liked, and that was unusual. Just the same, he didn't want to get into his past, including his stint in the United States Military Academy at West Point.

"Trust me when I tell you tracking them ain't gonna be that easy. Guarantee."

"Just so he ends up dead."

Altar looked back at Shepard.

"I'm with ya," Altar said. "But we gotta find out where those outlaws are headed."

Shepard rode for a time without saying anything. Then he looked at Altar.

"Just as soon see him dead myself," Shepard said with a shake of his head.

At the top of the ridge, Altar and Shepard dismounted and tied their horses to a scrub pine just short of the ridgeline. They walked up the last of the slope that was steep and rocky, the soil eroded by the ever-blowing winds. They scooted over the top and Altar showed Shepard where Smith was, though the outlaw was out of sight at the moment.

"Come around over by the low pass." Altar pointed along the ridgeline as it dropped out of sight. "Go ahead and make some noise so as to let him know you're coming. The one thing he ain't expecting is a lone rider. But stay outta rifle range just the same."

Shepard looked hard at Altar.

"And what're you gonna be doing?"

"Why," Altar said, "I'm gonna come up behind him and take him prisoner." He didn't add that since Shepard would be a ways off, that would give him time to get his brother's whereabouts from the outlaw.

"I'll holler at you when all is clear."

Shepard nodded, and they went back to their horses and climbed into their saddles. Both men removed their rifles from their scabbards and levered rounds into their chambers. They split up, with Shepard moving along the ridge just short of its peak, while Altar waited to go back over the top and take a more direct route to the outlaw below.

After having given Shepard enough time, Altar clicked his tongue and nudged his mount with his knees to get the beast moving. He rounded the rock outcropping and started down the slope, keeping as many trees and other vegetation as he could between him and Smith's camp.

Altar stopped a couple of times and took a look with his spyglass but couldn't see Smith or his horse. When he was a hundred yards from where he thought the camp was, Altar dismounted. He tied off his horse and crept through the rocks and scrub pine, his rifle in his hands.

The scent of the pine was nearly overpowering as he pushed slowly through the needles that scratched at his face and tugged at his clothing.

A rifle shot barked from somewhere in front of him. Altar hunkered down some but didn't think the shot was aimed at him.

Another shot from farther away answered the first. That time, though, Altar thought he could hear the bullet passing through the branches off to his left. If it had been aimed at him, they were way off, but he figured it was Shepard's return fire at Smith.

"Give yourself up, Smith!" Shepard said, sounding like he was far away. "I'll see to it you get a fair trial for what you done to Conner."

Altar took a deep breath and shook his head. Not exactly how'd he'd planned it but plans never stayed the same once you got to acting them out and let other folks have their say.

A shot from up ahead of Altar was the only response Shepard got for his trouble.

Altar crouched and edged forward. He knew about where Smith was, but didn't know for sure, and since he didn't need to worry about Shepard, he went slow.

A minute later, another rifle shot sounded like it was just in front of him. He tried to peer through the branches of a pine, but they were so thick and green. He felt almost overwhelmed by the heavy scent of the tree filling his nose. He pushed down a branch laden with green needles and was surprised to see it wasn't Smith shooting at Shepard.

This man was white, looked clean and freshly shaven, in what could only be new clothes. He had on a starched white shirt, and a black striped vest over pants of a similar cloth, with ornately tooled brown boots with a Mexican heel. He had a pistol rig tied to his leg and cartridge loops on his belt filled with fat brass bullets. A gambler's style hat was on the rock to the man's right; it looked as if it was made of beaver. And he was shooting a Winchester that was so clean it had to be new.

Altar glanced around. Were they bracing the wrong cowboy? Had he been following the wrong man?

That just wasn't possible, he was damn sure that had been Smith he'd seen bathing earlier. Someone could fool him, maybe, but not Dog. There had to be another explanation, but he'd be hard-pressed to provide one at the moment.

Off to his right, Altar saw someone move past a rock into a stand of birch.

Smith.

He was flanking Shepard.

A whinny and movement on his left caught his attention. Altar turned his head and saw there were three horses tied under the trees forty yards off.

Was there a third cowboy?

Had Smith met up with the whole damn gang? If he had, Altar and Shepard were in for a world of hurt.

Altar couldn't see where Shepard was laid up, but if the third cowboy was working his way around the other side opposite Smith, Shepard didn't have long.

Altar brought his rifle up and took aim at the back of the new man's head. He waited for the man in front of him to get ready to shoot, slowly drawing the trigger back. When the man pulled his trigger, Altar finished his own pull at the same time. The guns went off together.

The man's face exploded into the rock in front of him and he dropped to the ground like he'd been poleaxed, leaving a trail of gore on the stone. Altar didn't see or hear anything, not that he could hear particularly well after the shot. He moved up and still couldn't see Shepard, Smith, or the third cowboy, if he existed.

"Shep!" Altar said. "There's more than one! And they're flanking you!"

A shot followed on Altar's last word, but the bullet didn't hit anywhere close to him. Another shot rang out.

Altar looked back at the horses to ensure he wasn't being flanked himself. He saw some heavy canvas bags on the ground by the tree, stuffed full of something that could easily be gold.

There was no third cowboy, he thought. The extra horse was carrying the gold.

Another shot rang out, followed by a cry of pain.

Altar took off in the direction he'd seen Smith take.

He was close to where Smith had gone into the branches when the outlaw stumbled out and stopped. Blood streamed down Smith's shirt from a wound high up on his chest. The outlaw's eyes went wide, and he raised his rifle.

Altar shot him and was pissed that he'd been forced to kill the man so quickly.

The heavy .44 caliber rimfire bullet hit Smith square in the chest. His rifle fell to the ground as the outlaw staggered backward. He grasped at the branches and trunks of the birch, the bark peeling off in his hands as he sank backward to sit on the ground.

Smith grasped his pistol but only had the strength to pull it halfway free before Altar stepped forward and kicked Smith's gun hand. The revolver's report was loud. The toe of Smith's boot burst open as a cloud of smoke rose from the round's concussion.

Smith's gaze slowly rose from his boot to Altar.

"Shot my own goddamned toes off." Blood leaked from the corner of Smith's mouth. "Never would've guessed another Altar would be the one killed me."

Altar took the Colt from Smith's weak fingers and stuck it in the back of his own pants.

"Where's Bobby?" Altar grabbed Smith's shoulders and shook the outlaw. "Do you know where my brother is?"

"Just ain't right." Smith's voice was growing faint. "Another yella-bellied fucking Altar. Munther'll never believe this."

"Altar?" Shepard wasn't far away, from the sound of his voice. "You all right?"

Altar patted Smith's face to keep him grounded in the moment.

"Where's my brother?" He kept his tone to a whisper.

"Goddamned like to blown my own foot off," Smith said with a strangled laugh. "Be just like your fucking brother."

Altar slapped Smith hard as the outlaw's eyes were closing. Altar could hear Shepard getting closer.

"What do you mean, 'be like my brother'? Where's Bobby?"

Smith looked blankly at Altar's face.

"Who?"

"My brother," Altar said low and willful. "Bobby."

"Can't feel my legs," Smith said. "Bob's always bellyaching about his."

Shepard broke into the clearing and stopped in front of them before Altar could ask Smith any more about his brother. "Where are they going?" he asked instead, hoping Shepard hadn't heard any of his earlier questions.

Smith's head rolled back, his eyes half closed. The outlaw's hand twitched. It took a second movement before Altar realized Smith was beckoning him closer. Altar leaned nearer.

"Bet you'd like to know —" Smith spat a blood-streaked spew into Altar's face. The outlaw's back arched, and whatever else he said in dying rose up out of his throat in red-tinged bubbles and froth.

Chapter 9
Spring Creek

Mounted on his own horse, Altar led the two animals with the dead bodies. The outlaws were tied over their horses' withers to save the saddles from being stained and reducing their resale value. Shepard led the horse with the gold. Dog ran ahead, always foraging for something to eat or piss on. Since Shepard knew the way, they'd ridden all night and now the two men were bone-tired.

It was late the next afternoon, almost evening, when they came through the pass above Spring Creek. The town had two roads going north and south and two more east and west, though only one road in each direction led into the countryside. The buildings were constructed of wood, except the one that Altar figured to be the bank, which was made of fieldstone and some brick.

Verandas ran in front of most of the buildings. The main thoroughfare seemed to be the north and south streets, which accounted for a couple of hotels and saloons. Altar saw that virtually all the windows had been broken out, but whether from gunfire or something else, he couldn't tell. There appeared to be a couple of different stables as well. Smoke rose into the blue, cloudless sky as they followed the road, through the deepening late afternoon shadows, into town.

Houses, and a couple of churches too, made up the outskirts of Spring Creek, and homes continued to dot the open ground outside of town, along with some tents, until plowed fields spread out to the forest.

"Where's that dog of yours?" Shepard asked.

"He'll find us," Altar said. "Always does, scents me out, or my horse."

Shepard shook his head. "Damnedest thing."

Shepard led the way to the marshal's office, where a hand-painted sign over the single door of the log building read, *JAIL*.

A crowd had gathered in the street. Gulliford, in a shirt, trousers with suspenders and no gun rig, spoke to the men. He had a gaggle of rough-looking deputies half-ringed behind him. The marshal stopped midsentence when he recognized Altar and Shepard, his eyes trailing along to the horses being led.

"I take it one of those is Smith?" Gulliford took a puff on his pipe.

"Yep," Shepard said. "And another one of their bunch fancied a ride back as well." Shepard was hoarse, his voice dry from lack of water. Altar had insisted they push hard, except when they had to allow their animals a little relief, but their canteens were long dry. He didn't want to miss riding out with the marshal's new posse. If he was going to save Bobby, he had to be with them.

Gulliford stepped from the gallery into the street. Dean, who had been one of the deputies behind him, hesitated, but followed; his star pinned to his shirt cockeyed. The crowd of men parted to let them through. Gulliford stuck his pipe in his mouth and gripped it with his teeth as he strode up to the trailing horses.

His features set in a grimace, the marshal went to the stranger first and pulled his head up by the hair. He immediately reared back from the dead man's ruined face.

"Hey, Hermann," someone from the crowd said. "Ain't he a-wearing that suit you kept in your window?"

"Sure enough," another said.

A portly man, wearing a starched white shirt and a bow tie under an apron, stepped from the crowd. He was nearly bald and had a waxed mustache looping in curls above his mouth. He moved toward Gulliford slowly like his feet were mired in molasses. The man nodded toward the body when Gulliford looked at him. The marshal stepped back, giving the man access.

The shop owner gasped when he raised the stranger's head.

"Ruined the whole suit," the shopkeep said after a few moments' examination. "Blood and brains all down the shirt and trousers."

"How 'bout them fancy boots?" someone asked. "I'll give ya two bits for 'em?"

The shopkeeper spun around. "Why, those boots are from Mexico City, I'll have you know," he said, sputtering. "They're twenty dollars, I'll thank you very much."

"Not with all that blood on 'em, they ain't," another said, eliciting a guffaw from the crowd.

The shopkeep kept trying to catch the man speaking. "Is that you, Pete?" he said. "You wouldn't know a good pair of boots if they bit you on the —"

"Hold it down," Dean said. "Y'all forgetting what happened here?"

Gulliford walked around the horses to Smith's body. Grabbing the outlaw by the hair, he lifted the dead man's head to look at his face. He turned to Shepard, then looked at Altar.

"Had to kill the both of them?"

"Yep," Altar said. "Afraid so."

Gulliford looked back to Shepard.

"That the way it was, Shep?"

Shepard stared at the marshal for a moment before answering.

"Afraid so, Marshal. Altar here," Shepard nodded toward Altar, "was trying to get Smith to tell him their meeting spot, but the good-for-nothing son of a bitch died too quick." Shepard spat on the ground. Altar was surprised the former deputy was able to muster enough saliva.

"Nothing?" Gulliford asked.

Altar shook his head and pointed to the horse laden with the bags of gold. "Got some of the gold back," he said. "Where do the gang's tracks lead?"

Gulliford looked at Dean.

Then someone from the crowd spoke up.

"Seems like they all left out in different directions," the man said. "Taking two or three horses and wagons with them to spoil the tracks."

Altar looked at Shepard, who met his gaze.

"Guaranteed," Altar said, knowing these outlaws weren't going to make anything easy. He faced the townsman who had been speaking. "Wagons?"

The man nodded. "Sure enough. They rode one in and lit out with two or three."

"More like four, Vern," another person said.

"Four, then."

"What now, Marshal?" a different voice from the crowd asked.

Gulliford took a long pull from his pipe, letting the smoke trickle out of his nose.

"We're gonna form up a posse and go after them, of course." Gulliford exhaled the rest of the smoke from his lungs.

"So's they can come back 'round and rob us some more?" someone else said. "We need to have some men ready for 'em in case they come back."

"Reckon they took all they wanted the first time, Roy," yet another townsman said.

"Now, men." Gulliford raised his arms. "Any a' you want to come along, go get your traps. Bring enough food for a week on the trail. And what guns you can find."

Looks like the gold wasn't all they took, Altar thought.

"When we leaving, Marshal?"

"I reckon it'll take us a spell to get the supplies together," Gulliford said. "Maybe in three hours."

"But the sun's going to set right after, and we ain't going to be much more'n an hour out of town," someone said.

Gulliford looked at the sky as if the time of the day hadn't occurred to him.

"Be here at dawn, then," he said. "We ride shortly after."

The crowd broke up, with the men leaving for their homes or the saloons. Gulliford went into the marshal's office, with Dean trailing behind in his cloud of smoke like a tender railcar following a locomotive on the tracks.

"Trade you." Shepard held up the reins to the horse with the gold. "I'm going to the undertaker if you want to talk to the marshal."

Altar slipped off his mount and tied the animal to a hitching rail. He handed the reins of the horses laden with the bodies to Shepard and took the reins of the other horse, tying it off alongside his own.

"Dean," Altar called. "Gimme a hand."

He had the bags of gold pulled from the horse and on the ground before Dean came out of the office and down from the veranda.

Altar hefted two, while Dean took the third. They carried them through the deputies still standing on the porch, none of whom offered to lend a hand, then into the marshal's office where they dropped them onto the rough-hewn floorboards.

Gulliford was in the back of the first room, pouring a cup of coffee from a pot he'd taken from the stove in the corner. An empty rifle rack was on one wall, a desk and chair across the room from it. The crossbeam that would have secured the weapons in place had been broken, the two halves dangling effetely. The marshal's pipe lay on a tin plate on the desktop. A heavy door, open, led into a back room where iron bars could be seen.

Gulliford set the pot down and turned. "Where's Shep?"

"Undertaker," Altar said, "dropping off Smith and the dandy."

Gulliford didn't say anything, just stayed in the spot where he stood, feet splayed shoulder-width apart. He brought the tin cup near his nose and smelled the steam rising into the stove-heated air of the room. From the aroma, Altar figured it was coffee and was perturbed the marshal hadn't offered any to him.

"Does he know?" Gulliford asked.

Altar crossed his arms and leaned in the open doorframe leading out onto the porch. "Know what?"

Gulliford glanced at Dean, who was propped against the back wall, close to the door leading to the jail cell. The men exchanged knowing looks.

"Did something happen to his family?" Altar asked.

Neither man spoke, but Dean nodded as if in agreement.

"His wife?"

Dean renewed his head motion as if the words weren't utterable.

Gulliford cleared his throat.

"Bess is dead. And his sister, Elizabeth, and her daughter, Molly, were taken."

"Taken?"

"Apparently, the outlaws said they was going to sell them to mountain men," Gulliford said.

"Shep's about to learn of his wife's passing at the undertaker," Altar said. "And that's just not right. How many people killed altogether?"

Gulliford shrugged and looked at Dean.

Dean looked at his feet. "Twenty or so."

"Hope he don't see his wife displayed in a box," Altar said. "Or worse yet, in a pile of bodies."

114

"Lids should be on them boxes," Dean said.

"Not when you got a whole bunch of people to keep straight." Altar turned from the door. "Where's the undertaker?"

"Over east side of town," Gulliford said. "Can't miss it with all the damn coffins they been building."

"If he ain't there," Dean said, "he'll be next door."

"What's next door?" Altar asked, looking over his shoulder at the deputy.

"Saloon."

Chapter 10
He's the Duly Elected
Official for *All* the People

Altar stepped off the boardwalk into the street and glanced about to get his bearings. Sounds of hammering and sawing came from various directions as the townspeople fixed their homes and businesses.

Too bad it wasn't as easy to fix people, he thought.

"C'mon," Gulliford said, having followed him out of the office and off the porch. "I'll walk with you."

They crossed the expanse that was wide enough for a wagon team to completely turn around. The dirt of the street was mostly dry and sprinkled with road apples. It smelled of woodsmoke with the faint hint of horses, and churned earth.

All this death. Altar wondered if the town could recover — and Bobby — could he have been part of this?

No, Altar thought. *He couldn't be. Not my little brother.*

"How is it you came across the second outlaw?" Gulliford asked as he packed his pipe with tobacco.

Altar couldn't decide if he didn't like the marshal or just didn't respect him. He certainly didn't find him to be a particularly good leader of men, and he wouldn't be taking much direction from him if things got thorny.

"We thought we'd caught up to Smith morning before last," Altar finally said. "But when we went to wrangle him, we were surprised by the second dandified outlaw. He was actually the one doing the shooting at your deputy while Smith worked to flank him."

"Wasn't no deputy of mine, he quit, remember?" Gulliford struck a match and held it to the bowl of his pipe. He drew in his breath as he held the flame to the leaf.

"You'd be making a mistake," Altar said. "You don't take him back. He's a good man."

"Now there's a surprise." Gulliford waggled the match out before he flicked it into the dirt. "You thinking I'm making a mistake. I reckon it's a good thing you weren't around for the election, or I might be still panning them streams up yonder in them hills."

"I ain't no lawman," Altar said. "Nor do I have a mind to be."

"And why's that?" Gulliford asked.

"I wouldn't like collecting no tax money," Altar said. "That, and there's too much telling people what to do."

"I reckon you make an exception telling me," Gulliford said. "When you ain't looking for your brother, what is it you do?"

Gulliford stopped to draw on his pipe. Smoke streamed from the man's mouth and nose. The scent reminded Altar of summer berries.

"Farming," Altar said. "But mostly, up until recent, I was soldiering."

"Which side you fight on?"

Altar looked at him. "The Union. You?"

Gulliford ignored the question. "You mostly fight the Confederate States of America or the Indians?"

"Both, depending on which year."

"You get out when the war ended?" Gulliford held his pipe in his mouth with one hand as they continued to walk.

"Nope," Altar said. "Stayed in until my enlistment run out."

"So, after the war was over you took to fighting Indians?" the marshal asked.

"More or less."

"Kind of tight-lipped, ain't you?"

Altar walked a few more steps. "Guess so."

He turned the corner and recognized the change in the town. As they moved down the road, Altar noticed a couple of deputies trailing behind and they weren't bothering to hide what they were doing. Young Dean and another rougher-looking fella, a few days' growth of dark beard on his face.

He and Gulliford seemed to have stepped over a demarcation line of some kind. Low buildings, looking like homesteads, ran the length of the east-west street. Most of the doors to the places were thrown open. Several women, wearing garish dresses or just their undergarments, were sitting in front of one establishment in the shadows of the gallery. A heavyset, dark-haired woman, in a dress that pushed her bosom out, stood when Altar and the marshal got closer. She leaned on the railing into the sunlight, her breasts seemingly defying gravity. She waved.

"Hey, Marshal," she said. "Why don't you visit me no more? Am I too much woman for you?"

Gulliford ignored her, his eyes glued to something on the horizon in front of him.

"Who's that good-looking cowboy?" Her voice was high-pitched and had a nasal twang Altar associated with Southern folk.

"He got any money, or is he a tightwad like you?"

Gulliford's face reddened, and it seemed his teeth would snap his pipe's stem, but his eyes stayed fixed straight ahead as the other women on the porch laughed, sounding like a bunch of honking geese.

The woman pulled one of her ample breasts from her dress and waggled it up and down. "It's almost dinnertime, Marshal. C'mon back, I got your favorite." She pulled the second from the low confines of her dress. "Or was it this one, I don't rightly remember. Don't matter no ways. Y'all come back now, ya hear?"

It looked like Altar wasn't the only one who had little respect for Marshal Gulliford.

"That one of your constituents?" Altar asked, displaying the first grin he'd worn for some time.

"I'm a duly elected official," the marshal said. "I gotta be there for all the people in this town."

"Sounds like you were there for a couple of them ladies, all right."

"You're twisting things, Altar."

Altar shook his head. "I couldn't do that, no sir. There's some people I just don't like and I ain't good pretending I do."

"Why?" Gulliford asked. "You'd just as soon shoot them, I expect."

"I could be wrong," Altar said, with the grin spreading into a genuine smile. "But ain't that the kind of thing she's looking for you to do to her? Shoot her, but not with no six-shooter."

The redness of the marshal's face deepened into crimson as they walked. His pipe trailed a thin cloud of sweet fragrance.

Altar's stomach growled and he was aware he hadn't eaten in hours, nor had any water for that matter. He promised himself he'd get something after they'd seen Shep, maybe get him something too.

Gulliford pointed ahead to a stack of coffins down the street in front of a two-story unpainted frame house with a whitewashed picket fence running around it. "There's the undertaker."

Three horses were tied to the hitching post in front of the mortician's place. One was Shepard's and the other two were the ones the dead outlaws had been riding.

"You think Shep knows about his family?" Gulliford asked.

"I wonder if someone's had the gumption to tell him by now," Altar said.

"I reckon so." Gulliford fidgeted with his pipe. "Should've told him my own self."

"On that we agree, Marshal."

Gulliford's gaze peeled away from the undertaker's place to hold Altar's.

Altar removed his hat and knocked the trail dust from it as he started off down the street, figuring he could take a look-see in the mortician's on the way to the saloon. He could feel the marshal a step or two behind.

Those two deputies, Altar thought, *are sticking closer to us than a couple of ticks on a hound dog. Were they worried I might shoot the marshal?*

There was a row of coffins propped up on the picket fence along the home's front. Some of the wooden boxes were lidless, and others had the lid tacked in place only exposing the head of the deceased. A stack of empty coffins stood at the end nearest to Altar and the marshal as they walked up.

Some of the lids had names hand-painted on, including the ones that were completely closed. One in the middle of the row had *Bessy Shepard* painted in white on the fully closed lid. The paint dripped, as if it had been done too quickly.

Altar looked at Gulliford.

"Some of the folks weren't too comely after," the marshal said. "So, Hans closed them up like he done with Bess."

Altar nodded, looking for whomever was working that he could talk to. On the side of the home, a short, shirtless man with spectacles, wearing pants held up by suspenders, was stooped over, lining up a couple of boards on a sawhorse.

Gulliford pointed to the man. "That's him, Hans Schultz, should you want to talk. He can figure what you're saying, but he don't speak English too good. He mostly talks German." Gulliford took his pipe from his mouth and spoke loudly. "Hans."

The man kept looking down the length of a board he held up along its long axis, holding a shorter piece perpendicular to it.

"Hans," Gulliford said, louder. Then, to Altar: "You got to speak up on account that Hans can't hear too good. The war, you know." The marshal didn't offer any other explanation.

Altar stepped forward and waved his hand. Hans Schultz glanced toward him and straightened, pushing his spectacles off the tip of his nose.

"*Ja,*" he said.

"I'm with Shepard." Altar nodded toward the backyard where he could see the business of building coffins was taking place. Hans's eyes followed. "Where are the bodies Shep brought to you?"

Hans pointed to the backyard, and wiped his face with a handkerchief he produced from a back pocket before stooping down and lifting the boards again.

In the back, Altar found Smith and the other outlaw laid out in boxes, though the dandy's legs were sticking out because he was too tall. A saw in the grass told Altar all he needed to know about how Hans was going to get the man to fit.

The two outlaws were still dressed, but no longer wore any of their firearms, and their boots had been removed and were nowhere in sight. Smith's front was covered in blood, now a crusted brown, that seemed to be sourced from several wounds, while the blood covering the other outlaw all came from his face or what was left of it.

"A .44 makes a man right ugly." Gulliford puffed on his pipe.

Altar didn't take his eyes off the two dead men and was thankful for the alternative scent the marshal's pipe brought along.

"Reckon it does, at that," Altar said.

The marshal walked around the dead men. He puffed on his pipe and studied the bodies, leaving a ring of smoke around the open coffins.

He took the pipe from his mouth and pointed the stem at the unknown outlaw.

"Looks like this fella was shot in the back of the head."

Altar nodded. "Looks that way."

"Wasn't you the one shot them both?"

Altar nodded, before looking at the marshal. "Shepard shot Smith some, guess I was the one who done him in, though."

"Well, we don't look kindly upon back-shooters around here," Gulliford said.

"Back-shooter?" Altar glanced at Gulliford. Had the people of Spring Creek elected the village idiot to be marshal? "Seems to me," Altar pointed at the dead outlaw next to Smith. "I recall this here fella was fixin' to shoot Shepard, like he'd already tried to do three or four times before I shot him."

Gulliford puffed on his pipe.

As Altar was about to continue, Hans patted him on the shoulder.

"Bist du der Mann." Hans made the shape of a revolver with his hand and mimicked shooting it at Smith and the other dead man. *"Der diese beiden getötet hat?"*

Altar turned to face the undertaker, seeing only sincerity in the other man's gaze. Was Schultz asking if he'd been the one who killed these two?

Altar nodded. "Yes, sir."

The undertaker took Altar's hand into his

two calloused ones and shook them vigorously.

"*Danke, mein Herr,*" Hans said. "*Danke.*"

Gulliford frowned.

Altar half-turned to face the marshal. "Don't seem to bother your undertaker none, whether I back-shot him or not."

"Don't reckon it does," Gulliford said. "But neither is he a duly elected official of the people of Spring Creek with an expectation to uphold the law."

Altar waved the marshal's words away. "Shep could've been up here alongside his poor wife, wasn't for me."

Altar stepped closer to the unidentified dead man and crouched. He took the man's chin and turned his head to see his profile, then he turned it to see the other side. With his free hand, Altar fingered a flap of skin back to the man's cheek. There was a blue powder burn beneath the blood-soaked flesh that obviously preceded their shootout. Altar turned the wound so Gulliford could see.

"Want to get a better look at this here burn," Altar said. "Maybe we can figure who he is on account of it. You got some of those Wanted posters in your office?"

Gulliford smirked and nodded. "Might have a few." He drew on his pipe. "Why?"

"To go through them for descriptions." Altar gestured toward the two dead outlaws. "Maybe we can put a name on this here burn scar fella or see if Smith's that one's real name."

Gulliford's mouth puckered around his pipe's stem as smoked leaked from his nose.

"Maybe there'd be some reward money," the marshal said. "Is that what you're really driving at?"

"Any reward money can go to the townsfolk for all I care. We figure out who one or two of these guys are, we might know who we're dealing with, as they tend to run in packs."

Altar shrugged as he stood. He'd already gone through the men's pockets looking for any clues as to who they were, back when he and Shepard first loaded their bodies on the horses, and found nothing.

"Don't you reckon." The marshal blew out a cloud of smoke. "These outlaws would've probably burned up any posters we had after they killed Deputy Cobb." Gulliford cleared his throat. "They sure enough emptied the rifle rack and the cartridge locker."

"Still be worth a look-see," Altar said. "Be good to know who these boys are." *Except of course, leaving my brother out of it.*

Gulliford nodded and called to one of the deputies standing on the other side of the street. When the man came over, the marshal instructed him to go back and look for the Wanted handbills. If he couldn't find any, Gulliford said to have Eppley go to the telegraph office to see if they had some and wire for wanted outlaw descriptions, and to have some handbills brought up on the next stage or with the mail carrier.

"Won't do us no good if we don't have them handy in the office," Gulliford said. "But they might be helpful should we bring some of them boys back to town with us later."

"Might at that." Altar shifted his attention back to the dead outlaws, but he didn't find anything other than the powder burn and Smith's facial scar that might help identify them. But right now he had to check on Shepard.

Chapter 11
It's time to ride

The front door of the saloon was propped open with a woodcutter's axe. A side door was also ajar, though Altar couldn't tell how it was being held open. The saloon was dark and stuffy and hot. It took a few seconds for his eyes to adjust to the shadows. Altar took his hat off, though it didn't help his being able to see.

Shepard was standing at what served as the bar, a wooden rafter board with a slight bow resting on sawhorses. He had several men grouped around him, and one woman. Shepard's head hung low, his shoulders drooped, and his elbows looked to be resting heavy on the wood. A bottle sat on the beam in front of him; it only had a couple of fingers' worth of brown liquid left. Several small glasses were scattered around.

Another beam ran against the wall behind the sawhorses, stocked with a few liquor bottles. A fat man in a bowler and a grime-stained apron prowled between the two surfaces, wiping a short glass down with a towel.

Altar hoped the bottle hadn't been full when Shepard arrived. He, along with the marshal, stepped over to stand near the group. Someone looked around, and then whispered something to those gathered. They dispersed without saying anything, leaving Shepard and the woman, who was an arm's length away, alone.

Altar stepped to the bar, close enough that his arm nudged Shepard's. When the man in the bowler caught his eye, Altar raised his hand. He glanced at the marshal, who shook his head. Altar displayed one finger, and the man set the glass in his hand down in front of him.

"Mind if I have me a swig from your bottle?" Altar asked.

Shepard's head swiveled an inch, far enough so one eye could see Altar.

"Ain't my bottle."

Altar knew Shepard's voice was gravelly from miles of caked dust because he'd eaten the same. But now Shepard's tone had the edge of alcohol to it. Altar poured himself half a glass of the liquor, leaving a finger's worth at the bottom. He held it to his nose.

Whiskey.

"I'm sorry to hear about your family." Altar assumed the former deputy had been told already. He belted the firewater down his gullet, feeling the excruciating burn all the way to his toes.

Shepard nodded. " 'Preciate your kindness."

"But now, get sober," Altar said. "Let's go get them girls of yours back."

"I'll be sober right enough when time comes to ride after them sons of bitches," Shepard said in a low growl. "Ain't nobody gonna run off with my baby sister and her daughter. And any who got the gumption to try better be prepared to meet the Lord Almighty right quick."

"I'm fixin' to go," Altar said. "Right now, if you're interested." He poured himself another splash of whiskey, emptying the bottle, more to keep it from Shepard's glass.

Shepard looked at him with both eyes from under heavy brows and trail-stringy hair.

"Don't pull my leg none, John," he said.

"Not much of a leg puller." Altar drained the whiskey glass. The second wave was every bit as substantial as the first, especially on an empty stomach. "Got our work cut out for us, though. I got a suspicion this is a right slippery bunch of cutthroats."

Shepard turned onto an elbow, facing Altar, and stared. After a moment, he nodded.

"Okay," he said. "I'm sober right enough, count me in."

"Count you in on what?" Gulliford asked as he pushed forward. "On what?"

Shepard strained a little as he stretched to see the marshal.

"Going after those murdering, raping sons of bitches."

"At first light," Gulliford said.

Shepard shifted his gaze back to Altar, who shook his head.

"This afternoon," Altar said. "Soon as I can rustle up some supplies." He fished in his pocket for a coin to pay for the whiskey as the barkeep stepped over.

"You're Altar, right?" The man grabbed the bottle and fingered the glasses together into a bunch. "The one who shot them two ne'er-do-wells over to the undertaker's?"

Altar nodded.

"Then don't worry about it none," the barkeep said. "On the house." Hands full of empty glasses, the man walked away.

"We're riding out first thing in the morning," the marshal said around the pipe in his mouth.

"Don't you think we'd better get on that

trail right away, on account of those women they took?" Altar asked.

"Don't fret none," the marshal said. "People said the outlaws were gonna sell them girls to mountain men, but they got to keep them pristine so's they can get top price."

Altar shook his head. "So, you're expecting outlaws to keep their word?"

"What's a few hours when they have a couple of days on us already?" Gulliford said. "Besides, they've at least one wagon, probably two, maybe even three. We should be able to catch them right quick."

"Regardless of what they've done," Altar said. "These men are seasoned veterans and are more dangerous than your average outlaw. Do not underestimate them."

Gulliford waved him off. Then he pulled something small from his pocket and rubbed it with his thumb as if he wasn't sure what to do with the object. After a couple of moments, he held it out to Shepard, while he looked at Altar, his eyes seemingly daring Altar to say anything.

It was Shepard's badge.

Shepard stared at the dull star. Then he looked up and waited for Gulliford's gaze to return to him.

"All due respect, Marshal," Shepard said.

"But I'm throwing in with Altar here, on account of I seen him work and I reckon he knows what he's doing."

Gulliford stared at Shepard, then shifted to Altar as the color in the marshal's face reddened once again. He hitched up his pants.

Altar wondered, since the man wasn't heeled, what could be making his pants droop so's he needed to keep pulling them up? Maybe the responsibility of being the duly elected marshal?

"And exactly how're you going to throw in with him," the marshal said, "when I'm gonna lock him up?"

"Don't seem too locked up to me," Shepard said.

Altar stifled a laugh, not wanting to aggravate the marshal any further than Shepard already had, but he couldn't help grinning.

"I'm headed to Judge Black's house as soon as we're done here, to enter into conversation with the good magistrate surrounding the circumstances of my investigation to this point, and I suspect I'll be swearing out a warrant lickety-split."

"You're serious," Shepard said. "And just what in God's name would you lock him up for?"

"Back-shooting," the marshal said.

"You mean back-shooting the fella that was fixin' to shoot me?"

"One and the same," Gulliford said. "And we don't know for certain that was what the feller was up to, he might well have been trying to scare you off. Fact is, you don't know, ain't no one knows."

"He came mighty close to putting a hole in my ass more than once." Shepard's face colored as bright as Gulliford's.

"But he didn't shoot you, did he?" Gulliford blew twin geysers of gray-white smoke from his nostrils as if to the emphasize the point. "Seems that reflects some on his intentions."

"Wasn't for no lack of trying," Altar said.

"What about Smith?" Shepard said. "You gonna say he didn't kill Conner?"

Gulliford took a deep draw on his pipe. After a moment in which he stared at Shepard, he blew the smoke from his lungs.

"Ain't nobody saw who cut Conner," Gulliford said. "Just as easy could've been Altar here done it and blamed it on Smith."

"I recall Conner saying that Smith was the one who gutted him."

Altar stepped forward to stand in between the two men, a grin on his face.

"Marshal," he said. "Why don't you go

talk to your judge and leave Shep and me alone to commiserate and plan."

Gulliford took another puff on his pipe, his face now crimson. He looked from Altar to Shepard.

"Be a disgrace to your lovely wife's memory throwing in with this no-account backshooter," Gulliford said. "Guess you ain't the man I thought you was."

Finally, he spun on his heel and walked out the front door, his lone remaining deputy steps behind.

Shepard pushed off the bar to follow, his mouth turned down and his nostrils flared. Altar put a hand on Shepard's chest and held him back.

"Let them go," Altar said. "Why don't you get us something hot and I'll go to the mercantile for the rest of the supplies."

"I been knowing that man for a long spell," Shepard said. "He ain't got no call to speak to me like that."

"Shep." Altar's palm stayed on the man's chest, which was heaving with his emotion. "I'm hungry. Get us something to eat before we're back on trail rations."

Shepard stood his ground, his weight against Altar's hand. After a moment, something dark passed behind Shepard's eyes, then his mouth twisted into a grim line beneath his mustache.

"Let me see what I can fetch up." Shepard grabbed his hat from the bar and strode out of the side exit, with a loud bang of the door. As Altar was about to follow the marshal out the front, he felt a hand on his arm, pulling heavily.

He looked down into the eyes of the woman who'd been an arm's length from Shepard the whole time they'd talked. She'd mostly had her shoulder turned away from them, and Altar hadn't noticed before that her face was bruised and she had a fat lip. She was plump, had long hair the color of a dun horse tied up on her head, and wore a dress with a high neck and a skirt with a dirty hem that rustled on the wooden floor. The woman seemed younger than Altar had originally thought, maybe twenty.

"Excuse me," she said.

He didn't respond but held her gaze.

"I couldn't help but overhear you talking with Deputy Shepard." She kept her hand on his arm, her grip tight, supporting her weight. "I was wanting to tell you something."

"Yes, ma'am." Altar leaned toward the door, so she understood he was in a hurry.

The woman shifted as if scanning the room. "You mind stepping over there?" She pointed at the far corner of the saloon, dimmed by shadows.

Figuring she must've suffered at the hands of the outlaws, Altar took a deep breath and nodded. A few moments wouldn't matter none. He followed her over to the dark corner. The woman limped and Altar couldn't tell what she was wearing on her feet, if anything, as she made her way to the corner.

When she got to the wall, she leaned on the wainscoting's top edge. Altar was worried that it would give as she settled on it.

"What's wrong with your leg?" he asked.

"Oh, it's nothing," she said. "Don't fret none about it, it'll pass."

"I'm sorry about whatever those men did to you," he said.

"They done a whole lot worse to other folks," she said. "I got off easy compared to a few, like Mrs. Shepard." Tears brimmed in her eyes. "I sure do hope Deputy Shepard will be all right. He's such a kind man, and to lose his wife like that, her a God-fearing woman and all, just ain't right."

"What did you want to tell me?" He squinted at her. "I don't even know your name."

"It's not important." She sniffled. "What's important is you get those men and make them pay for what they done. Someone's gotta stand for all the dead townsfolk."

Altar nodded. "That's what we're fixin' to do, all right. Soon as we get some supplies."

The woman glanced around, and Altar was taken again with how young her face looked, yet her eyes were burdened and haunted, underscored by dark circles more expected on someone nearly twice her age.

Was she even eighteen, he wondered?

Her gaze hardened and she looked him in the eye.

"I overheard those men talking some when they was in here." She darted glances around the wall.

Altar followed her gaze and realized the spots on the wall, until now unnoticed, were actually bullet holes. That got him wondering if the rafter board had always been in place, or did the townspeople improvise?

"They was talking about the mountains, going across them or into them or some such."

"All right," he said. "You know where?"

"One of them kept saying he didn't want to ride into Indian country," she said. "He was downright bellyaching about it."

He waited for her to go on as she grew pale in front of him, and her hand on the wainscoting seemed to twist as if her grip had slipped. He reached out for her and she fell into his arms. He glanced about and saw a chair. He hooked a toe around one of the spindle legs and pulled it over, then lowered the girl down until she was sitting.

"Pardon me, ma'am." He knelt in front of her and lifted the hem of her dress to reveal a bare foot, swollen and discolored a purplish blue, with toes bloated and black, oozing blood from around the embedded nails.

It was Altar's turn to reel back. He hadn't seen much worse in the war, except maybe what wasn't still attached to a leg.

She sobbed.

"They said I was a bad bar girl," she said. "And they commenced to stomping and kicking me 'til I can't remember. Afterward, they —"

"Shhhh." Altar stood and glanced around the room. "Somebody get the doctor."

The voices hushed.

Then the barkeep in the bowler said, "You heard the man."

A young boy, maybe nine, ran from the saloon.

Altar knelt again, unwilling to raise her skirt any further for fear of what he might see. He already knew the likelihood of her keeping the foot was largely dependent upon the skills of the town's surgeon.

"What more can you tell me about those men?" He needed to know the information, but also wanted to keep her mind off her ruined foot. "Anything you can remember."

"Just that one of them was scared of the Indians and they were headed to the mountains."

"And you don't know which ones?"

"Afraid not." Her face grew contorted from what he could only surmise to be pain.

He leaned into her and lowered his voice. "Did you hear anything that would make you think one of them was called Bobby or Bob?"

"No, sir," she said with shallow, winded breath. He'd heard many a wounded man on the battlefield talk so breathlessly, some right before they died.

"Robert, or any names at all?"

"No, sir."

The fat man in the bowler came over. "What's wrong with her?"

"Outlaws stomped on her," Altar said. "Her foot's busted up real good, probably all sorts of broken bones."

The man knelt and took the woman's hand. "Sent Pedro to get the doc," he said to her in a surprisingly soft voice. "I suspect he'll be here right quick." He looked toward the bar and stretched his neck as if to get a better view. "Bristol."

A short man standing at the front of the bar turned.

"Bring me a bottle of whiskey."

The short man retrieved a bottle from behind the rafter bar and brought it over, handing the bottle to the man in the bowler.

"Thank ye," the man said, uncorking the whiskey. He held the bottle up to the woman's mouth. "Have ye a swallow there, Maggie."

She took a sip. When she swallowed, she convulsed and coughed, covering her mouth with her hand.

"You should've told us," the fat man said. "Ain't no need to suffer like this."

After she'd quit coughing, she said, "People a lot more important than me need the doctor's attention." She took another pull from the whiskey, smaller this time. "I'll be fine."

"Like hell, young lady," said an older man who had walked up. "Make room." The man elbowed his way past Altar and knelt next to the guy in the bowler.

As Altar stepped out of the way, the young woman reached toward him.

"I think they said something about Merritt," she said. "Does that sound like it could be someone?"

"I'll sure find out," Altar said. "Thank you."

The man who'd just arrived lifted the hem of her dress up above her knees. The black and blue and purple marks climbed her leg and Altar wondered how the hell those men had done that much harm. Looked more like a herd of horses had stomped her.

With the young girl getting assistance, Altar decided it was as good a time as any to go. With his hat still in his hand he stepped around the swelling crowd and walked toward the front door.

How the hell did Bobby get wrapped up with a bunch like this, he wondered. What else had they done that he didn't even know about. It like to make him sick. He hoped he could save Bobby, and not have to put him down like a rabid dog. He was glad his mama didn't know.

This was getting more and more complicated. He took in a deep breath and stepped onto the porch, looking for the general store.

And then a voice behind him called out.

"Altar!"

Chapter 12
Change of Plans

He turned to see the marshal standing by one of the veranda posts, Deputy Dean and another deputy he didn't recognize behind him.

Altar was about to speak when something hard and heavy smashed into his skull just behind his ear. The porch swirled and blurred as he sank to a knee. Someone planted a booted foot with a sharp heel in his back and shoved him down the steps into the street.

"Get his gun," the marshal said.

Altar felt someone tug the leather thong from the revolver's hammer spur and pull his Remington from its holster.

"What're you doing, Gulliford?" Altar spoke through clenched teeth, forcing the words out.

"Placing you under arrest."

"For what?" Pain radiated from the back of his head like ripples in a lake, except these ripples felt like they were twelve feet tall and all aflame.

"Suspicion." It sounded as if Gulliford was still on the veranda and not on the street, like he couldn't get himself dirtied. "Don't need no warrant to arrest you. Judge Black will see it my way sure enough."

Altar felt hands take his arms and lift him to his feet. He swayed, the ground spun.

"Bind his hands right quick," Gulliford said. "If he gives you any trouble, tap him on the head some more. Just be careful not to kill him."

Altar's hands were brought in front of his body, and someone looped a coarse rope around his wrists and bound him tight before he could get his mind straight.

A hard shove from behind pushed him forward.

"When's his trial, Marshal?"

"I reckon once we get back from chasing down them outlaws," Gulliford said. "I'll see where things stand then."

"My hat." Altar tried to turn around, swaying, and feeling his stomach roil. He was afraid he was about to vomit.

"Ain't gonna need no hat where you're going," a man said. "Sun don't shine up in that cell none."

" 'Sides," Dean said. "You don't want to

get no blood on it."

Altar's gait was unsteady, especially with his eyes closed to slits against the bright sun and the ever-pulsing pain in his skull. The trip back to the jail took longer than the trek to the saloon in the first place. The undertaker stopped hammering long enough to watch the little procession trundle by, the whole time shaking his head as if in disbelief.

The marshal led with Altar and another deputy next, followed closely by the deputy directly behind him, always pushing and shoving for him to quicken his pace, and then Dean.

Altar fought down the nausea that threatened to unleash the whiskey and whatever water he'd taken in recently. As they rounded the corner close to the jail, he saw Dog curled up on the porch asleep, where his horse was tied off.

"We ain't gonna have any trouble with your dog, are we?" Gulliford asked. "Hate for my men to have to shoot him."

When Altar stepped on the stair leading up the veranda, Dog's head lifted. He growled deep in his chest as he took in the four men.

"I'll shoot the son of a bitch, he give me a reason," the deputy directly behind Altar said. "Blow the top of his head clean off."

"Quiet," Altar said to Dog.

The growling lowered but was still a rumble as they passed the animal. Gulliford remained in the street as if he was uneasy passing too close to Dog.

"If you harm this animal, Deputy," Altar said. "There won't be a place you could hide that I wouldn't find you."

The deputy pushed Altar against the log wall of the jail. "Stay," he said.

Another deputy, this one tall and lanky, stepped over from farther down the veranda.

The deputy directly behind Altar said, "If he makes to run, Eppley, shoot him." The tall lanky man nodded.

The deputy stepped from behind Altar and fumbled with some keys on his belt. The man was short, had a tangle of orangish sweaty hair plastered to the back of his neck that was visible from under his dusty black Stetson, and wore boots with an extended Mexican heel. Altar figured he was trying to look taller than he really was. The deputy thrust the key into the lock and opened the door, stepping into the jail.

As the short deputy walked into the office, presumably to open the cell, Altar felt another presence lurking behind him. Then someone leaned in close. It was the tall, lanky deputy called Eppley, who couldn't have been more than eighteen.

"I ain't ever shot no dog," Eppley said. "Not about to now, but Harmon there will, probably enjoy it."

After a few long moments, Deputy Harmon stuck his head out of the open door. "Bring him."

"What were you standing on when you hit me?" Altar asked as he stepped past Harmon. "A crate?"

Eppley gently pushed Altar's back as they moved past the deputy into the marshal's office.

Harmon watched with hard eyes, his mouth set in a thin pale line like a scar, as Eppley marched Altar across the office into the second room where the cell was located. A pile of Wanted posters was stacked on the desk, a fist-sized stone on top to keep them from blowing away. He saw the beat-up Stetson was hung on a peg in the wall.

Altar walked into the second room, which was dark from a lack of windows or any other light. The smell was fetid with the odor of sweat and fear. He went into the cell and turned, holding his bound wrists out.

Eppley closed the cell door with a clang, ignoring his offered hands, and locked the mechanism, withdrawing the iron key. Altar stuck his wrists out from between the bars. Eppley stuck the key in his belt, then pulled a knife from a sheath and sawed through the rope.

"I wouldn't recommend teasing Harmon none about his height," Eppley said in a whisper as he cut through the last strand. "He's kind of sensitive about it."

"As a matter of fact, that was my hope."

Eppley shook his head. "Ain't no good gonna come of it you keep it up." He found a long kitchen match from somewhere and took to lighting several sconces on the wall that held a candle each.

"Appreciate your concern, friend," Altar said. "Think I'll take my chances."

He crossed over to the bunk and lay down despite the smell of mold emanating from the mattress of straw. The ache in his head pounded to the rhythm of his heart, threatening to blast his skull in a hundred pieces. He was careful to tilt his head to keep the injury from touching anything. With his arm over his eyes, Altar tried to sleep, which he knew to be futile, as long as his head hurt like it did.

Before Eppley left, he relit one of the candles that had gone out. All the sconces were well out of arm's reach.

After a while, Altar heard boots on the floor outside the door.

"The guilty always sleep," Harmon said. " 'Cause they ain't got no decency."

Altar moved his arm and cracked open an eye to see the deputy standing in the doorway.

"Ain't a whole lot else to do," Altar said.

"You hungry?" Harmon asked.

Altar was reluctant to admit anything to Harmon; he'd known any number of men like him in his life. Harmon was a bully, even being so short. But truth be told, Altar was hungry, and it might prove a good insight into the diminutive deputy's attitude toward him.

Altar nodded.

"Good." Harmon slammed the door closed.

Altar almost smiled, or would have if it wouldn't have hurt. Harmon didn't leave much uncertainty as to how he felt. Though it had never been much in doubt, Eppley was right. Altar hadn't met too many short cowboys who weren't carrying that heavy chip on their shoulders.

Altar must've dozed off. Sometime later, he awoke to voices coming from the other side of the door. He thought he recognized

Shepard's voice, and maybe the marshal's. The door swung open. Shepard stood in the doorway.

"You all right?" Shepard asked, stepping into the room.

Gulliford walked over to the doorway and leaned against the jamb.

Did he not trust Shepard?

Altar sat up and instinctively reached for the lump on his head. He winced and felt a sticky mess behind his ear.

"Yep." Altar stood. He no longer felt dizzy or nauseated, but the inside of his head rang with the hammers of a dozen blacksmiths.

"Marshal." Shepard turned from Altar. "You know this ain't right, locking this man up like this. He was protecting me, for God's sake."

"If that's the case," Gulliford said, "he'll be a free man once I've conducted my investigation."

"Conducting an investigation?" Shepard asked. "Wait one cotton-picking second, you done already conducted an investigation."

"The hell you say," Gulliford said.

"Well," Shepard said. He ticked off on his fingers. "You talked to me. And you talked to Altar. The only other two people that were there is laying in boxes over to Hans's place. Me and Altar told you how it was, which should be good enough. So, just what're you investigating?"

"Shep," the marshal said. "You don't understand."

"I worked for you for what? Five, six years?"

Gulliford nodded.

"What don't I understand?" Shepard asked. "I ran this office when you wasn't here. What don't I understand? Tell me, please."

Gulliford glared at Shepard. Nothing passed between the two men except hard stares.

"My little sister and niece are out there." Shepard's long arm shot out and he pointed with a gloved hand. "Out there somewhere with those two-legged animals and you're putting an able-bodied man who could track these monsters in jail? And you're gonna have to leave a deputy or two here to keep an eye on him?"

"Shep," Gulliford said. "I think your emotions got the better of you and I'm going to forget this lapse in judgment."

"Lapse in judgment?" Shepard's hands balled into fists. "If you wasn't the marshal I'd knock you on your ass faster than a hog would jump on slop."

"Get out of this office before I have you

locked up," Gulliford said, his face deepening into a shade of crimson that bordered on purple. "You can't see past that nose on your face." Gulliford pointed at Altar. "Way I see it, he's likely part of that gang. He ain't been around here until after they passed through. He's not army. He's not anything, just a drifter who says he's tracking them outlaws. Now, ask yourself, why's one man tracking a pack of twelve or thirteen outlaws? Don't make no sense. What's he going to do when he catches them? Join them, I say."

The marshal stepped up to Shepard, whose chest heaved with emotion, and put his hand on the man's shoulder.

"Go home," Gulliford said. "Mourn Bess. If you want to be in on the posse, be here at first light."

Shepard smacked the marshal's hand off his shoulder and strode from the office without looking back.

Gulliford stood in place as if he was affixed to the floor, but his eyes followed Shepard out the door. After a few moments, Gulliford stepped to the door leading onto the porch.

"What're you doing, Shep?"

Shepard's voice drifted in faintly, muffled by the log walls. "Taking his horse and kit down to the stable. Ain't fair to the animal to just leave it here saddled."

"You taking the dog, too?" Harmon asked.

"That's up to Dog," Shepard said.

Chapter 13
Lord, let not Bobby
be among these

Gulliford returned and leaned against the doorjamb once again, his tin cup in his hand. Altar sat back on the bunk against the log wall and practically salivated to the aroma of coffee wafting from Gulliford's cup. The two men held each other's gaze for a long moment until the marshal finally looked away. He turned to look over his shoulder as if something had required his attention.

Altar grinned. The marshal wasn't much of an actor, nor a lawman for that matter.

Gulliford returned his gaze to Altar, who was staring right at him. The marshal's eyes quickly lowered.

After a few moments, Gulliford looked up.

"Marshal," Altar said. "I was hoping you'd let me glance through those posters you got on your desk."

"They're handbills," Gulliford said. He turned and walked to his desk, then came back with the stack of papers clutched in one hand and his coffee in the other. The marshal offered the stack through the bars. "Or postcards, though I suppose you could call them posters of a sort, if you didn't know any better."

Altar stood and took them. Much of the dizziness he'd experienced earlier was gone. If he were a praying man, which he wasn't, he'd sure be down on his knees praying that he didn't find his brother's name or description on one of these postcards.

It'll sure kill our mama if she were to find out, he thought.

And if he did find Bobby among those described, he wouldn't be the one to tell her.

The smell of the coffee made him forget his nausea, and his stomach growled.

"Smells good," Altar said before he could even think, as if he couldn't hold it in. He was hungry, and very thirsty for that matter.

"It sure does," Gulliford said. "Tastes even better."

Altar looked at him — so the marshal had a sadistic streak, which would go a long way to explain why he acted the way he did. Altar's academy commander all over again.

He sat and started to leaf through the

handbills, trying not to show any aggravation on his face. Who knew when he'd get something to eat or drink, but he wouldn't beg.

Hell, he wouldn't even ask.

Most of the postcards had names on them, and others contained descriptions of the men and their crimes. Maybe he'd come across the outlaw the bar girl, Maggie, had mentioned, named Merritt, he thought. What was that son of a bitch's name Smith and the camp guards had talked about? Munther?

The cell took up most of the room, and what illumination didn't come from the door, came from the candles whose light flickered and danced. The shifting of what little light there was made it hard to read, and his head hurt so bad it made him squint half the time. The papers were dirty and had been handled by who knows how many men, most of whom worked outside with their hands.

"So, I'm trying to reckon this out in my mind, maybe you can help me," Gulliford said. "When we first met, you told me you were looking for your brother Robert or some such. And then, you're telling me you're following this pack of killers."

The marshal took a sip of his coffee.

Altar didn't say anything as he searched the postcards. He sure didn't want to find Bobby's description, but Altar was hoping to find Smith's description or name, or the man with the powder burn. That would help him identify the outlaws beyond what he'd learned from the Camp Douglas guards, that the leader was supposedly named Charlie Munther.

Gulliford continued.

"You got me to thinking. Is it one or the other, or now, I'm thinking, maybe both?" He waited and watched Altar. The marshal took another sip. "Maybe your brother is one of those outlaws? Maybe you're looking to join them?"

Altar kept reading the postcards. He bent the corner of one describing a big killer who was called Grapeshot Charlie, on account of his penchant for shooting people with a revolver that used buckshot instead of bullets. He stopped. Was that something he'd heard about before? He couldn't quite remember but thought he should.

"I have lots of questions," Gulliford said.

Altar focused on the papers in front of him. He didn't want to give the marshal any tells to feed his already damn accurate suspicions.

And just when I figured this man wasn't any

good at his job, Altar thought, *the son of a bitch surprises me.*

Just like his mama had always said, "Don't jump to no conclusions about nobody."

"I know you killed two of them." Gulliford spoke low. "And you certainly didn't like Smith, and he didn't like you. That was right apparent. But these gangs are known to have squabbles amongst their rabble, ain't that so, Harmon?"

Harmon's strong voice came from the other room as if he was in front of a congregation. "That's right, Marshal."

"I know Shep's thinking you saved his life," Gulliford said. "And maybe you did. But I sure would be feeling a stitch or two better if I had the chance to ask a couple of these no-accounts if they recognize you, or your name."

Altar put the handbills down on his lap and finally looked at Gulliford.

"That's a right lot of thinking you done, Marshal." Altar interlinked his fingers and rested them on the postcards as if he were in church. "But what I told you was that I left Missouri looking for my brother, which is true."

He waited to make sure Gulliford was following his speech. The marshal just stared at him.

"But — and this is where your thinking takes a wrong turn. I told you I was looking for my brother when I came across the massacre. After seeing all those people murdered, I was just following the outlaws. I'll take up the search for my brother later."

"Why's that?" Gulliford asked. "You didn't know any of those people. They were all strangers to you."

"I seen a good many more dead people over the years than I care to count," Altar said. "And in the war, so much of it was brutal and seemed so senseless. But what happened out there." His head bobbed once in the direction he thought lay the remains of the wagon train. "Those people didn't have nothing worth taking, didn't even have a herd of cattle, but those murdering sons of bitches killed every last one, and now they got to pay. Someone has to stand for the dead."

The marshal nodded but his face gave no tell of whether he believed the story or not.

"You sure did have a lot to say about what I should do, and still do, for that matter. You keep telling me what the outlaws are going to do and such, how they stuck the arrow in by hand, and led the posse out of town so they could rob it. It's like you know this gang that you claim not to know."

"All I said was that I recognized the tactics being used as being like those used by some of the guerrilla fighters I fought when I rode with the First Missouri."

"Gorillas?" Gulliford's eyebrows rose. "And exactly what is a gorilla? Ain't like we got hairy apes roaming these parts."

"Local partisan fighters who engage in irregular warfare."

"They teach you that in the First Missouri, too?"

"No sir," Altar said. "The United States Military Academy."

The marshal's eyes widened as if he wasn't expecting that answer. "So, you're a graduate of the United States Military Academy at West Point?"

"Not so much." Altar lowered his voice. He returned to his search of the handbills, not wanting to get into that discussion. "Not a graduate, though I went there for a time."

Chapter 14
Decisions

"Now, you being a graduate of that there institution, *that* would've surprised me." Gulliford stood there for a moment, then he turned and walked out, closing the room's door behind him.

After a time, long enough to plant a mighty ache both in the front and the back of his head, Altar put the handbills down. He'd read enough descriptions in the shadows of the cell about the men and their crimes that he'd just as soon go to sleep. There'd been no discernible sign of Bobby anywhere. But the longer he sat there, the farther away that band of outlaws, and possibly his brother, got with those poor women they'd taken. Was it just Shepard's daughter and her child, or were there other women, and if so, how many?

At some point, Altar heard voices in the front office, but he was unable to discern what was being said or by whom, though he suspected Gulliford and Harmon had left. Surely, there was someone keeping an eye on him, or at least the door leading into the cell room. The three candles in the sconces had all burned out, and with the sundown, the only light came from a lantern in the other room that drifted in under the door.

Voices roused Altar just before the door was yanked open. Shepard stood in the doorway, something under his arm, and with a lantern in his hand, saying something about being quiet to whoever else was in the room.

"Checking on ya," Shepard said, turning to Altar. "Was told you took a pretty good lick in the back of the head."

"It's all right," Altar said. "My head's harder than Harmon's pistol butt."

Shepard stepped in toward the cell and held out the object he'd cradled under his arm.

"Cowboy shouldn't be without his hat." Shepard handed Altar's hat to him. "Eppley done searched it already, ain't got no firearms, knives, or cell door keys in it."

"Thanks." Altar set it on the bunk, thinking his head was a tad bit tender as of yet. Shepard backed up to the doorway.

"Scoot me one of them chairs, Dillon." Someone out of Altar's line of sight slid a chair to Shepard. The former deputy put the lantern on the floor, pulled the chair around, and sat. Looking over his shoulder he said, "Is this far enough away?"

"Yes, sir," Eppley said.

Shepard turned his attention back to Altar.

"Is Dog all right?" Altar asked.

"Yep," Shepard said. "Took him home and he was asleep in the shed when I come down here. That critter can eat, let me tell you." Shepard laughed, though it rang hollow.

"Thanks for looking after him and my horse." Altar rubbed his face, feeling a little of the tension wash from his body knowing his animals were seen to. "He don't get along with many, but seems to take to you fine. He sure does eat more than his share when he's a mind to."

"Well," Shepard said. "It's kind of nice to have the critter around since the house is so goddamned quiet, what with Bess dead and Elizabeth and Molly shanghaied."

Altar sat silent, not knowing what to say.

"Speaking of bellies," Shepard said. "They feed you?"

"Nope."

Shepard turned in his chair again. "Run over to Maple's and get this fella something to eat. Ain't civil to not feed him."

"Sir, you know I can't do that," Eppley said. "With all due respect, why don't you go get him some food."

" 'Cause," Shepard said. "I ain't a deputy no more and she'll charge me a pretty penny, where she won't charge you none."

"Sir, the marshal told me he had to stay under my control," Eppley said. "I go across the street and he's not going to be, is he?"

Shepard nodded. "We could always put him in irons and take him over there. He'd still be in your care."

Eppley laughed. "I don't think so, sir. Do I look slow or something?"

"Don't reckon you really want me to answer that, boy." Shepard rubbed his chin. "How about keep the front door of the jail open and go knock on Maple's door. I'll stand on the porch so as you can see me. Give Maple the order, she can have one of the girls run it over. Bet you're hungry too, ain't ya? I know I am and it's well past suppertime."

Eppley didn't say anything for a bit. Finally, Altar heard a chair being pushed back and the floor creaked under boots.

"Matter of fact, sir." Eppley stepped into Altar's view. "I'm hungry as a hog in heat. Give me your keys to the office door and stand on the porch where I can see you, while I go over and order up some vittles." Eppley shooed a protesting Shepard out of the office and onto the veranda, followed by the sound of the door closing. Then Altar heard the lock as the two men yapped about something he couldn't make out.

After a quarter hour or so, Altar heard the key in the lock again. The door opened and Shepard came in holding a steaming plate in each hand. Eppley came in behind him, a plate in one hand, and a small wicker basket in the other. They crossed out of Altar's sight, presumably for the desk. Eppley crossed back and put a hunk of pig iron in front of the door to hold it open.

A few minutes later, Eppley walked into the cell room holding a pair of shackles. He stared at Altar for a few moments before speaking.

"Mister Altar," Eppley said. "I been knowing Mister Shepard my whole life." The deputy jangled the shackles in one hand. "He's telling me you're a man of your word. Is that a fact?"

"I am," Altar said.

"If you give me your word that you'll not try and escape, I'll let you eat by the desk with one hand shackled to the chair."

"You have my word."

Eppley shackled Altar's hands in front of him through the bars before he opened the cell door. Then he led him out into the front room and sat him at the desk, freeing his right hand. Eppley fastened the open manacle to the chair leg.

There were three plates arrayed on the desk in front of him, each brimming with a steaming serving of what looked like beef stew. The basket in the middle of the table was filled with a split brown-topped loaf of bread, glistening with butter. Altar's mouth instantly started to water, as the scent was overpowering.

He sat, one hand shackled to the chair. He shoveled some stew into his mouth with a spoon and had to stop for a second. It was hot, but the taste that flooded into his senses practically made him to want to cry.

"Oh, Mama," Shepard said. "How that woman can cook."

Altar and Eppley grunted agreement but didn't seem willing to actually stop chewing long enough to say it.

"Bess," Shepard said. "I loved her to death." He shook his head, and it appeared his eyes teared up. "Couldn't cook a lick, God rest her gentle soul."

"Gentle?" Eppley said with a cough as if he'd swallowed something down the wrong pipe. "I like to remember her to taking that broomstick to you a time or two right before you came over to hide out with my daddy in the barn . . . sir."

Shepard's mustache turned up at each end as he smiled.

"Wasn't hiding out," he said. "More like we was talking about plowing, about the difference with an ox or a mule pulling the confounded thing."

"That ain't what I heard," Eppley said with a grin.

"Beats pushing it your own self," Altar said.

"Damn straight." Shepard shook his head. "But she could swing a mean-assed broomstick, ain't that the truth of it. She tanned my hide once or twice right enough."

"My mama said you had it coming, sir," Eppley said between mouthfuls. "And it was a good many times more than once or twice if she had the right of it."

"I guess she would at that," Shepard said. "I guess she would at that." A tear broke from his eye and ran down his cheek. "Should've treated that woman a good deal better than I done."

"We all got things in the past we'd like to be able to take another shot at," Altar said.

Eppley looked from him to Shepard as he

chewed a heaping spoonful of stew.

"Like, for my part," Altar said. "I sure would take the opportunity to treat my little brother a mite better before I left for the war."

"Why's that, Mister Altar?" Eppley asked.

"We was arguing from different sides is all," Altar said. "Just so happened our dad, who was still alive at the time, took with the Union side like me. But Bobby was against us, and he was such a hothead. Hardheaded, too."

"You all own slaves, Mister Altar?"

"Hell no," Altar said. "Nothing like that, just Bobby thought the government didn't have no business telling people how to live their lives is all. And he felt mighty strong about it. Said the government could just butt out."

"What happened?" Eppley asked.

Altar could see that Shepard was still struggling through some emotions as he ate and pretended to be listening to their conversation, but Altar suspected memories that he'd just as soon keep to himself were at the forefront of the man's mind.

"Everything came to a head and my daddy threw Bobby out, said not to come back 'til he was thinking right," Altar said. "And I didn't do anything, and I wish to God I had."

"Then what happened?"

Shepard was still wrestling with whatever shadows were haunting his thoughts, so Altar figured he'd patronize the younger man for the time and give the older man a spell to collect himself.

"Well, it about tore up our family, my mama was heartbroken," Altar said. "I lit out and joined the Union Army first chance I got. Plumb run away. Only fight I ever turned my back on."

"What did Bobby do?"

"Cut me a slice of bread, would ya? Hard to do one-handed."

Eppley set his spoon down long enough to saw off a hunk of bread. He spread a dollop of butter from a small crock hidden under the loaf, then handed the bread to Altar. It was still warm and fragrant.

Am I in heaven? Altar wondered. He couldn't remember a time he'd had such a tasty meal. At least not within the last year or so. He glanced at Shepard. The man certainly wasn't in any good place, if the grimace on his face meant anything.

"Way I hear it," Altar said as he chewed the bread. "Bobby went and joined Johnny Reb. And that's the last I heard."

"And your daddy," Eppley said. "You said he passed?"

"Yep," Altar said. "I guess not long after Bobby joined the CSA. Mama always said it was the guilts killed him."

Shepard took to shoving the stew in his mouth, spoonful after spoonful, like he was possessed. Eppley laid his spoon on the table and stared.

"Might enjoy it better," Altar said, "if you took a second to chew it."

"I'll be goddamned if I'm going to sit here and enjoy this while my baby sister and her Molly are out there at the hands of them animals." Shepard scraped the now empty plate. Setting his spoon down, he ripped a chunk of bread from the loaf and mopped the plate of what gravy was left.

"Quite a few hours yet 'til the marshal plans to ride out," Eppley said.

"Like hell I'm going to wait around."

"Sir, you gonna go out all by yourself?" Eppley asked.

Shepard caught Altar's eye. The unbridled passion in the man's stare like to broke Altar's heart. The moment seemed to last forever.

"Nope," Shepard said. "I need Altar to go with me."

Eppley looked scared. "But sir, I can't allow that."

Shepard started to say something, but Altar spoke up.

"The three of us can go," Altar said.

"What?!" Eppley sat back. "How?"

"I'll still be in your charge," Altar said. "If you're along. And I'll even come back and let the marshal investigate if you want. But we gotta get on that trail and soon."

"Mister Altar, I don't —"

"Dillon Eppley," Shepard said. "Like you said earlier, you've known me your whole life. I ain't going to steer you wrong, but I need this man with me." He pointed at Altar with his thumb. "If bringing you with us is the only way to achieve that, then fine. Getting those women back is all I got to live for at the moment. That and killing every one of those sons of bitches."

"I don't —"

"I'll tell the marshal I made you," Shepard said. "If that's what you want. Hell, I'll knock you on the head and lock you in the cell if you want. If that'd make you feel like you're doing your duty and all." Shepard held his hand out for the shackle key. "Or you can come with us and help to make things right."

Eppley pondered the situation a moment more and then threw his lap cloth down on his plate and splattered what little was left of his stew.

"Well, shit," Eppley said. "Hold on just a cotton-picking minute, sir. It's dark out, how're you gonna know which trail to follow since they left so many?"

"We know which way Smith lit out when he run from the posse. He went west," Altar said. "That alone lets us ignore a quarter of the directions. Plus, the man was angling north, which I think eliminates another quarter. So, the only ones we really have to pay attention to lead north and west."

Eppley nodded, while Shepard stared at Altar with a gaze so intense in its need and pain that it was hard to return.

"Then," Altar said. "This young gal over to the saloon, she said she heard the men talking about heading into the mountains in Indian country."

"That'd be Maggie, I suspect," Shepard said. "Glad she's all right."

"Wasn't so all right when I left her," Altar said. "She'd been hiding a god-awful beating those bastards gave her. Like to stomped her leg off."

Eppley shook his head. "North and west would put you in Indian country right enough."

Shepard rubbed his face, grown older by

years in a day. "And mountains."

"Sure would," Eppley said. "But things have been kind of quiet since the army pulled out."

"Has," Shepard said.

"Army?" Altar asked.

"Sure," Eppley said. "President Grant closed the Bozeman Trail through the Dakotas to Oregon and gave it to the Indians. White men ain't welcome. I'd be plumb nervous if I was about to go riding in there."

"That's where we're headed, Dillon," Shepard said. "You're welcome to stay in town."

"Like hell, sir," Eppley said.

"What's your mama gonna say?" Shepard asked.

"She knows I'm a deputy," Eppley said. "The worries ain't killed her yet."

Altar cleared his throat and mostly looked toward Shepard but with an occasional glance to the younger man. "The name Merritt ring a bell to either of you? Maggie heard the outlaws talking and thought one of them might be named such. I didn't find no mention of the name in the handbills."

"Merritt," Shepard said.

"Wasn't there a Candy Merritt?" Eppley said. "That old captain."

"That old fool wasn't no captain, only liked to pretend to be. Thought he could woo some gullible girl out of her unmentionables," Shepard said. "But what I think them boys were talking about was that fort. It was way up in the mountains, Fort Wesley Merritt, named after some general from one of the Indian wars. But I remember hearing from trappers and such, that the Indians liked to burn down all of them abandoned forts. Guess it reminded them too much of the U.S. Army."

"Would Fort Merritt be north and west?" Altar asked.

"Yep," Shepard said. "And a good deal upslope too, at the foot of what the Indians call White Eagle Pass."

Altar looked at Eppley. "And that, I reckon, is where we're headed."

Chapter 15
You're the Tracker...
And the Fugitive

An hour later, the three men walked their horses from the alley behind the jail. Altar led a pack mule as well. They mounted and Shepard started off through the streets lit brightly by the full moon. Dog joined them once they were out of town.

"Sir, why we going south?" Eppley asked. "I thought we was headed to White Eagle Pass?"

"Had a talk with Abner Link down to the mercantile store." Shepard adjusted himself in his saddle. "He said the marshal and the posse's gonna be headed north and west too, on account he had riders out since early this morning ferreting out the trail."

"But," Eppley said. "I thought the outlaws had gone all the different ways outta town? And that was going to slow the posse down."

"They did leave by the cardinal points and then some. Them riders the marshal sent out eliminated those other directions, like we done, but they had to do it by eye." Shepard tapped his head. "What we got going for us, is that we know to head for White Eagle Pass and don't have to worry none about the trails, whether false or true."

"Oh." Eppley flashed a dumb-looking grin. "I get it."

Altar didn't think the deputy did quite get it, but it didn't matter.

"Why you think they took wagons with them?" Eppley asked. "For the gold? But the rider you all shot had gold and no wagon."

"Could be they were splitting off?" Shepard said. "Going on just the two of them and already had their cut."

"Don't think so," Altar said. "The other dandified outlaw didn't have any extra provisions for being on the trail, and certainly didn't have enough for both him and Smith."

"Huh," Eppley said. "I don't follow you."

"Makes two of us, if they wasn't splitting off, then what?" Shepard turned to look at Altar who trailed behind. "Did they steal a wagon from them Mormons?"

"No," Altar said. "They been having one for a spell, maybe since Missouri." He hurriedly added, "I just think they split up the gold, so it wasn't wholly in one place is all."

As soon as the words were out of his mouth, Altar knew he'd made a grave error. He suspected the lie wouldn't slip Shepard's notice, though the man might not call attention in front of Deputy Eppley that Altar had just admitted he'd been following the outlaws from the beginning, not just Bobby. Altar waited for a break in the path to cut in front of the other men and ride ahead to avoid any further questioning.

Shepard shifted his horse a little to block Altar's way. "Kind of strange for outlaws to be riding in a wagon. You think one of them was hurt?"

"Don't rightly know." Altar remembered Smith making reference to his brother's leg. "They could have someone injured, I suppose. But I suspect they're hauling something or they got a good many more men than horses."

"What do you reckon they're hauling?"

"Didn't rightly know until I spoke to Maggie." He blew out a breath and decided to just face the mistake head-on if that was what Shepard wanted. "When she mentioned Indians, I figured they're hauling rifles to trade for safe passage."

" 'Bout the only thing that makes sense to me too." Shepard turned in his saddle.

"What kind of rifles do you suppose they're carrying?"

"Muskets, most like," Altar said. "Missouri was filthy with them after the war, Enfields mostly."

Shepard spat. "That's a shame. In the Dakotas, Indians been shooting repeaters for years and muskets'll likely just piss them off."

Altar never would've been able to follow the trail through the forest that blocked the moon's light without Shepard. It was hard to see and most times his horse followed on Shepard's, though not too close as it was an ill-tempered animal when crowded. Eppley followed behind the pack mule and was mostly out of earshot, but Altar didn't want to chance the younger deputy hearing anything that might make him question the wisdom of Altar's being free.

"There any town between here and White Eagle?" Altar asked already suspecting the answer. Spring Creek had every sign of being that last stop before you were in the godforsaken wilderness.

He didn't figure the women were destined to be sold off to any mountain men, as he didn't think the outlaws had saved any of the Mormon women. Altar figured there was as good a chance as any that they'd come across the women's bodies when the outlaws tired of them, or they were saving them for something or someone else. Maybe the Indians?

"No, just a couple of homesteads occupied by settlers more brave than smart," Shepard said. "But you know how these little towns pop up, like a pimple on a whore's ass."

Altar heard the hope in the man's voice. The marshal must've made up the whole mountain men business to keep Shepard from falling off some kind of emotional cliff.

Who was Altar to rob the man of that hope?

"You figure them for selling them women to the mountain men?" Shepard asked with a shake in his voice. "Or you think the marshal was being kind?" Shepard wiped at his face with his forearm as if wiping sweat away, but Altar suspected it was more for his eyes.

The man was a glutton for pain, Altar thought, though he'd be the same way if things were reversed. Might as well tell him the truth, at least as far as he had it reckoned, because his hope and suspicion weren't much different than the whole mountain man story, and it was a good deal better than the darker alternative that had to be unspoken in Shepard's thoughts.

"I don't rightly think they're selling no one to any mountain men," Altar said. "I suspect Elizabeth and Molly and whoever else they shanghaied are being taken to someone in that fort. Whoever's running the show."

It was the darkest of the night, not long before dawn, when they heard the pounding of hooves coming down the road that was off to their left. They steered their horses into a group of trees.

"Who do you think they are?" Eppley asked.

"Gulliford, I suspect." The weight of his worry settled on Altar's shoulders like a boulder. He'd been hopeful that if they could stay ahead of the posse, it would be easier to find the outlaws and give him a chance to cut Bobby out of the group before any shooting started.

"Think he discovered you was gone?" Shepard asked.

"Be my guess." Altar looked at Eppley.

"The marshal must not have put much stock in that letter Dillon wrote about you still being in his custody and all." Shepard shifted in his saddle.

"I reckon not," Altar said.

They couldn't see the horsemen who

thundered past in the dark, as the road was too far away. But it was clear there were a good many, and they seemed in a hurry.

After the group had passed, they rode on in silence as the trail drifted farther away from the road. Even the insects stopped their chirping as they passed by, leaving their horses' breathing and the clopping of their hooves as the only sound to be heard on that dusty trail. The path widened and climbed into a rocky area, more strewn with boulders than wooded. It wasn't long before Altar detected the scent of a wood fire. He glanced at Shepard, who nodded.

"I smell it too," Shepard whispered. He caught Eppley's attention and motioned for him to stop.

Eppley reined his horse in. "Who you think it is, sir?"

"Don't rightly think the marshal would've been riding that hard only to stop to build a fire this time of the morning," Shepard said.

"That'd be my surmise," Altar said. "Maybe he posted a couple of guys to keep watch?"

"Might have." Shepard shrugged. "Be quiet."

Altar nodded and glanced at Eppley, who put his finger over his lips. Shepard nudged his horse forward, back into the trees, and

Altar and the deputy proceeded behind.

They hadn't gone a hundred yards when light danced through the sparse woods ahead to their left and downslope a little. Shepard held his palm out. They stopped. Shepard turned in his saddle and silently shooshed them. Apparently convinced they understood, Shepard turned and walked his mount forward. They followed with Dog in the rear.

The trees weren't dense, given the rocky nature of the ground, and the undergrowth was practically nonexistent. They were able to move their horses through what trees were scattered about without much difficulty or noise. Finally, as they approached the edge of the wood, Shepard stopped. Beyond the shadows, Altar saw that he was motioning him forward. He nudged his mount up next to Shepard, who leaned closer.

Before them, maybe thirty or forty yards away, was a campfire. A lone man, his back against his saddle, sat a few feet from the flames, nursing a bottle. His horse was a shadowy presence on the other side of the fire, illuminated by the flickering radiance cast by the sputtering flares against the velvety darkness of the predawn night.

"Only one," Shepard said in a low whisper.

"And he's here a good piece off the road."

"I don't know," Eppley said. "I reckon them men smelled the fire like we done. They coulda rode over."

"Sun's damn near about to rise and I don't see any sign of anyone else." Altar squinted at the shadows all around the man's camp. "Ain't but the one."

"C'mon, I might know him," Shepard said. "And he ain't likely to be riding hard anywheres. But stay back so he don't get a good look at ya, just in case. Ain't nobody gonna think twice about seeing me."

"All right." Altar took his hat off and wiped his forehead with a gloved hand.

Shepard moved forward and hadn't gone more than twenty yards when the man's head jerked over to look at them. He stood and his pants dropped as if they hadn't been fastened. He reached down with his empty hand, but instead of his pants, he came up holding a big revolver. From that distance, Altar couldn't tell what brand.

Shepard yanked his reins hard, stopping his horse on the spot. Altar did likewise and thumbed the thong from his Remington's hammer spur.

"Whoa! Tom," Shepard called out. "Is that you? It's Merle Shepard. Take it easy with that hogleg."

"Shit," the man said. "Y'all startled me." He stood still, the bottle in one hand and the revolver in the other.

"Sorry, Tom," Shepard said. "You must've been concentrating mighty strong on . . . on your early breakfast to not hear our clopping down this trail."

The man laughed and dropped his revolver next to the saddle. "Ain't no vittles got my attention, but some whiskey."

Shepard chuckled. "That'll dull any man's senses."

"Sorry to hear about your Bess." The man pulled his pants up and looped one suspender over his shoulder.

"Thank ye," Shepard said.

"It's a goddamned shame," the man said. "And taking them women too, what's the world a-coming to?"

"Going to hell in a handbasket I reckon," Shepard said. "You out here all by your lonesome?"

"Sure am," the man said. "Most a' them others went home last night. Who ya got with you?"

"Just a couple boys looking to join the posse that already rode out."

"Rode out, you say." The man looked at the sky. "I thought they was riding after first light."

"Guess the marshal changed his mind some." Shepard edged his hat back a smidge.

When the man didn't say anything about the earlier group of riders, Altar sighed and slipped the thong loop back over his revolver's hammer. The man mustn't have heard or seen them.

"Why don't you slide off those goddamned horses and have yourselves a taste?"

"I'd love to," Shepard said. "But we gotta push on. Anyone farther down the trail? I don't want to startle no trigger-happy cowboy."

"Naw, you're good," the man said. "You ain't gonna find nothing unless you go over to the road south of here. Them murdering bastards left some tree limbs they was using to cover their wagons' tracks. Like I said, everybody else went back to town, wanted to sleep in a bed another night before this thing got started in earnest."

"Didn't you want to snuggle up to the missus one more time?"

"Hell, no." The man's laugh was deep, settled somewhere in his belly. "I'd just as soon cuddle up to one of them timber rattlers. This here genuine bottle of whiskey is all the company I need." He threw back his head and took a quick swig as if in demonstration, and staggered back a step before sitting hard on the ground. He took another pull from the bottle, maybe to ensure it hadn't spilled, and then wiped his mouth with his sleeve.

"The marshal figuring on following the trail from the road, then?"

"Can't say for sure," the man said. "Dean said he had to talk to the marshal, as there sure is horse sign leading on north, but he said another track over west of there had a wagon heading that way too. But they didn't try and cover them tracks. Goddamnedest thing — never seen anything like it."

"Well," Shepard said. "Thanks for the warning. I'll be sure to take a look-see."

"If I had more whiskey," the man said, "and I don't. I'd send some with you men, but this is all I got, and I'm cherishing it."

Shepard laughed. "Don't give it no never mind."

He rejoined Altar and Eppley. They continued down the trail, the sunrise painting the horizon.

"I'd like to see what Old Tom was talking about on the road," Altar said.

Shepard looked over at him.

"Wouldn't that be taking an awful big chance, Mister Altar?" Eppley said.

"Might run into that posse," Shepard said.

"Well, let's be quiet then," Altar said. "Besides, seems them town riders were hell-bent on where they was going, not stopping in the middle of nowhere."

And maybe, Altar thought, he'd get some clue who they were. He still needed to know a whole lot more if he was going to be able to help Bobby.

Shepard shrugged. "Suit yourself, you're the tracker . . . and the fugitive."

Chapter 16
Time isn't our friend

Shepard directed them through the graying morning back toward the road. They didn't see or hear anything of the other riders who had passed previously until they got to the lane, where they found horse tracks aplenty. And a good many of them deep in the soil, having thrown a lot of dirt, which spoke to the speed at which they were traveling.

With dawn's first rays beaming over the horizon, the three riders surrounded a tussle of maple branches that were connected with rope lying in the middle of the road. No attempt had been made to hide anything. Even with the shrinking gray shadows of the sunrise, it was apparent that the branches hadn't done a decent job of masking the wagon's tracks.

Hell, Altar thought, the hoofprints of the passel of riders had done a better job of obscuring the wagon track than the branches had.

"Being that it's been drier than a scorpion's lair," Shepard said, "this here contraption wasn't terribly effective."

Something didn't sit well with Altar. Back in Missouri, he'd seen attempts the guerrillas had made to cover wagon tracks. This attempt was adequate, but he'd seen much better. And these fellows, being Missouri guerrilla fighters, would've been familiar with those superior tactics. He was surprised this one was so sloppy.

But, he asked himself, what good would it be if they weren't fully covering the tracks? Why do the job at all if you couldn't do it right? Maybe they didn't have the men who knew how to do it? Or maybe they wanted to be followed, but didn't want it to be too obvious. But then, according to that fellow Tom, that other wagon hadn't made any attempt to cover its trail. Maybe they hadn't had time to cut down enough branches?

Maybe. Maybe. Maybe.

It was a conundrum, to say the least. Good thing the three of them were headed to the pass and didn't have to puzzle it out. But he wasn't happy that he'd wasted time in catching up to this group of killers. As far as he knew, every minute counted in keeping Bobby's neck from wearing a noose or his corpse out of a pine box.

"I'm glad to be off that road," Shepard said as they rode back to the trail they'd been on earlier. "It runs through a couple of canyons that always give me the twitches."

"Why's that?" Altar asked.

"I always figured them for a good place for an ambush." Shepard followed Altar's gaze to the rear where Eppley's heavy eyelids were closed more than open. "Or robbed, maybe, it's not like I've been ambushed before."

"Once you have." Altar felt the little pinches from the starburst scars on his back and shoulder. "You're not like to forget it."

"You speaking from experience?" Shepard asked.

Altar didn't answer.

"Well, while that boy is half asleep on his horse." Shepard glanced back again, apparently to double-check. "Let me ask you something."

Altar said nothing.

Shepard continued after a moment. "I only been knowing you a couple of days, and after that initial shock of you creeping up on me with that rifle the day we met, I got a good feeling about you."

Altar shifted in his saddle, as Shepard was making him physically uncomfortable.

Shepard continued in a coarse whisper.

"I'm usually pretty good at sniffing out the no-accounts, that's mostly why the marshal keeps me around. But I was hoping you might enlighten me as to why you're lying about how long you been on them outlaws' trail. Seems you been dogging them a far spell longer than you told us."

Altar was torn. But he really didn't have a lie that would make any sense; anything he could come up with would've been told long ago when he'd first been questioned. And like Shepard, he'd always had pretty good hunches about men, and he felt Shepard was as solid as they come.

"It's a long story," Altar finally said.

"We got time."

Altar fetched his tobacco plug from his saddlebag and sawed off a chunk with his knife. He chewed it and spat. Chewed and spat, the tobacco juice pitch-black against the darkness of the night.

"Let me think on it awhile."

Shepard didn't ask again.

They rode mute until the sun was completely free from the eastern horizon before they set up camp. They picketed their animals and lay down to take a quick nap. No one was set on watch other than Dog, who lay between Altar and Shepard.

■ ■ ■ ■

Altar startled awake. His hand instinctively went to the Remington six-shooter perched on his flat belly. Everything had become clear to him while he slept.

Ambush, he thought. The posse was riding into an ambush. Rising to his feet, Altar rubbed what little sleep he'd gotten from his eyes with his free hand.

The sun hadn't moved far in the sky.

Was Bobby part of the group left back to do the ambush? If so, how was he going to cut him from the group?

"Shep," he said. "Dillon. Get up. We got some riding to do. And right quick."

Shepard stirred, but Eppley snorted and rolled over, his hat slipping from over his face to roll on the ground. Dog raised his head, alert.

"What're you hollering about?" Shepard's voice was hoarse and throaty from sleep.

"I'm thinking the posse that rode by last night is gonna find a warm welcome waiting in that canyon you was talking about."

Shepard stood. "You think them no-accounts are gonna wait for days to ambush the posse after they done escaped already?"

"Yes siree," Altar said. "I seen them do it

in the war. Shoot up who's following behind. Tends to slow the pursuit when you're looking around every bush to keep from getting back-shot."

Shepard grunted and gently booted Eppley.

"Get up, young'un, we got work to do."

They were saddled and mounting their horses within minutes.

"What's the fastest way to that canyon you were talking about?" Altar asked.

"There's two," Shepard said. "Which one?"

"I don't rightly know," Altar said. "Did you get the twitches, as you called them, more from one than the other?"

"No." Shepard took his hat off and scratched his head as if thinking hard made his brain itchy. "One's 'bout as good as the other as I remember, though one is bigger. Didn't like either so I didn't come up this way much."

"So," Altar said. "You don't know anything about how best to get up on top of the canyon rim?"

"Just what I seen from the road."

"Sir, you talking about Snake Canyon and the other, I think people call it Buzzard Gulch?" Eppley asked.

"Yeah," Shepard said.

"My pa used to bring me hunting up that-away," Eppley said. "I know 'em both. What ya wanna know, Mister Altar?"

"Which one is better for an ambush?" Altar asked.

Eppley sat on his horse and glanced up into the sky as he thought.

"I guess they'd both be pretty good," he said. "Though I don't got no army training. They both got steep sides and plenty of places where a smart shooter could dig in and be hard to root out."

"Does the road run through both of them?"

"Well," Eppley said. "Kind of, on account that the gulch gets flooded during a good rain, mostly in the spring."

"Where's the road go when it's flooded?"

"Around and up to the top." Eppley shook his head. "It's rough, so people try and brave the water and mud unless it's just too deep."

"So, it should be dry this time of year?"

"Should be, I reckon, Mister Altar."

"How about escape," Altar said. "Would one be easier for the bushwhackers to skedaddle toward White Eagle Pass?"

"Why sure," Eppley said. "That'd be Buzzard Gulch, especially since it's the second one you come to from this direction. And it's closer to the pass by a far piece."

"Is there a way we can circle around and come from the backside?" Altar looked at Shepard.

"Don't look at me," Shepard said. "I don't rightly know."

"Now you got me thinking of it," Eppley said. "I do know a way we could go. Miners, especially them with some gold, used to take this trail back toward Spring Creek that kept them off the road for a spell. We'd use it sometimes coming home. Ain't never gone up that way, don't see why you couldn't."

"Show me." Altar motioned for the young man to take the lead.

Eppley looked around as if getting his bearings. Finally, after a few minutes, he reined his horse about.

"C'mon." The young deputy urged his mount forward with a flick of the reins and a cluck of his tongue. "Kind of steep in some spots."

"All right." Altar followed behind. Shepard brought up the rear with the pack mule as Dog ran alongside.

The first hour wasn't bad, but the incline increased once they veered off on a thin trail and began to climb the slope through the pines and birch trees that grew amongst the large stone outcroppings. The sun winked in the sky as the leaf-laden branches slid by to hide the burning disk of the sun.

"You think Gulliford stopped to eat?" Altar asked back toward Shepard.

"Most likely," Shepard said. "They was riding them horses pretty hard. I imagine he'd want to give them a rest."

"Hope we don't have to do the same." Altar shifted in his saddle, leaning into the gradient. "Time isn't our friend." His thoughts drifted back to his brother.

How in the hell was he going to save his little brother's butt this time?

"We been pushing these beasts pretty good our own selves," Shepard said.

"True enough," Altar said. "If we have to stop, we'll make it quick."

Real quick, he thought.

An hour later, the horses were lathered from crisscrossing their way up the mountainside. Altar recognized that they would have to stop to give the mounts a breather, and they needed water.

"Dillon," Altar said to get the young deputy's attention.

Eppley turned in his saddle to look back at Altar.

"We need to get the horses some water;

we gonna come across a stream any time soon?"

Eppley took his hat off and ran his sleeve across his forehead.

"If memory serves me correct." Eppley snugged his hat back on. "I reckon we're gonna find a small lake the other side of this ridgeline we're climbing. My pa and me would fish it if we had time on the way home." He peered through the branches toward the sky. "Half hour, maybe, to get over and down the other side."

They reached the top and started down the incline with Dog ranging up ahead and the mule having to be coaxed by Shepard to keep up. Altar figured Eppley was pretty near his estimate when they stopped by a feeder stream emptying into the little lake with water as clear as a newly poured bath.

"Don't let them drink too much." Altar swung his leg back from the other side of the saddle and let himself down. He led the animal to the stream, and it dipped its head into the water and began to drink. They didn't have time to pull the saddles, but he would have liked to cool the beasts down. The stream wouldn't get them wet past their knees and he wasn't about to wade them into the lake.

He pulled his horse's head out of the

water and looked up at the smooth surface of the lake as it reflected the sun and the trees ringing the far bank. He was struck by the majesty of the water stretching out like glass to the other side, which was surrounded by trees, an occasional crooked brown branch visible through the wall of green, some even hanging into the lake. Altar heard the distant plop of some fish leaping for a bug near the surface.

Bobby would love fishing this lake, he thought.

Maybe in another time, the two of them could come back and see how their luck would hold. Of course, their luck would first have to hold at Buzzard Gulch, and Altar was thinking that was already quite a stretch for their fate.

"Oh, Mama," Altar said, then suddenly realized he was speaking out loud.

"What's that?" Shepard asked.

Altar shook his head. "Nothing."

Dog ran through the water of the lake close to shore, then waded deeper and splashed around, biting at the sprays of water.

Shepard nodded toward Dog. "At least one of us is having some fun."

Altar removed his hat and used it to scoop and toss water onto his horse's flank to cool the beast down. Shepard and Eppley both watched him, then did the same, while Altar shifted his effort to the mule.

After a few minutes, Altar patted his horse and the mule down, then mounted.

"We got to get back at it," he said.

Shepard and Eppley both climbed atop their mounts without complaint. Eppley led the way from the lake. Dog stayed in the water until they were almost out of sight, then he jumped out and shook his coat as dry as it would get and came bounding after them.

A couple of hours later, Eppley warned that he thought they were getting close.

"How close we gonna bring this mule?" Shepard asked.

"Till we figure we better stop, I reckon," Altar said. "I'd like to know what's in front of us, can't very well tie her off miles away."

They continued behind Eppley, who'd slowed down and was picking his way through pine trees on a flat. The tinkling of their bridles' brass was about the only sound since the bed of pine needles kept their horses' hooves silent.

It was into that silence that the first muffled rifle shots erupted. Followed by the screams of men and animals.

Altar recognized the shots came from

somewhere in front of them and there was a dullness to them that made him think they weren't directed their way. He got off his horse and looped the reins around a branch, then slipped his Henry from its scabbard. He levered a round into the chamber and stalked forward, aware that Shepard was following. He had to glance around to find Eppley, who was still astride his horse, the whites of both man and beast's eyes visible in their blood-drained faces.

Altar nodded toward Eppley. Shepard's gaze followed his nod, then the former deputy moved over to the younger man. Shepard grabbed the reins and quickly tugged them from Eppley's grasp.

That seemed to jar Eppley from whatever trance he was in. He got off his horse. Then more shots roared out from up ahead. These louder, and from a different position, closer. Eppley stumbled backward a step and reached out, grabbing his saddle's cantle to keep on his feet.

Shepard seized Eppley's shoulder.

"Get a hold of yourself," Shepard said. "They ain't shooting at us just yet."

Now the shooting had smoothed out to a steady bark of shots as opposed to what had sounded like a couple of choruses of synchronized cannon fire. In his mind, Altar could see the billowing clouds of white-gray smoke drifting over the battlefield obscuring the dead and dying somewhere in a no-name county of the South.

Chapter 17
Forgive me for what I'm about to do

Altar prowled ahead, his rifle out in front of him. How was he going to pick out Bobby if he was ensconced among the shooters? He hadn't seen Bobby in years. Then, what if he did see his brother among the bushwhackers? Shoot everybody but Bobby? But he couldn't keep Shepard or Eppley from shooting his little brother. He could try to wound him, put him out of the fight but not kill him, but he knew that wasn't likely. Anytime someone got shot, it could be fatal. Wound him, then some other posse member might finish him. And it wasn't like Bobby would be looking for his big brother to stick his nose in his business again.

Lordy, Altar thought, Bobby was going to be madder than a bushel of wet hornets.

Though he wasn't a religious man, Altar found himself saying a prayer as he pushed through the pine trees, into the den of gunshots and screaming men and beasts, the likes of which could only be ripped from the throats of those being killed. He shook his head and decided it was time someone started paying for what they had done to the Mormons on the trail and the good citizens of Spring Creek. Altar couldn't bring himself to believe Bobby would be embroiled in the kinds of things these outlaws had done.

But, he resolved, if Bobby had been, then he too would have to suffer like his ill-gotten brethren.

The icy chill of what he was about to do snaked down Altar's spine. It was as if he was back on the battlefield, whether against Confederates or Indians, it didn't matter. It was the same. He stalked forward with the intention to kill those opposed to him, and those who would do harm to the men at his side.

Woe be to he who stands against me, he thought.

Altar prayed again for forgiveness for what he was about to do.

The ledge of the gulch was before him. He tapped his hat back off his head to hang behind him by its leather cord. The sunlight, now unleashed upon his unprotected eyes, made him squint. He crouched and approached the edge of the outcropping.

Below, the side of the gulch dropped beneath him, and he saw what the marshal had unwittingly done.

The outlaws had set up a classic L-shaped ambush, with a wagon blocking the road below their positions. One group of outlaws was in front of the posse, on the other side of the wagon, more or less at the base of the gulch. Those men were behind felled trees, boulders, and the like. Altar suspected they'd opened the ambush when the posse rode up to move the wagon out of the way — an assumption supported by the writhing body of a posse member in the churned mud by the wagon.

Another outlaw element was positioned in front of the first group, but high up on the side of the gulch. Each man was either behind a substantial rock or a tree, or engulfed in a depression in the earth, making it nearly impossible for the posse to return any kind of effective fire up the slope. So, when the posse reacted to the first cascade of shots from the outlaws in front, they moved back into the firing lanes of the second group who had let them pass initially. The posse was completely outflanked and taking withering volleys of fire from their unprotected side.

Whoever had set up this ambush, Altar

thought, knew what the hell he was doing. Even though the South had capitulated, he suspected for these bushwhackers, it was definitely still a shooting war.

Then he remembered a little something those Union soldiers had told him at Fort Douglas.

"That brother of yours, Bobby, was a right nice fella for a grayback," the one camp guard had said. "But he fell in with a group from Missouri, like Bobby was, and they were real troublesome."

"Especially that big guy," the other guard said. "Called himself Munther, or some such. I don't rightly think he was from Missouri. Maybe Louisiana, to hear him talk. Anyway, that big mean son of a bitch was supposed to be some kind of war genius and had taught those Rebs all sorts of tricks. But, boy, he was as mean as any pit viper ever hoped to be."

"He sure enough was," the first guard said. "I'd hate to meet up with that one unless I had a whole squad with me. They called him Scattershot Charlie and one time, I seen him like to twist this other prisoner's head clean off with his bare hands. Killed him dead, lickety-split."

Altar saw this ambush wasn't the product of a genius, but it sure was well laid out, and he thought it had a bit of a meanness to it. It was set up to kill every member of the posse. The outlaw element in the front advanced from their cover and had started moving forward. Gulliford and his men were being cut to pieces.

Altar knew he and Shepard and Eppley had to alleviate one prong of the ambush if anyone from the posse was going to survive, and right quick. From their vantage point, they would be more effective if they engaged the element high up on the gulch side. Once they eliminated the cover fire keeping the surviving posse members' heads down, those men could repel the advance of the front group of outlaws with a little luck.

Altar turned and caught Shepard's eye as the ex-deputy set up to shoot at the advancing outlaws. Altar shook his head and pointed at the men up on the side of the gulch. Shepard held his gaze for a second as if he didn't agree, but then he swiveled his rifle around and took aim at the outlaws on the slope.

Altar held up his hand for Shepard to wait. Then Altar looked for Eppley and finally saw the young man behind Shepard. Altar waved him over. When Eppley drew near, Altar leaned close to him.

"We're engaging the outlaws on the slope.

Make sure you got a bullet in your firing chamber."

Eppley swallowed, his eyes wide, but the young deputy finally nodded and worked his rifle's lever, seating a round in the firing chamber but ejecting a good cartridge at the same time. He'd forgotten he'd already readied the rifle. Altar pointed to the closest outlaw.

"He's your man. Wait for me to start shooting."

Eppley nodded and swallowed again.

Altar patted Shepard's shoulder and pointed to two outlaws lower on the slope.

"You take those two closest to the bottom. Wait for me to shoot first."

Shepard didn't say anything as he adjusted his aim and waited.

"After our first volley," Altar said, "we're moving to the right and come at them from a different direction."

Altar took the pair farthest away, one of whom was shooting a .52 caliber Sharps rifle, his rear ladder sight up, and he was taking his time looking through it. From previous battles, Altar knew that rifle, in the hands of a man who knew what he was doing, could be decisive. He would be the first one Altar addressed. And he hoped it wasn't his brother. From this far away he couldn't be sure, but if he had to guess, he'd say neither man was Bobby.

Altar edged closer to the precipice and rose to one knee. He tucked his rifle into his shoulder and took careful aim, knowing he wouldn't have this kind of uninterrupted opportunity once the outlaws knew their position. He squeezed the trigger.

The rifle's percussion was a surprise as it bucked back into his shoulder and spit smoke and lead. His hearing deadened even while his eyes stayed downrange, and he levered another round into the chamber, which he felt more than heard. The Sharps shooter fell away and disappeared behind the boulder he'd been aiming around. The man standing next to him looked around in bewilderment and wiped at the blood on his face.

Two more deafening blasts sounded around him, Altar's face registering the heat from their muzzles. Shepard and Eppley had joined the fight. Altar didn't take the time to see how they'd fared. He brought his Henry back up and took aim at the man who was staring down, presumably at the shooter of the Sharps now on the ground.

Altar pulled the trigger, sending the Henry back into his shoulder again and spraying another column of smoke into the air. The second man had just ducked behind the boulder and the bullet chipped a hunk of stone from the rock behind him. Altar didn't know whether the man had been shot or not, nor could he tell if it was Bobby. Another blast sounded from behind as at least one of his companions contributed. As Altar again worked the lever on his rifle, his face was peppered by hot shards of stone from a nearby ricochet.

A powerful hand grabbed his shoulder and yanked. Altar fell backwards and saw Shepard hunker down as more rock sprayed and bounced around them.

"Git your damn fool head down," Shepard said. "These boys can shoot."

"I thought I'd get one more shot." Altar wiped at his cheek. The back of his hand came away a little bloody, but it didn't feel as if there was any wound of significance.

Shepard shook his head. "We definitely got their attention, but we're gonna need to move like you said."

Altar got to his feet in a crouch, his rifle in one hand, and made his way to the right, being sure to stay away from the ledge. *Let them think they have us pinned,* he thought.

He was almost to the other spot where some trees encroached upon the lip of the outcropping when he noticed Eppley wasn't with them. Turning, yet keeping low, Altar saw the young man on one knee behind a stone ledge, his shoulder bent into the rock as if it was helping him stay upright. Ricochets pinged off the boulders around Eppley, the stone shavings bouncing soundlessly on the ground.

Altar picked up a rock and flung it at Eppley. It hit him in the leg. Eppley looked up, his face pale and his eyes wide as if he couldn't get enough light. Altar summoned him with a wave. Eppley hesitated. Then he lurched forward. Just as the young man started to rise, Shepard knocked him down.

"Stay down, fool!"

"Sorry, Mister Shepard."

"Sorry ain't gonna cut it when I have to tell your pa you stood up when folks was shooting at you," Shepard said.

"I been hunting my whole life," Eppley said. "But ain't nothing shot back before."

"Does take a certain amount of adjusting, I'll admit." Shepard pushed the young deputy in between him and Altar. "Keep your damn fool head down."

They reached the trees and turned toward the edge once again.

Altar peeked downslope and saw that the outlaws were alternately shooting up where they'd just left, but a couple were scanning the rest of the gulch's edge as if anticipating their move. A quick glance at the floor of the gulch showed the posse rallying around someone Altar didn't recognize, and they'd stopped the advance of the other element of outlaws.

The men Altar had shot at weren't visible, and Shepard's two had disappeared as well. The man Eppley had been assigned was still upright, and shooting, a sneer on his face. Altar lifted his rifle and took aim.

"You got a target?" he asked Shepard. "I got that guy shooting."

"Yeah," Shepard said. "I got someone, all right."

Altar pulled the trigger. Shepard's shot roared a split second later. The man with the sneer dropped like a sack of potatoes, his rifle clattering over the rocks to roll down the incline. Altar scanned the slope for another target.

"There they go!" Eppley pointed to a washout that slashed across the rise at an angle. A handful of men scrambled down into the depression, their rifles all but forgotten in their grasps.

Altar brought his Henry up and took a quick shot. Shepard's gun followed. The outlaws vanished from sight.

"You get them?" Eppley asked.

"Don't think so," Shepard said.

Altar scanned for where the washout ended but didn't see any sign. He took another look at the battle at the bottom of the gulch. The outlaws had retreated to their original placements. The posse was rallying, returning fire, but their shots weren't killing any of their opponents. Altar thought he could make out some of the outlaws' faces looking up at him, but he didn't recognize anyone, nor did he think Bobby was among them.

"Think you can hit them from here?" Shepard asked.

"Maybe," Altar said. But he knew he could with the Sharps rifle. He looked down the slope of the gulch and didn't see any outlaws within easy range. "I'm going to where the guy had the Sharps. Make sure no one sticks their head up to shoot me."

"You think that's a good idea?"

"It's better than taking potshots at those guys down there," Altar said. "I get my hands on that rifle, I'll kill every last one of them."

Altar slid over the edge and started for the spot where the shooter had fallen. He carried his Henry rifle at the ready should a target jump out, like the other man who'd been next to the Sharps rifleman.

When he'd shot the man, it had been from a different part of the ridge. It took him several seconds to identify where the shooter had been from this direction. When he finally came into the little nest — for lack of a better term — that the Sharps man had made for himself, Altar found him crumpled on the ground, the back of his head a pulpy mess. There was no sign of the man's companion.

He lifted the Sharps rifle, wiped a swath of blood from the stock, and checked the breech. It was still loaded, but the percussion cap had been dislodged when the weapon was dropped. He found the cartridge box on the ground with two more flat-based paper cartridges. And he saw the shooter still had the cap box slung around his shoulder.

Altar retrieved a cap and placed it on the nipple, then cocked the hammer back. He straightened the ladder sight and rested the barrel on a sandbag the previous shooter had been using from the top of a boulder. He snugged the rifle's butt into his shoulder and used his free hand to pull it even tighter. He fingered the trigger and sighted just above the head of one prone outlaw who was still firing at the posse. He tightened his finger until the rifle thundered.

The Sharps bucked into his shoulder something fierce as the muzzle rose, and smoke erupted from both the muzzle and the breech. The shot spattered stone shards from the rock next to the heads of several outlaws.

Altar reloaded the Sharps with a paper cartridge and retrieved another cap, which he placed on the nipple. He resettled the barrel onto the sandbag and adjusted his sight on the previous target.

He took a deep breath and let it out real slow like, holding his aim a hair lower and a smidge to the right of the man he'd previously shot at. He pulled the butt into his shoulder and squeezed the trigger. Once again, the rifle kicked back hard and the muzzle rose, smoke spewing from the front of the Sharps and from the breech. Altar felt some settle on his face.

The outlaw he'd been aiming at rolled over away from him, his hat and large clump of hair flying off. The man's one arm flailed upward and then was quiet as the rifle fell from his grasp.

Several of the other outlaws' gazes moved upward, as if that shot had brought them all awake. Before Altar could reload with the last bullet, they scrambled from their hidey-holes and moved quickly away from the posse, running deeper into the gulch and to their horses, more than likely.

The battle was over. Everyone waited a few minutes, then started to peek out from their places of concealment. Altar wanted to search the side of the gulch for a wounded outlaw so he could interrogate him, but he couldn't do that with Shepard and Eppley around.

He caught sight of Shepard and waved to get his attention.

"Get the horses," Altar shouted. "I'll meet you below."

Shepard waved at him in acknowledgment.

As Shepard disappeared from sight Altar set about the grim task of checking the fallen bodies.

Chapter 18
Be accountable to your own skin

Please, Altar thought. *Don't let any of these be Bobby.* But Bobby wouldn't be a drygulcher — there was no way. Or would he? The realization of how long it had been since he'd seen his younger brother, talked to him . . . war changes a man.

It had changed Bobby. What had it done to him?

If he didn't find his little brother, he'd need time alone with at least one of the outlaws, preferably one inclined to talk. If any had survived.

With Shepard and Eppley getting the horses below, that at least would give him some time on the slope.

There were voices from below. Several members of the posse were walking around, checking on the fallen men. A couple of other men came over to the bottom of the slope and peered up the incline.

"Harv!" Shepard waved over his head as

he hollered down from the edge of the ridge. "It's Shepard!"

The gesture was returned, and one of the two men at the base of the slope pointed toward something out of Altar's sight about halfway up the incline.

What was the man pointing at — dead men, or outlaws that were still alive and dangerous? Altar had to assume someone was on the slope, someone waiting to kill him, because that way of thinking had kept him alive for a long time.

Switching back to his Henry rifle, Altar ensured it had a round chambered. He stepped from behind the boulder and started to make his way down the incline, his eyes and ears alert for any movement or sound. Dog silently scrambled down to join him and scampered along off to Altar's right, the animal's nose low to the ground.

The incline was very steep in places, making it necessary to use one hand to grip one of the many jutting boulders, or the raspy trunk of a scrub pine. Where it wasn't sheer, it was a bushwhacker's paradise of hidey-holes and depressions, screened by vegetation and smaller stones.

It took him close to five minutes to work his way to the first outlaw, the one Eppley was supposed to have dropped. The one he knew wasn't Bobby, as he'd gotten a good close look at him before he'd ended up shooting the man.

When Altar found him, the man's back, a bloody rent in his shirt, was facing toward Altar. He was twisted on the ground, partially hidden behind a stone outcropping. The sporadic rise and fall of the man's chest told Altar he was still alive. Altar scanned the slope downhill and saw the man's rifle lying on the scree, barrel pointed upslope where it had fallen. Altar knelt and pulled the man's shoulder toward him. The man gasped, his head rolled over, eyes unfocused, blood dribbling from the corner of his mouth.

No one else was around, so Altar figured this was his best chance.

He bent closer and slapped the man's face. "Hey, where's Bobby Altar?"

The man's eyes rolled up into his head, and his breath sucked in hard and ragged.

There was a hole in the man's chest, a handsbreadth down from his collarbone and opposite the wide irregular, blood-soaked tear in his shirt where the bullet had torn out the cloth along with a fist-sized chunk of flesh and bone.

No use talking to him, Altar thought. *He's at the end of his trail.*

Altar pulled an old, rusty Colt from the man's pants belt and emptied its cylinder of the remaining rounds, then tossed it down by the man's rifle.

One of the posse members at the bottom of the incline was now pointing below Altar, to his left, vaguely where he remembered the other men Shepard had shot at to be. A glance showed no other heads looking up from anywhere but the bottom of the incline.

Dog started to bark and growl back where the posse member had been pointing, where Shepard's targets had been. Altar saw the two cowboys at the bottom of the gulch working their way toward Dog, whose snarling was growing more vicious. Altar couldn't see any other danger just yet, so he started over and down to see what had Dog's hackles up.

As he got closer, he thought he could hear a voice. He stopped and listened. Dog's growling kept him from hearing what was being said, but it was a voice sure enough. He clucked and Dog stopped his incessant barking and swung around, ambling to where Altar squatted behind a flat boulder. The animal lay down, but the thick fur ridge along his spine was still high.

"Is it gone?" The voice had a Missourian

twang laced with pain.

"Shut up," came the harsh reply in a coarse whisper from behind a rock so close to Altar that he was startled. He froze. The voice continued. "I thought I heard something. Wish the damn thing had ripped out your throat, you talk as much as any girl I ever knowed."

"By God," the first voice said, but quieter. "I sure wish it was you all shot up. You'd sing a different tune."

"Shut your mouth, Cooter," the second voice said. "I'm all shot to hell too."

"You gotta help me," Cooter said.

"Help you?" the second voice said. "I'm accounting to my own skin."

"Don't leave me," Cooter pleaded.

A figure in a blood-soaked shirt rose from his hiding spot to Altar's right, a little downhill from where Altar squatted. The man had a rifle in his hand and took a shaky step away from Altar, toward where Dog had been barking. The man took another tentative step.

The blast took the man square in the chest and knocked him off his feet and backward to fall on the ground in front of Altar. His eyes were open and sightless. He was dead.

"Serves you right, you double-crossing son of a bitch."

After a moment, the ringing subsided in Altar's ears.

"Cooter." Altar let some of his Missourian accent come through. He'd spent a good deal of time trying to lose it, considering how many of his countrymen had fought for the South. "Cooter."

"Who the hell are you?" Cooter asked.

"John Altar. Bobby's brother."

"The hell you say!"

"I am," Altar said. "I got to find Bobby. Where's he at?"

"You gotta help me."

"Tell me where Bobby is first."

"Let me see you," Cooter said. "I gotta know you is real."

"Throw your iron away, I can't say I like how you treat your friends," Altar said.

"Wasn't no friend of mine, that good for nothing son of a bitch was turning his back on me. And after all I'd done for him."

Altar saw a scattergun pitch away from a clump of brush, followed by a revolver.

He crept up closer to Cooter, who lay against a short stone. Still from a safe distance, he said, "Tell me about Bobby and I'll help you." Altar had lost sight of the posse members working their way up the slope, and knew he didn't have much time before they got near enough to overhear the conversation.

"You'll get me outta here and to a doc?" The man coughed, a wet and ragged sound.

"Said I'd help you." Altar took notice of several rents in Cooter's clothing and flesh. "Not that I'm a miracle worker. But I'll make sure you get seen to and that you'll be treated well."

"Guess I can't ask for much more than that," Cooter said. "Bobby always said he had a bushel of fine Southern sisters and a no good layabout brother who was a Federal."

"Where is he?" Altar asked.

A rifle report caught Altar by surprise, as did the warm splatter of Cooter's blood and skull fragments across his face.

Damn, Altar thought, stunned as Cooter's eyes rolled reflexively back into his head. Whatever answers the outlaw had were forever gone. He'd been so close.

One of the posse members had shot Cooter. The other posse member poked his head up over a nearby boulder.

"Ya got him," the man said, a wide grin spreading across his face. "Clean through his damn skull."

Chapter 19
Though I fear you go to your deaths, Godspeed

The outlaws that Altar and Shepard had shot at had apparently made their escape through a deep, dry streambed that slashed across the face of the incline. He'd followed their dusty tracks and figured them for four. The gully let them out behind where the rest of their gang had been lying in wait for the posse at the bottom of the rise.

Altar had to bite his tongue to not harangue the two posse members who'd shot Cooter, but it didn't appear they'd heard any of what he'd asked the dying man. He'd just as soon not let anyone know.

Shepard and Eppley came into the gulch from the trail. They were leading two extra horses. Altar walked over to them, still fuming about Cooter.

"Hope my horse didn't give you any problems," Altar said. "Sometimes he bites after a gunfight."

"Now you tell us." Shepard dismounted.

"But it was Dillon who nearly got bit, not me."

Altar laughed, feeling some of his anger leave through the mirth. "That figures, he don't like tough old meat."

Since Altar had gotten to the bottom of the gulch, he'd learned that none of the women had been found, but he didn't think that would be the case here. He caught Shepard's eyes and shook his head. The man's gaze dropped to the ground.

"At least two of them fellas rode up to the top, Mister Altar," Eppley said, still astride his horse and unaware of the tension present. "Mister Shepard looked. There weren't nothing worthwhile to be found."

Altar laid his palm on the first spare horse's shoulder and walked the length of the animal. It was thin and tremors ran through its muscles even though it had been at rest for who knows how long.

"The second horse is in better shape than this nag," Shepard said, apparently having regained his composure. "But it's plain they've both been rode hard and underfed."

"Guess they was too busy robbing the town to feed their horses," Eppley said.

Shepard pointed to Altar's face. "You get cut some?"

"Mighta been a shard nicked me," Altar

said. "And one of them boys up yonder bled on me a bit."

"The audacity of some people." Shepard's crooked smile pressed across his face. His teeth were bright against his lead-smeared skin, the smudges divided by sweat lines running down his cheeks. Or maybe they were from tears.

"Altar!" The shout came from behind him.

Altar turned to see Marshal Gulliford's tall, lean frame steaming in his direction, a filthy rag wrapped around his head, blood from his ear staining the cloth.

"What in tarnation are you doing up here, out of your cell!" Gulliford stopped in front of Altar. "I want you in shackles. And by God, I want to know who let you out?"

Eppley, who was still mounted, hung his head low, while Shepard looked as if he was about to speak.

"I'm still in the custody of young Eppley here." Altar nodded toward the deputy. "He only set me free so we could attack those outlaws that had you pinned down and was picking y'all off."

Gulliford compressed his lips. They grew white and disappeared beneath his mustache.

"Seems to me," Shepard said. "The man darn near single-handedly saved your hide, and the hides of all them other fellas that rode with you right up to that ambush without a lick a' sense."

The marshal glowered at Shepard as if he thought he could shut the man's mouth with his stare alone.

Shepard met the lawman's gaze. "Any sign of Elizabeth and Molly?"

Gulliford's stare dropped, and he shook his head. He looked like the defeated man he was, saved by circumstance and the man he'd ordered locked up.

"We'll get 'em," Altar said. "If we have to ride to hell and back."

Gulliford raised his head. "I'd advise against making promises you can't keep."

"I'll keep that one, Marshal." Altar pulled his hat down to just above his eyes. "Or die trying."

Muttering to himself, Gulliford turned on his booted heel and stormed away, his scowl even deeper than before.

"Dillon," Altar said. "Get these horses seen to."

Eppley clucked and walked his string of animals to where a younger member of the posse was trying to gather the few loose mounts still nearby.

Shepard shook his head. "Some of them horses are halfway back to town, I reckon."

"Yep." Altar pushed his hat off his brow.

"I'm gonna see who's hurt and who's dead," Shepard said. "Figure I know 'em all one way or the other."

Altar went over to the wagon that was still canted across the gulch's trail. The heavy stones that had been in the back were discarded by the side of the path leading through the gulch. A couple of men were laying out the dead outlaws and throwing their rifles in a pile next to the bodies.

Thank God, Bobby wasn't among the few dead.

Altar couldn't see the Sharps rifle; it might still be on the slope amid the scree. Or perhaps it was already stuck in someone's saddle scabbard. Either way, he didn't have it.

A good long-range rifle could come in handy, he thought. But the other question was whether there were enough cartridges to make it worth lugging around. He knew he'd left one in the cap box. Was there another box, or two or three? The old boy who was shooting hadn't seemed concerned for his ammunition situation. It might be worth the climb.

He went back up the slope, to where the Sharps rifleman was. The rifle still lay by the corpse. The Sharps man had more cartridges, and the pouch of caps, though Altar didn't bother to count them. He figured it was enough for his troubles. He slung the pouches over his shoulder and then the rifle by its sling, then hoisted the body over his shoulder as well. The corpse weighed him down, but he managed to keep from falling as he descended the rocky incline.

After he laid the outlaw near the others, he went to find his horse. The rifle slid behind his Henry in its scabbard. It was a tight fit, but mostly out of sight, keeping the Sharps from wandering eyes. When he got back on the beast, he would have to find some other place to keep it, so it wouldn't rub the animal's shoulder and ribs.

When he came back to the wagon, he heard someone coming up behind him and turned.

Shepard was approaching, dragging his forearm across his red eyes. He offered a canteen to Altar. It sloshed when Altar took it. The water was warm, almost hot, but still slaked his thirst.

"Can't understand how the marshal didn't see that ambush a-coming when he set eyes on that wagon." Shepard pulled a bloody glove off one hand. "Lost some good men today."

"He should've known better," Altar said.

"If I would've been with him," Shepard said, "this wouldn't have happened, and those men might still be alive."

"Only if that hardheaded bastard would've listened to you."

"Shep!" a voice called. "Step away from that prisoner."

Altar and Shepard glanced around, thinking one of the outlaws had been found hiding, only to see the black Stetson-wearing Harmon holding a side-by-side down by his hip, both barrels pointed at Altar's belly. Gulliford towered behind the deputy, with Dean an arm's length to one side, holding shackles and a chain.

"Dean," Harmon said, "get him in chains."

"Take his gun first," the marshal said.

Dean hesitated.

"Deputy," Gulliford said. "Move your ass."

"Marshal." Shepard took a step toward Harmon. "This is some horseshit, and you know it."

Harmon shifted his aim toward Shepard.

Altar lunged and slapped the shotgun barrels down. The blast as they discharged sprayed gouts of earth into the air, showering Shepard with clots of dirt and turf. Altar drove his fist into Harmon's face. As the diminutive deputy fell backward, Altar grabbed the long gun by the hot barrels and ripped the weapon from the man's hands.

He raised the shotgun over his head and brought the stock down, not far from Harmon's prone figure, as if he was swinging a sledgehammer. The wood cracked with the first blow and separated completely with the second. Altar glared at Harmon, and then at the marshal before heaving the receiver and barrels into the trees.

Gulliford had stepped back as Harmon fell, his hands raised. Then, as if it dawned on him what was happening, the marshal tried to tear his revolver from its holster, but the thong was still looped around the hammer spur. The belt rotated until the holster served as an iron loincloth. And still the man tugged on the handgun, but it wouldn't clear the leather.

Dean dropped the shackles and drew his revolver.

Shepard pulled his Colt and held it by his side.

"You don't want to do this, Dean," Shepard said.

Finally, Gulliford drew his gun out and pointed it at Shepard.

"Drop that gun!" Gulliford shouted. His

hand shook so that the bullets in the revolver rattled in their cylinders.

Altar's Remington was in his hand, leveled at the marshal. He pulled the hammer back with a sharp click, which stopped everyone.

"Lower your gun." Altar took a step toward Gulliford.

Gulliford looked at Altar without turning his head, his eyes bulging.

Eppley ran up to the group of men, his revolver in his hand as well. He looked around as he breathed hard, like he couldn't catch his breath.

"I'm right tired of your marshaling, Gulliford." Altar took a step closer until his muzzle was practically touching the marshal's temple.

Gulliford's head rotated a little and his eyes crossed looking at the dark hole at the end of the weapon's barrel. His arm drooped, and his revolver finally pointed at the ground.

Altar leaned closer; the cold iron pushed against the marshal's forehead.

Gulliford let go and his gun dropped to the ground with a thump. He took a step back.

Altar let the hammer down and then lowered his Remington.

Then he stepped over to Harmon, who was still lying on his back. Altar took Harmon's revolver as the man groaned. He threw it on the ground by Gulliford's. Altar searched both men one-handed and didn't find any other weapons.

"You're going to hang for this," Gulliford said.

"For what?" Altar asked.

"I'm the duly elected marshal of Spring Creek —"

"If I hear that one more cotton-picking time . . ." Altar holstered his Remington, staring at Gulliford. "You're liable to hurt someone, you keep to trying to draw that hogleg. And Harmon there ain't no better."

Gulliford stared at Altar, his mouth open for a few moments, and then licked his lips.

"As the chief lawman here." His chest swelled as he spoke like a rooster puffing up for the hens.

"Put a cork in it, Gulliford," Altar said. "You're a long way from Spring Creek and well out of your jurisdiction, I suspect. You got good men killed today on account of either your arrogance or stupidity."

"Or both," Shepard said.

"You can't talk to me like that." Gulliford straightened as if his full height would change his predicament.

"I just did," Altar said. "And will, as long as you keep on being a horse's ass."

He put a boot on Harmon's shoulder as the man tried to sit up, keeping him down. "Stay there, Harmon. You're less dangerous to yourself and everyone else on your back."

Harmon moaned.

"The two of you together don't add up to an effective lawman, you ask me." Altar picked up the two discarded revolvers and hefted them. Both were oiled, and clean except for some dirt clinging to the iron frames, blown up from the discharge of Harmon's shotgun.

Maybe there was some hope for them yet, he thought. *A man who keeps his weapon clean can't be all bad.*

"Shepard," Gulliford said. "Are you going to let this man do this?"

"Do what?"

"Disarm me," Gulliford said. "I'm the marshal of Spring Creek."

Shepard shook his head. "By God," he said. "You are the duly elected marshal of Spring Creek. That's a fact."

"And you're going to be an accomplice to his law breaking?"

"And what, pray tell, laws has he broken?" Shepard asked. "You been bleating this whole time about this man being an outlaw, but you got nothing to show to it. Nothing but your speculation, and last I heard, according to Judge Black, it takes a good deal more than your surmise to lock a man up."

Gulliford glared at Shepard, but the former deputy merely returned the stare.

"Marshal," Altar said. "We're all on the same side here."

"So you say," Gulliford said. "I'm far from convinced."

Altar sighed. "A damn stump's got more sense than you." Though, in truth, the marshal was a good deal more perceptive than Altar cared to admit. "I'd just as soon you be armed and ready to fight as we ride on after this gang."

"Ride on?" Gulliford guffawed. "And how in the name of the good Lord are we going to do that?" He gestured with an arm behind him, toward the injured and dead posse members. "We have to get these men back to Spring Creek."

"What about my sister and niece and the other women?" Shepard asked. "You just gonna forget about 'em?"

"We ain't got enough healthy men to go on." Gulliford crossed his arms. "Ain't gonna do any good to get more men killed and shot up. This here is a ruthless bunch."

"That didn't occur to you when we was

looking at them butchered Mormons?" Altar shook his head. "Well, me and Shepard are following this through like we said."

Shepard cleared his throat. "They're down to maybe six. This posse can still follow on. Send Harmon and a deputy to bring the wounded back to Spring Creek."

"The hell you say." Gulliford stomped his booted foot. "This here is my posse and we're all going back to Spring Creek."

"Last I checked," Altar said, "Shep and me ain't part of your posse."

"You're my prisoner!"

Altar grinned. "Seems the tables have turned, Marshal."

"You said earlier that you were still in the custody of Deputy Eppley. Were you lying?"

"Not hardly," Altar said.

"Well." Gulliford smiled. "He's in my employ and I'm ordering him to bring you in."

"And he can do that," Altar said. "Just as soon as we see this through."

"I'm ordering Eppley to return with us."

"Can't do that, sir." Eppley's voice, very low, cracked as he stepped forward. "Shep and me will bring him back with the women. Promise."

Gulliford stared at the young deputy. "What'd I just say about making empty promises."

"Riders!" someone yelled, from beyond the wagon at the north end of the gulch. Another man ran from the bend leading to the gulch's mouth, pointing behind him. "Riders coming!"

Men scurried to grab their rifles from wherever they had stowed them and find some cover.

"Who are they?" Altar yelled to no one in particular.

"Can't say for sure," someone answered. "White men, looks like."

"Gotta be the outlaws coming back to finish us." Gulliford's voice trembled as much as his outstretched hand. "Gimme my pistol." He stared at Altar. "Please."

Altar held the marshal's gaze a moment.

"I don't take to having firearms pointed at me." He hefted the marshal's pistol. "You do it again and you're liable to lose that hand. *Comprende?*"

Gulliford flinched, but said nothing.

"*Comprende?*"

"Yes, yes." Gulliford looked over his shoulder, past the wagon. "Now, please."

"I'd rather have you to fight, if need be." Altar gave Gulliford his revolver, grip first.

The marshal nodded, holding the large weapon down by his leg as if it was too heavy to lift. Harmon was still on his back moaning, so Altar stuck the man's pistol in the back of his belt.

Altar wished they were on the plains where he could see a great distance. Much could be learned from watching your enemy's approach. But alas, in the gulch everything was much closer. Altar stared toward the north, where the riders would appear as they rounded the bend. It didn't make tactical sense for the outlaws to return by way of the gulch's road. No, the better strategy would have been to work their way up to the top of the walls and shoot down at the posse. Yet, who could it be? Indians? That made no better sense than the outlaws. And the man who'd shouted a warning had said they were whites.

Gulliford cupped a hand by his mouth and yelled, "Open fire when they round the bend!"

"Belay that order!" Altar shouted. He glared at the marshal. "We have time to identify the riders, make sure who we're shooting at."

Little by little the approaching riders became visible. They rode in formation, orderly. These were no outlaws or Indians.

Moments later, a dust-covered column of Union cavalry rode into the gulch. Eight uniformed, bloodstained, weary men, leading another half dozen riderless horses, each horse burdened with the still form of one or two bodies. They approached the wagon and flowed around it like water around a boulder. The leader raised his hand, and they came to a halt. Their mounts hung their heads low with their mouths reaching for what little grass was left.

A rider from the front broke off and cantered toward the remnants of the posse. The man was dark haired and burly; the stubble shadow along his cheeks was thick and his hat cocked to the side to allow for a blood-brown bandage that was wrapped around his head. His uniform was covered in trail dust and dried mud and blood, with rents and tears in the fabric. His black boots were filthy-brown. A carbine rested across his lap, and a holstered pistol with its flap unsecured bounced on his hip. Three yellow-gold sergeant's chevrons were visible through the grime on his sleeves.

"And what do we have here?" the sergeant asked as he reined up, taking in the figures standing before his horse.

Gulliford stepped forward before anyone else spoke.

"I'm Willard Gulliford, duly elect—" Gulliford stopped for a second and glanced at

Shepard. "Marshal of Spring Creek and leader of this posse."

"Sergeant Cannella, B Company, Seventh Cavalry." The sergeant surveyed the gulch. "Surprised to find y'all up here." His voice had a twang to it that Altar couldn't place. Indiana maybe, or southern Illinois.

"We just fought with a gang of outlaws." Gulliford shook his revolver as if it were wet. "The gang fled from here a little more than an hour ago. I'm surprised you didn't see them."

"No one was on that trail." The sergeant shook his head and spat a stream of brown tobacco juice. "Not that we seen."

Gulliford lifted his revolver and aimed it at Altar.

"Sergeant," Gulliford said. "This man is an escaped prisoner. Take him into custody."

The sergeant's gaze lingered a moment on Gulliford, before moving to each of them. Altar thought he saw a spark of recognition in the man's eyes when theirs met, but from where, he couldn't say.

"Marshal." The sergeant laughed. "The U.S. Army don't take orders from local lawmen."

"I'm telling you; he's escaped."

The sergeant pushed his hat back, worked a finger under the bandage, and scratched.

"Maybe so, don't change the fact you're not part of my chain of command. And I got my orders."

Altar caught Gulliford's sideways glance and shook his head. Altar spat and said to the marshal, "I see your word is no better than your grasp of tactics."

Gulliford stammered, then looked up at the sergeant again. "Who . . . who is in command?"

"Well." The sergeant turned in his saddle. "That would've been Lieutenant Darby, back there on that tall bay with the white stockings." The sergeant spit, then picked at a fleck of tobacco on his tongue. "But he would've told you the same thing."

Gulliford stepped to the side to peer around the sergeant's horse. "I don't see him."

"That's because he's wrapped in a blanket, dead. Lakotas like to taken his head off with one of them war axes they're so fond of."

Gulliford spun around to look up at Cannella. "Then . . . who's in charge?"

"I am," Cannella said. "And like I said, we don't take orders from anyone outside of the army. Guess you're going to have to do it yourself." The sergeant turned his attention to Altar. "Is that really you, Sergeant Altar?"

Altar nodded. "Is. You look familiar, trooper, where do you know me from?"

"Bit south and west of here," the sergeant said. "Middle of nowhere, really. A few years back, I was part of a little ammunition restore when a group of Sioux figured they wanted our powder and scalps."

Altar nodded. The images of hills covered in tall plains grass, painted Sioux warriors, and desperate Union soldiers flashed in his mind. He grinned and remembered that the good Lord had smiled upon them that day.

"It's good to see you still in one piece." Altar took his hat off and bowed his head a little. "It's been a while. I'm surprised you'd remember me."

"I'm not like to ever forget what you done that day." The sergeant laughed. "Every morning when I wake up, I thank the Lord and you and them three Indian scouts you had with you. Damnedest thing I ever seen."

"You all done the real work, as I remember," Altar said. "It was fortunate that we came when we did, those Sioux were a mite persistent."

"Yes, they was," Canella said. "And thank the good Lord, you were more so." He turned back to face Gulliford. "Marshal.

This man." He pointed at Altar. "From my understanding, he is part of the army, and is under my protection. If you lift a finger against him, it'll be as if you were acting against the U.S. Army, and me personally. Understand me?"

Gulliford stood slack mouthed. Then he seemed to find some courage.

"But . . . but . . . he's an escapee." Gulliford slowly and deliberately slid his revolver into the holster still directly in front of his genitals, apparently aware that the sergeant was watching him carefully, hands on the carbine in his lap. "You can't do that."

"Get your wits about you, Marshal," Shepard said. "He didn't do nothing, except maybe hurt your feelings some. About time you got over it. We got some work to do if we're going to catch up to that gang of outlaws."

Gulliford shook his head and nearly dislodged his hat. "Our pursuit?" the marshal said with a screech. "There is no more pursuit, we're returning to Spring Creek just as soon as we can."

Shepard's face darkened to a blood red.

Altar laid a hand on the man's shoulder, but the former deputy shrugged it off and took a step toward Gulliford. "You would condemn Elizabeth and Molly to life with that lot?" His voice was low and as sharp as a freshly stropped razor.

"Easy, Merle," Altar said. "We'll follow sure enough."

The sergeant lifted his carbine and rested its butt on his thigh. "You mean to track this band of outlaws?"

His hand on Shepard's shoulder again, Altar looked up at the sergeant. "I do."

"I am loath to agree with your marshal here," Cannella said. "But in this, he has the right of the matter. The Indians are roused in the Dakota Territories, and I can't advise going any farther than you are here. We're headed back to get more troopers. We got to put this rising down before it grows too big. Perhaps we'll come across these outlaws upon our return."

Gulliford nodded but stopped short of smiling. "Let the army hunt them down."

"Can't." Altar patted Shepard's shoulder. "You see, the outlaws have a number of women taken by force from Spring Creek, including my good friend's sister and niece."

"You'll find the land awash in blood, I'm afraid," Cannella said. "I don't think the outlaws will have any better of it, especially the women."

"Ever the more pressing is our need, then," Altar said. "What can you tell me about what lies north?"

"Since President Grant closed Bozeman and gifted the territories to the Indians, they've burned most of the forts, and driven any white men from the land. Though we have heard some whispers that one fort still stands high in the mountains, astride the pass."

"White Eagle Pass?"

"I believe that's what the Lakota call it," Cannella said. "Fort Merritt was there, if the stories are true. I have no idea who holds it if it does exist. No soldiers, to be sure."

"That's where the outlaws are headed," Altar said. "We reckon they had a wagonload of rifles. Maybe to meet up with more of their kind."

"Or to trade with the Indians." The sergeant shook his head. "My orders are clear, and I got no men to spare." He spat his chaw to the ground. "Though I fear you go to your deaths, Godspeed."

"And to you," Altar said. He looked at Shepard, who nodded.

They started to leave and then Shepard spun around. He looked at Gulliford and spat.

"You lying, cowardly son of a bitch," he said, and then joined Altar in walking away.

Chapter 20
There's Them Need Killing

Altar, on his haunches, studied the torn earth. He stayed low for a long time trying to decipher the different tracks. Certainly, several horses had been headed up trail, but much of their sign had been obliterated by those of the larger column of soldiers coming down the trail. The two groups had to have met, or at least passed by one another. Since Sergeant Cannella said they hadn't seen anyone, the only possible answer was that the outlaws had laid up out of sight while the army rode past.

It was silent except for the call of birds, some insects, and Dog's snuffling as he sniffed the trail ahead. Shepard, Eppley, and Harmon — Gulliford had insisted he accompany them — sat silent on their mounts, awaiting his judgment, along with a mule with panniers filled with provisions, especially ammunition.

From what he'd seen at the ambush site,

Altar was fairly certain Bobby wasn't among the outlaws who had fled, unless there were some he hadn't spotted. And he knew his brother wasn't among the dead. Altar felt hopeful that meant Bobby was with the second bunch that had split off with the women.

Finally, Altar stood.

"Can't say for sure." He stuck a boot into his stirrup. "We know them that headed up this trail numbered more than our four."

"Ain't you counting Dog, making five?" Shepard asked. His crooked smile showed teeth through his growing beard.

"I'm counting Dog, all right." Altar stepped up onto his horse, settled in, and thrust his boot in the other stirrup.

"How do ya get four, then?" Shepard asked, looking at the two deputies.

Altar clicked his tongue to set his horse moving up the trail. "I seen Eppley shoot. And Harmon can't hold onto his damn scattergun. They only count as one."

"I put *you* on your ass." Harmon snorted. "I woulda had more trouble hobbling a lamb than what you gave me putting you in shackles. What's that say?"

"That you was on someone's shoulders when you coldcocked me, for one." Altar laughed. "How you breathing through that nose?"

"Any time you want." Harmon spit a bloody clot to the ground. "I'll fix you one just like it, and then some. Maybe feed you some of those teeth a' yours. You owe me for that shotgun you busted up."

"Gotta give the little shit credit." Shepard spat. "He got a set of balls on him, like to drag on the ground if'n he didn't have pants on."

"His legs is short," Altar growled. "Besides, balls'll more than like get you killed if'n you can't think."

"Guess so." Shepard looked at Harmon. "Marshal sent you along, but don't get to thinking you got any say in what we do or how we do it. And by God, don't get in the way."

"Don't you worry none about me, old man," Harmon sneered. "Maybe you the one need to worry 'bout getting in *my* way."

Shepard laughed out loud and nudged his horse ahead of the deputy's.

For several hours they worked their way up the trail through the forest of what had turned mostly into tall, straight pine. Their horses labored in the thinning air as they climbed. In the daylight, with the blazing sun, it got hot, but at night the temperature dropped so that they were wanting a fire and more blankets.

The mule was passed off between the men as they rode higher, but Altar stayed in the lead, watching the trail and everything else as best he could, looking for an ambush.

"Gonna have to give these ponies a break soon enough." Shepard's whisper was gravelly as if filled with sand when he came up behind Altar. "They're near tuckered out."

Altar clamped his hat lower on his head and clucked at his horse, which had stopped like it understood Shepard's words.

Turning in his saddle, Altar said, "Give it a bit yet, Merle."

"Can't we step it up some," Harmon said. "Ain't never gonna catch them bastards if we keep at this pace."

"I ain't looking to get bushwhacked," Altar said.

"I'm with you on that." Eppley, eyes downcast, glanced back at Harmon. "Can't really say I'm all fired up to be getting shot at again."

Harmon spat. "Every outfit needs a cook." His laugh was high-pitched and nasally.

"Don't suspect I'll shoot another living thing again." Eppley's whole body shivered. "Appears my hunting days is over."

"A man's got to eat," Altar said.

"Give it some time." Shepard pulled his hat off and ran his gloved hand through his hair. "Can't live on greens alone."

"And," Altar said, "there's them need killing."

"Amen." Shepard reined his horse around a fallen tree. The pack mule hesitated before following along after Shepard's tug on the rope.

Altar pushed them for almost another hour before holding his hand up indicating they were taking a break.

"No fire and don't get comfortable," Altar said. "And keep your horse from drinking too much out of that stream."

"They ain't had nothing to drink for a time now," Eppley said, his tone more astonished than argumentative.

"Listen to what ya been told," Shepard said. "We ain't on no afternoon jaunt. Our lives might depend on these ponies getting up a head of steam, and a full belly ain't gonna help none with that."

"Yes, sir."

Shepard tied off his mount and sidled up to Altar, who stood on the trail as it meandered ever upward. "What ya thinking, John?"

Altar stood quiet for a moment. "Can't put my finger on it. Something ain't right.

Feels wrong somehow. And I'd feel a mite better if I could at least figure what it was got me itchy."

"This is your first time in these mountains," Shepard said. "And we're dogging a pack of murdering outlaws. That's enough to make most men turn tail and skedaddle."

"Yep," Altar said. "But there's something I ain't recognizing, and it's bothering me."

It wasn't long before Altar had the men back on their horses and was leading them higher up the trail. They rode for an hour more before Altar reined to a stop. He'd worked his way in front of the rest of the riders. Shepard was closest and cantered over to him.

Altar looked back the way they'd come, seeing Eppley and Harmon, who was last, now leading the pack mule. He caught Shepard's eye and nodded back toward the other riders.

"Harmon seems kind of content all of a sudden to be riding as the last man."

Shepard stopped and twisted in his saddle to look behind him. After a long stare, he turned to look at Altar. "Does seem contrary to all his bellyaching."

"Does."

"You reckon," Shepard said, "he just got tired of whining?"

"Not hardly."

Shepard pulled his canteen from his saddle horn, uncapped it, and took a long pull of what had to be tepid water.

"Maybe he's just being careful, thinking he can ride for help if trouble breaks out." Shepard wiped his mouth on his sleeve. "When you figure on making camp?"

Altar could feel Shepard's stare on the side of his face, and spat.

"You are figuring on stopping, right?" Shepard looped the canteen's strap back over the saddle horn. "Be dark afore long."

Altar glanced around at the sinking light and the mountains.

"Look for something defensible, but we're gonna keep riding for now."

"That in case we should encounter any Indians while we're catching some shut-eye?"

Altar looked back at Harmon. "Or some such."

An hour later, they found an outcropping of boulders that provided enough shelter that Altar agreed to stop. They picketed the horses close by and ate cold fare and drank cool water from a nearby mountain stream. Altar posted Shepard high upslope, and he took low. "I want to be back on the trail before first light."

"We picketing any sentries?" Shepard asked.

"Nope," Altar said. "I'm low and you're high, and Dog's the best overseer we could have."

Something awakened Altar during the night, but he didn't know what. He stood after a time and walked around, keeping downslope from the others. His breath formed light wisps in the thin, cool air heavy with the scent of pine. Even straining his ears, he couldn't hear anything out of the ordinary. But something had roused him.

And Dog was nowhere to be found. Had that been it? Had he heard something that pertained to the animal's absence? Altar immediately looked to the horses. They were still picketed and calm. One of them snorted as he approached.

Must have smelled me, he thought as he rubbed the animal's dark muzzle. He whispered to the beast as he looked around. The overcast sky hid what little light the stars would've provided.

Had it been a mountain lion? But the horses would've been agitated to the point of panic.

Maybe it had been a dream?

No, it was no dream. His gut told him that.

After a time of wandering around down by the trail, even with his ear pressed to the cold earth, he heard nothing and gave up. He lay back down. But he kept his revolver on his flat belly, with his coat thrown over him, every bit as much to conceal the weapon as for the warmth.

The mountain peaks to the east partially blocked the earliest rays of the morning sun. But before the light would even brighten the horizon at its lowest on the plains, Altar was up and collecting his meager belongings that he'd spread out.

He left his saddlebags laid across the saddle horn and made his way upslope to where Eppley and Harmon were bedded down. He heard Shepard, further up the rise, moving about, cursing softly against the brisk morning and his aching joints.

Altar found both Eppley and Harmon awake and dressing. Eppley was on his ass, pulling his boots on, with his britches only half up themselves.

"Mister Altar, no fire?" Eppley asked, his face hopeful as his foot finally plopped into place. He stood and began to shimmy his pants up over his union suit.

Altar shook his head, figuring the kid

wanted some coffee. They all did, but they couldn't afford giving away their presence any more than they already had.

There'd be time enough for coffee, he thought. If they survived that long.

"Choke some biscuit down with water," he said. "We're late for the trail."

"Can't see no more'n twenty feet," Harmon said. "Seems we should wait a time."

"Waited long enough as it is."

They were saddling their horses in the graying morning light when Shepard gave a grunt. "John," he said. "That's Dog, ain't it? Not no wolf."

Altar looked over the withers of his horse to see Dog's form slinking down through the rocks in the barest of light. And he had something in his mouth.

Altar came from around his mount.

"What's he got?" Shepard asked, moving away from where he'd tightened his cinch.

"Who knows," Altar said. "Gopher or rabbit, maybe."

"Lemme see," Shepard said. "Beats the tarnation out of this hardtack."

Altar chuckled. "Not raw, it don't."

Dog loped up, dropped the object at Altar's feet, and turned away. He trotted over to the stream and started lapping noisily.

"Jesus." Eppley looked down from his saddle.

The young man's breath caught, then he gagged.

Chapter 21
These was some good boys

Harmon stepped over to where the dog had dropped the object. He stared down for a moment; his shoulders sagged before he moved away. The deputy removed his black Stetson and held it in front of his chest as if he didn't know what to do.

Shepard crouched, staring. He looked up at Eppley, who was retching, leaving clumps of biscuit to tumble down one of his pants legs. Shepard's gaze turned to Harmon, who snugged his hat back down on his curly red locks and stepped up to mount his horse.

Altar glanced down and saw an intact human hand. A left hand that had been shorn from an arm at the joint, the blood still a dark crimson in the early light.

"Ain't this Josh's?" Shepard pointed at the severed hand lying on the ground, four fingers curled up toward the sky, bloody nails dark. "He was in the posse, wasn't he?"

"I reckon." Harmon's complexion was pale as if he'd seen a ghost. He looked away as if to prevent his looking down once again.

"You reckon?" Eppley wiped at his mouth with a forearm. "I seen you two together with the marshal before we rode off."

"Who's Josh?" Altar asked. More importantly, why was he close enough for Dog to come across his remains?

"Another deputy," Shepard said. "Runs with Harmon here."

"How do you know it's his hand?" Altar asked, thinking of only one reason why members of the posse would be bird-dogging them.

"On account of this here." Shepard pointed at the nubbed joint of the thumb. The last part of the digit was missing, though the scar tissue indicated the injury had healed some years ago. "He smashed the tip off over at the blacksmith's when he was a young'un."

Eppley coughed.

"Who would've done this?" His voice was a hoarse croak. "The outlaws?"

"Lakota," Altar said.

Shepard stood. "What in the devil was Josh up this way for?"

Altar looked to Harmon, who glanced around as if he preferred to look anywhere but at Altar or Josh's hand.

"Fixin' to dry-gulch us, would be my guess," Altar said under his breath as he crouched and patted the ground by the hand. "Dog."

The beast stopped lapping at the stream and came over.

Altar patted the ground again and the animal's nose dropped. He sniffed, water from the stream dripping from his wet muzzle onto the cold flesh of the hand.

"Ain't he already got the scent?" Eppley asked.

"Yep," Altar said. "But I want him to take us to where he found it." He looked at the other riders, all mounted now.

Dog loped off, back from where he'd come.

"Gimme a empty sack," Altar said.

"What fer?" Harmon asked.

Shepard twisted in his saddle and yanked a couple of empty sacks from his saddlebags. "So's we can bury Josh with all his parts. Be my surmise."

He threw an empty sack to Altar.

"Yep, I reckon your buddy would like to be buried as whole as we can make him." Altar shook the crumbs out of the sack. He scooped the hand off the ground and dropped it into the bag, cinching the bag tight.

Altar was surprised when Dog led their group ahead of where they'd spent the night. It took them about forty-five minutes to finally find Deputy Josh, whatever his last name might've been, and the other deputies. They hadn't needed Dog's guidance for the last half mile or so, because they'd followed the carrion birds aloft and finally the squawks of vultures and crows as they got closer still.

They pulled their horses to a stop.

Dean's bloody eyeless sockets stared out of his severed head, resting on its side atop a boulder, where a couple of crows pecked at the flesh between screeching at one another.

Two more severed heads had left a gory trail from where they'd fallen off the stone and rolled on the ground at the base of the large rock. Crows fought over those as well. Their shrill cries made the hair on the back of Altar's neck stand on end.

He'd seen plenty of soldiers mutilated by the engines of war, bayonets, musket, rifle ball, and cannons belching cannister shot and flames and boiling smoke into masses of men. And then there was the kind that was done by hand, altogether more sinister and malignant, that he witnessed when he rode against the Indians. The carnage inflicted on one another from both sides. It made his soul sick, but the wounds no longer manifested upon his countenance. His compassion for his fellow man had been mostly worn from him by the corrosive nature of war.

Was Bobby gonna make a similar claim when Altar finally caught up to him?

How could all this death and violence not affect a man? How could it not profoundly affect a man to the point of making him no better than an animal?

But he could think of no animal as mean and cruel as man, not by a long shot, though he knew there would be those to argue for the badger. Mostly, critters did what came natural to them. Could one say the same for men? He thought not. The meanest men he'd known had been made that way by how they'd grown up, though he would certainly hold to some men being easier swayed to cruelty.

Vultures waddled from around the boulder, their wings flapping. One crow on the ground pecked and tore something from the head it had been working at and flew off, the fleshy morsel hanging from its beak. The other crow hopped away from the larger carrion birds, and then flew off without a grisly prize.

Eppley and Harmon drew their revolvers.

"Goddamn birds!" Harmon said.

"Holster your damn iron," Altar said. "You'd have the Lakota on us for certain."

He ripped his hat from his head and waved it as he spurred his mount forward. "Scat!"

The vultures burst into flight in a feathered wave, the deep thump of their wings beating their retreat as their bloated bodies labored up and away into the cloudless sky.

The scene on the other side of the boulder was as gruesome as any Altar could remember. The three deputies had been hacked apart and left to the scavengers. Their kits had been strewn about and there were no weapons of any kind to be found among the men or their trappings.

The only sound to be heard was the insistent buzzing of blue-green bottle flies and the screeching of the carrion fowl.

This was an Indian massacre, in every way authentic, as opposed to the staged scene of the Mormon slaughter. Altar wished Gulliford was here to witness this carnage. He looked to Shepard, who just stared at the butchery.

No doubt Gulliford had sent these men

ahead to effect Altar's capture. And, of course, Harmon had been forced into their party to that end. Sure explained why the deputy had been hanging back, waiting for the dead men to spring whatever trap they'd planned on setting. Like everything the marshal did, this was poorly planned and woefully undermanned.

Altar took a turn around the scene on horseback, looking for tracks. He would've been happy to find them coming or going. He found nothing. That worried him. There should be some sign of the Indians, but there wasn't any that he could see, and this being fresh. They were like ghosts.

Altar slid off his mount and began to gather the pieces of the men, laying the parts with the torsos best he could reckon. They didn't have any shovel and the earth was hard-packed. Even with an implement, it would take hours to dig three graves.

As he worked, he glanced over to the other riders. Shepard was now dismounted and moving stiffly, gathering the men together where Altar had dragged the torsos. Eppley sobbed quietly and Harmon's eyes were practically bugged out of his head. They sat transfixed, their horses skittish from the spilled blood.

"Start gathering rocks, you two," Altar

said. "Can't dig a grave, so's we're gonna build a cairn. Keep the critters from getting at them any more than they already have."

At least for the time being, he thought. The more persistent predators, the coyotes, would come later to dig and paw at the stones.

The men worked in silence and by late morning they had finished. Each of them stripped to the waist, sluicing sweat as if they worked in the desert.

They drank some water and then dressed and made ready to go.

"Wanna say some words?" Altar looked at Shepard, the only man not mounted, but he was speaking to all of them.

Eppley shook his head, his lips clinched tight. Harmon stared at the ground and didn't move, as if he hadn't heard the question. Shepard looked to the other deputies, then took his hat off and stepped to the head of the pile of stones.

"These was some good boys," he said. "Didn't deserve nothing like this here. May the good Lord have mercy on their souls."

Altar, on his horse, was adjacent to Harmon's mount. As soon as Shepard quit speaking, Altar reared back and kicked Harmon from his saddle. The smaller deputy crashed to the earth with a great thud and *humph* as the air was forced from his lungs.

Harmon's mount ran off. Altar reined his horse in a circle and he pulled his Remington from its holster in as fluid a motion as there could be. By the time Harmon recovered his wits and went for his own revolver, Altar's gun was aimed down at his heart.

"You son of a bitch," Altar said with a sneer. "I should shoot you now."

"What the hell are you doing?" Shepard spun around, surprised.

"Harmon here," Altar said, and emphasized the point by gesturing with his revolver at the ground farther out. "Had been planning on dry-gulching us with these three dead men. He might as well be buried under them rocks with his compadres."

Shepard turned to look down at the man on the ground.

"You want me to shoot you now, or leave you walking for the Indians to find?" Altar asked.

Harmon didn't say anything, but sat up, his gun hand in the air apparently to prevent Altar from mistaking his action.

"How do you want it?" Altar asked. "Head, heart, or belly?"

Shepard stepped closer but didn't get between the men. "You can't be serious?"

"I'm as serious as a snakebite." Altar stared at Harmon. "Ain't that what Gulliford told you to do? Why he insisted you ride along with us?"

Harmon's lips compressed into a pale scar across his reddening face. He said nothing, but wouldn't look Shepard in the eye.

"Ask him." Altar kept his Remington on target. "Ask him how they were going to take me into custody, Merle."

Shepard looked down at Harmon. "Is that the way it was gonna be?"

"Weren't supposed to be no gun play involved," Harmon said.

"But if we didn't cooperate?" Altar asked. "What then?"

"It wasn't supposed to get to that point," Harmon said. "They was gonna surprise you and I'd have the drop from the back."

Altar cocked his Remington.

"Hold on," Shepard said, his voice rising. "Just hold on a cotton-picking minute." His arms held out wide as if he was about to signal the start of a foot race at the county fair. He lowered one arm and pointed up at Altar. "What if he were to promise his loyalty, and even give up his gun 'til you feel like you can trust him?"

"I ain't never going to trust that sack of horseshit."

"Don't be too quick to say *never*," Shepard said. "We're gonna need all the help we can get to rescue the women, ain't we?"

Altar considered this but said nothing.

"Well," Shepard said after several seconds. "How about it?"

He looked back at Harmon.

"Don't seem much choice to me," Harmon said. "Gut shot and left for the Injuns, or give up my revolver and ride into surefire hell unarmed."

"At least you got a choice," Eppley said from behind them all. "Dean didn't seem to have been given much choice . . ."

The diminutive deputy's gaze went to the stone-stacked grave and a tear wound its way down his cheek. He slowly reached down, and with two fingers, withdrew his revolver from its holster and handed it to Shepard, who put it in his saddlebag.

"It weren't supposed to happen this way." Harmon's voice sounded brittle.

"But it did," Altar said. "And don't you forget it."

He kept the Remington pointed at Harmon for a few seconds more and then uncocked the revolver and rammed it back into its holster.

"The only reason you're still alive is my respect for this man here." Altar gestured toward Shepard. "That, and he's right about us needing all of us if we're gonna rescue those women. But know this. If you ever try anything like this again, it'll be the last mistake you ever make. Comprende?"

Harmon gave a quick nod, got to his feet, and brushed himself off.

Eppley handed him the reins to his horse.

Shepard and Harmon mounted, and the men rode off. Altar was in the lead, pulling the mule, and Dog was on the ground foraging ahead. Then came Eppley, nudged along by Shepard. Altar glanced back over his shoulder and saw that Harmon was still sitting on his horse at the cairn's foot, starring down at the gathered stones. He doffed his Stetson and wiped at his forehead, his bright orange-red hair stringy with sweat. Then he placed the hat back onto his head with great care before reining his horse around to follow the others. As he was about to pass from sight, he glanced around as if he expected to see someone following. With his hand on his empty holster, he quickly nudged his horse to close with Shepard.

It took Altar more than an hour to cut the outlaws' track, then it was back to bird-dogging the band who'd ridden off from the ambush in Buzzard Gulch. It seemed they were sticking to the overgrown trail headed up the mountain. Altar figured it had once upon a time been a road to resupply the fort.

Shepard had known Harmon for a whole lot longer than he had, but Altar couldn't help but think sparring the kid was a mistake. Hopefully not one that would cost them dearly.

Chapter 22
Some men are just plumb evil

They'd been following the tracks through and up the foothills for two days. Altar's horse stood at the point where the outlaws had veered off the overgrown two-track worn into the earth by the heavy wagons used to bring supplies to the fort. They hadn't done that before, and Altar wondered why.

Eppley pointed to the noon sky. "Look at that."

Altar looked up.

Buzzards.

He'd been staring so hard at the ground, he'd neglected the horizon. Sure enough, some ways off ahead, five birds wheeled in the brilliant blue sky, no clouds anywhere to be seen.

"What d'you think it is?" Eppley asked.

Shepard gazed up. "Something dead or dying, I reckon."

"I know that much, Mister Shepard," Eppley said.

"We going to see?" Harmon asked.

"Reckon we are," Altar said.

"Ain't that a waste of time?" Harmon spun his dancing horse around.

Altar shook his head. "No matter. Tracks are headed off the road that way."

It took them a while to negotiate their way through the landscape that wasn't too hospitable to their horses, but on they went. As they neared the place that the buzzards had been circling, Altar caught the wafting scent of what might've been a campfire, but he suspected was something more sinister.

Then a distinctive and unmistakable odor assailed them and the horses in the midday breeze. Death had caught up to them again.

Shepard looked at him.

Altar nodded and rode on, knowing Shepard had smelled it too.

"You boys," Shepard said. "Best stay here for a spell."

Eppley swallowed, while Harmon clucked his horse forward. "Like hell."

Altar led the way into a shallow valley of aspen and pine with a greensward of tall grass. Shepard followed close behind him, then came Harmon, trailed by Eppley holding the lead to the mule. Eppley didn't seem to be in any hurry to keep up.

It had been a small camp of old men, women, and children. Their bodies were strewn about, apparently where they had fallen. Their tipis trodden down, most likely by men on horseback. Outlaw men.

The children were clad in frock-like animal skins against the cold, while the women wore colorful beaded hide dresses, now covered in dried blood, but the blood wasn't that old.

Altar dismounted and examined the bodies. They were cold, but not stiff with rigor mortis.

One old man appeared to be an invalid. His throat had been cut, and he'd been scalped.

Altar saw two women, quite old. One had been shot in the face, the other clubbed in the back of the head with something heavy. They too had been scalped.

The children, two girls of perhaps five or six and a boy of maybe three, had been run down and trampled to death. Their scalps had also been taken.

He recognized some of the hoofprints, belonging to the outlaws they'd been bird-dogging. Not a surprise.

The others had stayed on horseback. Altar looked around and figured a close stand of trees would have to do. The buzzards weren't the only critters who'd come to the feast. He bent down and picked up the woman whose head was staved in. She was lighter than he thought she'd be. Malnourished.

He damned the white hunters that ravaged the buffalo herds, and the railroads that pierced the land without regard for anything other than greed in the name of progress.

He carried her to the trees and placed her body, birdlike in its brittleness, on the ground.

Pretty soon, these people would have nothing to eat and would be dependent on the government to provide meat. *Talk about being damned,* he thought.

The government claimed to have liked the men in the army, and they suffered wickedly. How would a people the government despised survive?

Maybe perpetual war wasn't so bad, he thought.

It sure beat starving to death.

"By God," Shepard said. "What in tarnation're you doing?"

"Got no time for a proper burial." Altar walked back to the other woman. "I've seen Lakota put their dead on platforms before they burn them."

"I thought you said no fires?"

"Ain't gonna burn them," Altar said. "Just get 'em off the ground."

He hefted the other old woman, even lighter than the first.

"These trees are gonna have to do." He strode toward the stand again. "We're going to build a pallet in the branches. Keep the bigger critters away until maybe their people can find them."

Shepard got off his horse slowly, as if he was being held back. He stopped at the small boy and shook his head.

"Don't make no sense, John. Why would they've done something like this?"

Altar was back and picked up one of the girls' bodies. "Sheer meanness, I reckon."

"But this is just —" Words failed Shepard. He wiped his face quickly and cleared his throat. "Some men are just plumb evil."

Altar laid the girl next to one of the women. "And I'd be right happy if I had a chance to put them down, one at a time, like a pack of mad dogs."

After the bodies were collected, they hacked some boughs that were two or three fingers thick and crisscrossed them in the lower branches.

"These old women didn't birth these

children," Shepard said when they took a rest.

"I reckon not." Altar wiped the sweat from his forehead with his sleeve. " 'Fraid the mothers were took, same as your Elizabeth and Molly."

They worked silently, Shepard handing the bodies up into the branches for Altar to lay out. After a while, Altar figured they done it best they could, given the time constraints they faced. Every minute spent here meant their quarry was getting farther and farther away, and they had been close.

He hoped the outlaws were taking the squaws to the fort like all the town women. Perhaps they had other designs, but then they could've done that right there where they killed all the rest. He hoped against hope they'd find the Indian women alive and still willing to live, which were his hopes for Elizabeth, Molly, and the other Spring Creek women as well.

He didn't figure his brother could be involved with this kind of atrocity. Not the Bobby he knew. But if he was, he'd go down just like the rest. Bobby had thrown in with a bunch of malicious men, but they'd proven that when they'd slaughtered the Mormons.

Why was he surprised? Because Bobby

was among them? That didn't seem to hold much water any longer. How could he tell their mama what he'd seen? What his younger brother had been a party to. He'd tell her only that Bobby was gone. That alone might kill her, with all the guilt she'd been feeling about not standing up to their pa.

This here, he thought, *she'd never be able to bear.*

Hell. He wasn't shouldering it all too well himself.

He set the last of the bodies in place and climbed down. He wiped the sweat from his brow and put his shirt back on.

It was time to get moving.

Chapter 23
God help us if you're wrong

A mile or so later, he noticed the outlaws had returned to their earlier trail, the overgrown road to the fort, he presumed. They'd added an unshod horse, most likely for the Indian women, which meant at least one was alive. But maybe that wasn't such a good thing, given the vicious nature of their captors. The thought spurred him onward.

Altar drank in the fresh air, trying to get the stink of death from his nose. He cleared his throat, hoping the sound would break the memory of the incessant drone of blue-green flies from his ears as they had buzzed around the carnage. And he spat, trying to rid his mouth of the fetid taste of death. He believed this group of outlaws was headed to the fort to join back with the other party of no-accounts that had the women of Spring Creek, and whoever else might be there. But what if they weren't? He, Shepard, and the other two would be losing precious time. Especially with the Indians in an uproar.

Shepard rode up behind him, leaving Eppley and Harmon back a ways as they fought and tugged the reluctant pack mule along after them.

"How far ahead are they, you figure?" Shepard asked.

"Couple hours, maybe less." Altar twisted around and pulled his plug of tobacco from his saddlebag. "You saw how fresh that blood looked." After unwrapping the tobacco from its cloth, he sawed off a hunk and offered the hard-packed leaf, balanced on his blade, to the older man.

Shepard shook his head. "And when we do catch up to them, what then?"

Altar put the chunk in his mouth and bit down. The dry piece crushed apart, and the taste of tobacco bloomed. He wanted to spit but didn't have enough moisture left in his mouth. He turned back in his saddle.

"Kill 'em, I suppose." He chewed more, the substance stealing what little wetness the trail dust hadn't dried up. "Take the women."

"And what're we going to do with the women?"

"Give 'em back to the Indians."

"And you got that all figured out somehow?"

"Yep." Altar finally had enough moisture and spat. "They'll find us sure enough. Guess it'll be a matter of whether we take possession of them women before they come 'round."

"You figure they'll be coming?" Shepard asked.

"Yep. Soon."

"And if we haven't recovered their squaws?"

"They'll lump us in with them outlaws and we'll be hard-pressed to stay alive."

"And if we have their squaws?"

"Then maybe they'll listen to reason."

A grim chuckle escaped Shepard's throat. "And just how do you propose to do that? Reason with 'em?"

"Figure we'll talk a spell."

"By God," Shepard snorted so hard his mustaches twitched. "You do have this all surmised."

"Reckon so."

"God help us if you're wrong."

They rode until darkness and the rocky terrain made their going difficult. Altar called a halt in fear for the welfare of the horses. The breeze blew in the direction that would bring the scent of their fire to the outlaws. Accordingly, it was another cold dinner, followed by a still colder night, the crisp mountain air drawing their breath out in wisps of fog.

Altar made clear the importance of staying alert when he told them of their sentry duty. He emphasized it with, "Unless you want to end up like that group of deputies we buried."

It felt as if he'd only just fallen asleep when he suddenly came awake. His hand slid over the butt of his Remington, warmed from its perch on his stomach, just as someone shook his shoulder.

"Mister Altar." It was Eppley's turn at sentry. He said quietly, "I smell smoke."

Altar sat up and laid his revolver on the bedroll before he pulled his boots on. Eppley led him from the camp, away from the sound of snores coming from Shepard and Harmon.

The scent of woodsmoke was subtle as it drifted in on the gentle chilly breeze that had changed direction since he'd lain down. And it came from the direction they'd been trailing the outlaws.

Had those fools started a campfire, Altar thought. Did they have a death wish? It would surely bring the Indians down on them.

He could detect no flickering light in the distance, though he didn't expect to see one. He turned to Eppley. "If I am not back in a quarter hour," he said quietly, "wake up Shepard and have him make ready to break camp, but be quiet."

"Yes, sir."

"And tell him he can give Harmon back his six-shooter."

Clad in his dirty white union suit and boots, and holding his Remington in one hand, Altar walked away from the young deputy.

He moved slowly, careful not to make much sound. His senses were alert, despite his having gotten little sleep. As his ears and eyes strained, not recognizing anything useful, his nose registered his own odor. And it wasn't good. When was the last time he'd bathed?

He wasn't afraid of snakes; the night was too cold. Should any be out in the open, they'd move so slow he'd have plenty of warning before any attack. Still, he did not want any unnecessary sound to give him away.

As he crept along, the scent of the fire grew stronger with every step. It wasn't until his mouth seemed overly moist that he realized he detected the scent of roasting meat. It seemed like a month since he'd had something cooked over a fire.

A faint hint of sound tickled his ears.

Laughter.

His pace slowed even more, knowing if he could hear them, they'd be able to hear him in return. Yet still he moved forward, knowing that Eppley, had he followed directions, should've awakened Shepard by now.

He also was aware that the cylinder of his Remington was loaded with only five chambers of powder and ball. He kept one empty under the hammer. Nor did he have his knife. Careless.

But he'd only intended to so some reconnoitering — nothing more.

Not only careless, he thought, but stupid not taking a weapon with a full load to a gunfight.

He'd walked away from camp to reconnoiter, he told himself.

He knew better.

In the old days he'd reprimanded troopers for less; you never knew what opportunity might present itself. Only one who was ready could take full advantage of those occasions. And this time he clearly wasn't ready.

Getting into a gunfight, dressed only in his union suit and boots, with five shots against six shooters seemed a little harebrained. But he'd done dumber things and had the scars to prove it.

Altar mounted the rise slowly, only planning on peeking over the topmost crown of the slope. The outlaws were not far away; the sound of their voices was very near, along with the scent from their fire, which was now mixed with the strong odor of their horses.

If the fools would have posted a sentry, Altar knew he'd have been discovered by now. But a shout or shot never came as he crept closer.

How had they survived this long? Just on meanness? He'd seen it, to be sure.

The sound of voices roused him from his thoughts.

"I'm mighty sick a' being told hands off on account of Munther. He owes me a bushel a' gold and ain't even here." The voice was gravelly, as if the man spoke with a throat full of river rock.

"You know what he said, Toad," said a second, equally gravelly voice. "Hands off if we were to come across any women."

"Hell, these ain't women," Toad said. "Since when is squaws women?"

"Maybe so," the second voice replied. "Just the same, I'd feel a mite better we let Big Charlie Munther decide. You know how he is."

"Nash, how's he to know if we were to have a taste?" Toad said. "Ain't like these bitches gonna tell him."

"All the same —"

"To hell with all the same!" Toad sounded closer, like he was moving toward Altar. "My pecker's so damn hard I can barely piss through it."

"The rest of us feel the same way, for Christ's sake," Nash said. "We should be there in a couple days. Can't you wait?"

"That might work for a reformed sodbuster like you," Toad said. "But, by God, I'm a man and an outlaw, and I don't stand for no rules."

"These here is Charlie Munther's rules, making them a whole lot different than government ones."

"To hell with Charlie Munther," Toad said. "I'm going to use this here one's mouth and feel on her teats some, it'll be quick like."

A different voice spoke up. "Good way to lose your equipment, you ask me. She's liable to bite it clean off, then you gonna have to squat to pee 'cause you'll be spraying like some bitch." A high-pitched cackle followed.

"Shut your mouth, Jasper," Toad and Nash said together.

Nash continued, "You ain't got the good sense God give a turnip."

"C'mere," Toad said with a guttural throatiness.

Altar heard a sharp intake of breath, as if from pain.

"Don't do it," Nash said.

"She gonna chew your pecker off," Jasper said with a laugh. "I can see it in her eyes."

"Toad, you'd better not," Nash said. "Charlie'll be madder than an old wet hen."

"Who's gonna stop me?" Silence, and then Toad added in a deep throaty croak, "You better keep your traps shut, know what's good fer ya."

Altar hesitated.

Should I intervene? he thought.

He thumbed his hammer back, with an audible click. But the sound of a fist smacking flesh drowned it out.

Five shots.

Six adversaries.

A slap reached his ears. An Indian woman grunted in pain.

Jasper's resonant laugh cackled into the night air. "I bet she take it clean off at the root with one chomp!"

Altar let his breath out slowly, knowing that none of the men speaking was his little brother, and stepped over the crown. He found himself ten paces from the back of a man who had a kneeling woman by the hair, yanking her closer to him as he fiddled with his britches.

Toad.

Chapter 24
I asked you a question

Altar raised the Remington. And pulled the trigger.

The explosion was muffled by the openness. The ignition of the burning powder pitched from the barrel. As the smoke spewed outward, the man fell forward as if he'd been axed.

One, Altar said to himself.

Across from him, on the other side of a small campfire, another outlaw stood with his red union suit half unbuttoned, his mouth agape as he stared at the fallen man.

The squaw scooted away from Altar, her eyes wide, pupils liquid black.

The man in the red union suit held his arms out as if to ward off a charge. Altar figured he must look like some kind of apparition in his own white union suit, now gray from wear.

Was this one Nash?

Altar shot him through his outstretched

hand, the bullet finding the man's chest. He twisted as he fell to the ground.

Two, Altar said silently.

A movement down to his right caught Altar's eye. One of the remaining outlaws was spinning in his bedroll, levering a cartridge into his rifle.

Altar thumbed the hammer back and shot the rifleman in the top of his head. He was pretty sure this one wasn't his little brother, either.

Three.

Only two more rounds, but he figured three more outlaws. He needed to keep one alive to talk to before Shepard and the others heard the shots and ran over to lend a hand.

Altar stepped over another Indian squaw curled on the ground and backed into the shadows. He heard the horses whinnying across from him, somewhere in the dark. He took another sideways step, looking for another bedroll, another outlaw.

"Jesus!" a man exclaimed from the darkness. "What're y'all doing?"

A tall rangy man stepped from the shadows that hinted of pine, with a yawning pitch-black path between the trunks. He strode into the light and stopped. He wore an unbuttoned checkered shirt over his long johns and boots. It wasn't Bobby. Altar was too far away to crack the man with his pistol, so he shot him in the side of the head. The man fell sideways.

Four.

Altar spotted a bedroll, lumpy with someone in it. He stepped over, keeping an eye on the figure for any movement or weapon. He crouched. No way was this guy asleep.

The man in the bedroll lay stock still, his face lax, and seemed bloodless.

Altar lifted the horse blanket and saw the bandages, dark from blood. It smelled like an outhouse. He was intimately acquainted with the smell from the war.

Gut shot. The man was dying from the sepsis.

Five.

Altar's eyes lifted.

In the shadows, flickering at the very edge of the light cast by the dying fire, he stared into the wide eyes of another, younger man. His mouth slack with disbelief, squatting. His pants around his ankles, his arms around his knees. Caught with his pants down.

"Mister," the man said, his voice a barely audible croak. "I ain't lifted no hand against you and I ain't aiming to."

Altar stood, his Remington held at his hip,

pointed at the man.

"I took no part in taking them squaws. And I ain't touched nary a hair on their heads."

Altar circled around until he was on the man's left side, more than likely opposite his gun hand, which would force him to come across his whole body to shoot.

Altar's voice was low, harsh. "You take part in riding their families down? Stomping those oldsters to death? Clubbing them children's brains out, did ya?"

The man swallowed; his lip quivered.

"They forced me to," he said, his voice cracking. "I ain't much more than a kid my own self. I'm barely seventeen."

"How many good men did you shoot the other day in Buzzard's Gulch? Or killed in Spring Creek? How many Mormon throats did you slit on that wagon train?"

"Mister." The young man shifted his feet as if he was uncomfortable. "Who are you to know all we done?"

"Boy," Altar said. "I'm like nothing you ever run across, I got no compassion for the likes of you for what you done. What's your name, boy?"

The young man twisted and started to raise his hand opposite Altar, which was gripping a dark iron-colored revolver.

Altar fired before he really knew what he was doing. It caught the kid in the chest and kicked him backward. His booted feet scattered his shit like slop.

Altar strode forward. He knelt alongside the kid, putting his empty Remington on the ground next to his knee. He grabbed the young man's firearm and tossed it away.

"What'd you do that for? I would've let you live."

The young man moaned. His eyes fluttered.

Altar grabbed him by his unbuttoned shirt.

"Where's Bobby Altar?"

The boy's mouth worked but no sound came out, only blood.

"I'm looking for Bobby, where is he?"

For a second the kid focused on Altar's face. The boy squinted; tears rolled from his eyes.

"Bobby?"

"Yes, Bobby! Where is he?" Altar shook him.

"Bobby's —" The boy choked and coughed. Blood trickled in a thickening stream from his mouth, reddening his teeth. "Bobby . . . went —"

A moist burp escaped, spattering Altar's face with flecks of warm blood. But the kid's eyes had glazed over and were unseeing.

Altar shook the body again. Then he stood and let it drop to the ground. He stared in silence; his ears still rang.

"Who's Bobby?" a voice behind him asked.

Altar turned as he glanced over his shoulder.

Shepard stepped from the shadows, his Navy Colt held by his leg.

Altar said nothing.

Shepard cocked the hammer of his revolver.

"I asked you a question."

Chapter 25
Clean of the dirt, clean of the sweat, and clean of the blood

There was no sign of Eppley or Harmon behind Shepard.

Altar remained silent. Was this it? Were he and Shepard going to have a showdown over his little brother? Was he going to have to shoot this man he now considered a friend? Which would be hard to do, considering his Remington was on the ground, empty. And he'd thrown the kid's revolver off to the side.

"He's my little brother," Altar said finally.

"Your brother?" Shepard's eyes widened in apparent sudden understanding. He gestured with his Navy Colt. "He's riding with the likes of them?"

Again, Altar remained mute.

What was there to say? This man had lost his wife, and had his sister and niece abducted, subjected to who knew what. Most likely subjected to unspeakable horrors at the hands of the monsters like those scattered about his feet.

How could Bobby be part of that?

"So, was Gulliford right all along?" Shepard asked. "That you were looking to join up with this pack of killers, be with your no-account brother? Was I wrong about you the whole time?"

"I never lied to you or the marshal," Altar said feeling naked now that he was essentially unarmed. "Like I said from the start, I'm looking to bring Bobby back to Missouri to see our mother. She's the one asked me to find him."

Shepard took a deep breath, stared at Altar, and then very slowly lowered the cocked hammer of his revolver and holstered the heavy gun. He started to turn away, then whirled back around to face Altar.

"Know this." Shepard pointed a finger shaking with anger. "I aim to kill every last one of those sons of bitches. No matter who they are. Comprende?"

Altar searched for the words to answer but could find none. He just stared at Shepard, who shook with rage.

Shepard turned and walked off into the shadows, not waiting for an answer. Altar guessed the answer didn't matter to the man.

He moved his head in the barest of nods as Shepard's form disappeared into the darkness. "Guess we'll cross that bridge when we get to it," Altar said in a whisper.

After Shepard left, Altar stepped over to the fire. There was a bowie knife, blade nicked from use, its metal dull, stuck into a log by the fire's rim. Another, thinner skinning knife lay on a dirty tin plate under a spit of half-eaten meat. He picked up the slender blade whose handle was slippery from grease.

The squaws looked at him with terror in their eyes.

The cords that held their wrists were tight and had cut into their tawny skin.

He was torn. Should he free the Indian women and let them ride off, or keep ahold of them? If he were to keep them, they'd have to stay bound in some manner to prevent them from running off.

And if their outfit encountered the war party without the squaws, Altar would have nothing to bargain with for their lives.

As much as he'd just as soon set the women free, that wasn't practical. They'd been bound too long as it was.

The squaws couldn't ride back to their camp; nothing was left for them except to add their number to the funeral pyre, all the food having been spoiled by the murdering outlaws, their weapons either stolen or broken.

The women had no implements with which to hunt, though he could give them the weapons and tools these dead outlaws had carried. With his experience, he knew the women could survive, had they the means. But first, he'd need to go through the supplies himself.

And now, he had to worry about Shepard knowing the truth about his brother. If their roles were reversed, what would Altar do? But he already knew the answer to that, didn't he.

The heated metal of his revolver had cooled to his touch, and he slid the Remington, its chambers empty, into his boot, careful not to scratch himself. He hefted the kid's gun and checked the cylinder to see how many rounds were left.

It was fully loaded. Apparently, the kid had every chamber primed without an accident, only to die with his fully loaded revolver in his hand when he was taking a shit.

Life can be cruel, kid, Altar thought.

He barked a laugh. With all the horrors he'd seen, the irony of this kid's death wasn't lost on him.

He shook his head. Could he ever return to the farm in Missouri? Would these musings drive him crazy were he to be toiling in a field with a middle-buster plow year after year until he died like his father? Years from now, would he forgive himself for keeping these women, their hands bound, fearful for their lives?

He couldn't abide the keeping of humans in any form. Prisoners of war or outlaws held for justice were one thing he'd stomach, but these women weren't of that ilk.

Carefully he cut away their bonds, trying not to injure the women any more than they'd already suffered. They were scared and he cooed to them softly, as one might to a skittish horse. Once free, they huddled together and stared wide-eyed at him.

Using a cloth, he removed the fire-heated bowie knife from the log. He laid both blades and the plate of roasted meat at the feet of the Indian women.

"Eat, little sisters." His Lakota was long unpracticed and broken, but he figured they'd understand. "Then you are free."

The women remained motionless for a time, then they descended on the hunk of meat, slicing off chunks with the knives, eating with an abandon spurred by hunger.

He began to rummage through the

outlaws' traps, looking for supplies to supplement their own. The rest he'd leave for the women.

After they'd finished eating, the women slid the knives in their hide dresses' cinch belts. On their knees, they looked around the camp, glancing at him out of the corners of their eyes. He continued to paw through a pannier of meager supplies but kept them in sight.

He saw the women pull a couple of saddle blankets from a pile just inside the fire's light. They wrapped themselves up and spun in a circle, staring at the sky. One of the women walked toward the picketed horses, while the other gazed at him. When he didn't do anything except to keep searching, she dragged two more blankets to where the first woman was bridling one of the mounts. Altar wondered if that horse was the Indians' horse the outlaws had taken with the women.

The second woman tossed one of the blankets across the mount's back and the two of them climbed on, one behind the other. They rode into the darkness bundled against the cold, as Shepard barged out from the shadows on the other side of the camp. There was still no sign of Eppley, Harmon, or Dog.

"Ain't we keeping them squaws?" Shepard gestured in the direction the women had ridden from camp.

"Reckoned it wasn't right." Altar emptied a saddlebag of filthy, wrinkled clothes onto the ground by the fire.

"Thought you said we was gonna barter with the Indians," Shepard said, spittle spraying from his mouth into the firelight. "Gonna trade their lives for ours."

"That's what I said." Altar kicked through the garments. "Know what I ain't found?"

"To hell with whatever you ain't found. Why'd you let them squaws go free?"

Altar looked up from his inspection of the scattered clothing.

"Changed my mind, Merle."

"And if the war party rides up?"

"I'll talk to them," Altar said.

Shepard scoffed.

"But I ain't found none of Spring Creek's gold." Altar kicked at a pile of clothes already searched.

"To hell with the gold, John," Shepard said. "Ain't gonna do us a lick a' good if we're dead."

Altar took a deep breath. He took it as a good sign that Shepard had referred to him by his Christian name. Maybe the revelation about Bobby hadn't been as disastrous as Altar thought it would be.

"I been fighting Indians for years, rode with 'em as a scout," he said. "Trust me, especially with the Lakota."

"Like you want me to trust you tracking down your brother amongst this murdering, thieving pack of outlaws."

"Something like that."

"You're asking for an awful lot."

Altar stopped kicking through the supplies.

"I suppose I am."

By late morning the group of riders, leading the six outlaws' horses, had put miles between them and the camp. Neither he, Shepard, nor Dillon Eppley felt particularly Christian towards the dead, and the bodies had been left where they lay. The memories of the staved-in heads of the Indian children and the scalped elders prevented whatever sympathy might've been left after the Buzzard Gulch ambush. The recollections of the wagon train and Spring Creek still loomed large as well.

Altar led them back along the overgrown two-track — the trail the outlaws had been using. He was confident it would lead to the fort.

As they had mounted after first light,

Harmon spoke up. "We just going to leave these white men laying like they are?"

"Yep," Altar said.

"You done special for the redskins. Why not them?"

"Critters gotta eat too." Altar tugged his reins over as his horse turned. "You want to bury them, go ahead. But we ain't waiting none."

Harmon frowned but said nothing, and that suited Altar just fine. He was tired. All he wanted to do was bring his search to an end. Find his brother.

But then what?

Fight Shepard?

After what Altar had seen, kin or not, did someone who'd done all those outrages deserve to be spared? He'd promised his mother to bring her youngest son home. But he'd put down a family dog gone mad without bringing it back among those he loved. Why take the chance with Bobby?

If Bobby was involved in any way.

He was having a hard time believing that the young, towheaded boy he remembered would be capable of doing the types of horrors they'd encountered. And then he thought about the other young men, many no more than boys, that he'd seen in the war, their stares vacant, wiped of their humanity by what they'd seen and had to do to stay alive. People change in that cauldron of war. Had Bobby?

Altar knew he'd have to find out, but what then? Where did he go from there? Could he put his brother down in cold blood? And then what?

Was he suited to the life of a farmer?

Was Bobby?

Would Bobby even agree to go back to Missouri if he was found, and wasn't killed by Shepard, or Harmon or Eppley or Altar himself?

Shepard hadn't said another word to him. Even Eppley and Harmon were quiet, apparently aware of the gravity surrounding all of them. In what had to be a first, Altar had been the most talkative breaking camp, barking out his short commands.

Dog had wondered off and was nowhere to be seen throughout their morning's ride. Maybe the tension, which was thick and pervasive, drove the animal away.

Altar paused at the top of a rise, turning his horse back toward the path they'd traveled. There was a horse some ways behind them. One which he suspected bore two riders.

It was the Indian women, certain enough. They had nowhere else to go.

He wondered how that would play out.
We all got a ways to go, he thought.

The sun overhead brought some warmth to an otherwise chilly morning. They'd traversed over a couple of dry creek beds and Altar wanted to find somewhere to water the horses. He'd a mind to bathe, having a sliver of soap left wrapped up in cloth. He'd smelled himself last night, and it was past time.

If I don't get clean soon, he thought, *they'll smell me coming.*

The seemingly endless trek continued as they rode right past time to eat their midday meal. No one spoke, no one complained, even the horses labored quietly, their snorting and whinnying held within, perhaps for want of water.

They climbed. Well after they should've stopped, Altar felt his mount quiver under him. He saw its ears twitch and the animal pulled against its bit, wanting to go off the path. Then he heard it too. A gurgle . . . Water . . . Somewhere close.

They'd found the swift-moving river, rather wide, over a small rise and through the pines, which broke open to reveal an ample clearing for the rocky riverbank.

Altar steered his mount toward the water

and let the animal drink while he dug his other union suit, less sullied than the one he wore, from his saddlebag. Keeping his horse between him and the other riders, who were all now dismounted and milling around their own horses, Altar stripped off his boots, and then his shirt.

He knelt in the ice-cold flow of water, its touch like jagged slivers of glass against his skin, and tried to wring the blood and grime from his shirtsleeves. Since he wasn't using any soap, he ultimately knew his effort wouldn't be particularly successful, but it would help to some small extent. Next came his trousers and he tried to do the same for them. Then he stripped off the union suit. Though he was going to change into the less dirty one, the sleeves and torso of the one he currently wore were particularly thick with blood from last night. The blood of the kid whom he'd been forced to shoot.

Once his clothes, still reeking like a charnel house, but somewhat less so, were laid out across some large rocks, Altar turned back to his horse. He hoped the sun could help with the smell as he dug the soap from the saddlebag, unwrapping the tiny sliver.

He stood with his back facing the river, still more or less out of view of the others. Even though the scars along his back were well healed, he still resented them and loathed talking about them and what they represented. He'd found the best strategy was to keep them covered and out of sight.

The water was cold, and looking down through the turbulent flow, his feet looked blue as they sought purchase on the slippery stones underneath the flowing stream. He waded out, naked as a jaybird, his teeth chattering against the freezing temperature, his skin bristling with goose bumps, the sliver of soap clutched in his now pink-stained left hand.

It was a test of his will to push himself to go out farther, deeper into the frigid, swirling current, but he wanted to be clean. Clean of the dirt, clean of the sweat, and clean of the blood. He'd collected enough of all three over the days past.

Back on the bank, Shepard and Eppley were digging in their saddlebags for something to eat. Harmon sat on a large rock and wrapped his arms around his bent legs. His Stetson pushed back, he laid his forehead against his knees.

When Altar had progressed far enough out, he began to scrub his hands. The sharp scent of the soap smelled clean at least, though his flesh had a ways to go, and his soul was probably permanently stained, if not lost altogether.

Aware of Shepard's stare, Altar turned away, the distance being great enough to blur the healed red lacerations on his back, but he was half afraid the man would see the desperation with which he scoured his soiled skin.

Dog had slunk back among them. First the animal sated his thirst, then he sank down and lay near the water, his massive head on his paws.

Altar worked the soap into a lather, focusing his attention on retaining his precious but slippery sliver. Half blue, he dunked his head and worked his hair into a sudsy froth that dripped white cloudy bubbles onto the surface of the river, then churned and floated away. He wished it carried away his sins as easily but knew better and suspected he'd answer for them one day, whether in this earthly existence or at the pearly gates, should those actually exist.

He rinsed and shook his hair free of as much moisture as he could. Still clutching his now much tinier sliver of soap, Altar began wading back to the shore where his clothes had hopefully dried somewhat in the sun.

The water was just above his knees when Dog's head jerked up, his teeth bared. A deep-throated growl emitted from his gullet.

What had dog heard or smelled? Altar looked to the other side of the river. Two horsemen pushed through the pines.

Indians.

Chapter 26
He sensed his skin grow hot with the blood rushing to his face

The two Lakota Indian warriors were mounted on spotted ponies. One rider was tall, the disparity made all the more obvious by the short stature of his mount. The man was so tall it seemed he could touch the ground if he had a mind to.

How many Indians of this height were there? Altar wondered. He knew of at least one, who was a noted warrior.

They were like statues. The tall Indian, whose visage had been baked by years of sun and wind, had long jet-black hair that hung loose around his head, his face painted with lines of white and red. His shirt was festooned with beads, and a bib of thin bones was strung together across his chest. Altar suspected a similar bib rested on his back.

The other rider was younger with smoother skin, his face streaked longways with white paint, his thick black hair braided with cords. He was dressed in skins adorned with tufts of human hair.

Both men held repeating rifles and had knives and tomahawks tucked into belts around their waists. The two sat still and didn't say anything or make another move.

Altar spun as four more horsemen erupted out of the forest not far from him. Their shrill war whoops threatened to pierce his eardrums and perhaps even his courage. They held their rifles high overhead as they rode all out from the trees.

Altar was alone.

Did it all come down to this? he thought. All the events leading up to where he stood, naked, flashed in his mind in the instant it takes for a single thought . . . his lost love, the war, the search for his brother, the wagon train, and this new and urgent search.

Was this how he was going to die? Naked. Weaponless. Up to his knees in the cold water of the river.

The look in the kid's eyes, squatting in the dark, his pants down around his ankles, caught unawares, was etched in Altar's brain as if chiseled in stone. As well as the image of the boy's cooling body, his chest rent wide, and his boots smeared in shit.

Would Altar be an afterthought to some

Lakota warrior, though he doubted they would see the taking of a life in such a fashion. Striking down a white man wasn't something to which a warrior would give a second thought; it wasn't in their culture. Not after what they'd been subjected to again and again at the hands of the white man.

He stood motionless, possum-like, then something stirred from behind the riders and caught his attention.

It was the squaws, still mounted upon a single horse. They rode out of the trees and stopped.

There was hope.

They must have talked to the warriors, told them of their rescue.

Hadn't they?

But would the warriors have listened?

Did their rage burn beyond reason?

The metallic clack of a rifle's action broke the unexpected silence.

"No!" Altar shouted at Shepard and Eppley, who had already grabbed their rifles and were leveraging cartridges into the breeches. They were inviting disaster. Altar knew they were all dead if he was wrong.

"Wait, Shep," he shouted over his shoulder. "Don't shoot!"

"What?" Shepard shouted, as wide-eyed

as Eppley had been at Buzzard Gulch.

"Let's see what they want," Altar shouted back. "We'd be dead already if that's what they wanted."

Harmon, whose red hair blazed in the light, had fallen off his rock and now looked over its peak, his revolver in his hand.

Dog stood at the water's edge, his hackles high along his spine.

Altar wanted to send him off but knew the beast would never abandon him in a fight. "Dog! Stay!"

The growling continued deep in the animal's chest, but he stood in his place and moved not a hair.

The four riders turned at the last second and rode around the white men. The Indian warriors plunged into the river. The ponies' hooves showered fountains of water in a high arching spray that twinkled in the sun like diamonds.

The riders split, two on either side of Altar and his companions, who had all shuffled around their respective, yet inadequate, boulders looking for cover.

Altar, still knee-deep in the water, naked, turned toward the river and the Indians. His hands were empty, aside from the tiny sliver of soap, and felt as heavy as if they were made of pig iron.

The four Indian warriors whooped more, then fell silent.

Across the river, the tall Indian slipped his rifle into a tanned leather sleeve, adorned with human hair, red cloth, and feathers, that he slung around his shoulder. Afterward, he and the other rider on the opposite bank kneed their mounts forward, splashing slowly into the water. The younger man's rifle butt still rested on his thigh, the barrel, whose muzzle was ornamented with feathers, toward the sky.

A glance over his shoulder showed Altar the women had not moved from where they had halted, not far from the forest from which they'd appeared. They sat motionless, though the woman in back, not much more than a girl, peered around the foremost rider so she could see the developments.

The younger rider stopped. The tall Indian continued until he was a horse length away from Altar. He suspected the Indian was taller even than himself, by several inches.

"Who are you that speaks our tongue?" asked the tall man in Lakota.

"I am called John Altar," he answered, in somewhat broken Lakota. "But I am known by some of your people as One with a Striped Back."

"Who was it give you this name?"

"Spotted Elk."

The large Indian's face broke into something akin to a grin.

"Could be," he said. "Spotted Elk spoke of one that he named such. Show me your back."

Altar slowly turned away. He felt so exposed standing naked, weaponless, his back to six Lakota warriors. He stopped and looked at Shepard, whose mouth hung open. Altar felt the scars that ran up and down his back seize and pinch as if they were all in a tight knot, like someone was thrusting darning needles into him. The scars were years old but seemed as inflamed as if they'd been whipped onto his torso just yesterday.

Looking over his shoulder, Altar saw the tall Indian nod.

After a moment, the Indian said, "It is as Spotted Elk spoke."

Altar turned to face him.

The tall man touched his chest. "I am Touch the Clouds, son of Chief Lone Horn, brother of Spotted Elk, Frog, and Hook Nose of the *Minneconjou Lahkota.*" The Indian's twinkling eyes hardened, and his mouth twisted into a grim smirk. "Why does One with a Striped Back trespass on sacred

Lahkota ground?"

"We hunt some wicked men." Altar pointed in the direction he believed the fort lay. "They who stole our women and killed our friends. And they now hide in your land."

"How do you know this?"

"We have tracked them. We believe the men who took our women are in the fort in the pass."

Touch the Clouds nodded, his face an impenetrable mask of grave portent.

"It was you who killed the men who slaughtered our elders and children."

It was a statement.

He had spoken to the women.

"We did."

"No," Touch the Clouds said. "It was you and you alone who did this. They told me you are a great *ozuye.*"

Altar nodded, knowing Touch the Clouds had not only spoken to the women but listened as well.

"And it was you who placed the elders and children in the *čhán*?"

"Yes."

Touch the Clouds stared at Altar unblinking as if weighing his words, his eyes revealing a cunning intelligence. After several moments of apparent thought, Touch the

Clouds reined his horse around and cantered back through the river to the other bank, to where a new rider, much older and nearly as tall, sat just outside of the pine trees.

The two men conferred.

After several minutes of conversation, both Indians gesturing with their long arms, Touch the Clouds returned. He again sat silent for several moments, the gurgling of the river the only sound before he finally spoke. When he did, his voice was low.

"One with a Striped Back is known to my people," Touch the Clouds said. "Known as a great *ozuye*. But that does not give One with a Striped Back freedom to walk our lands."

Touch the Clouds stared down at Altar. His face, with eyes as black as onyx, didn't reveal any of the man's thoughts. He continued.

"You did a service for our people," Touch the Clouds said. "By placing the bodies of our dead in the *čhán,* you have kept any from walking over their graves and have moved their spirits closer to the *wanagi makoce.* And it is for this, you have been given until Spotted Elk brings the rest of our nation to this place to take your *winyan* back from the *wašíču* in the *ča tipi* in the pass of the white eagle."

"How much time is that?"

"No more than two sleeps, perhaps one. There will be no *tipi* of *phê ča* come the sunrise following our attack." Touch the Clouds squinted to the extent Altar couldn't see his eyes clearly. "It will be consumed by the *phéta* of the *Minneconjou Lahkota.* If your *winyan* are not freed, they too will be consumed, and any left within its walls."

Altar nodded, feeling the chill creep up his legs to his spine, to his teeth, which started to rattle against the freezing temperature.

"Get your *winyan* and leave the sacred lands of our people." Touch the Clouds's chin rose perceptively. "For once the *phé tipi* is consumed, and the *wašíču's* bones are scattered, we will be on the hunt once again for those trespassing on the lands of our fathers. Our wrath is far from abated."

"Do we travel the true path to the fort, the *ča tipi*?"

After a moment, Touch the Clouds nodded once. "But know this. The *wašíču* there have a great gun, that spits many bullets."

"A cannon?" Altar hadn't heard or seen anything in his journey that would make him believe the outlaws had a cannon unless it had been disassembled in the wagon bed. Or perhaps the earlier Johnny Rebs had brought it.

"No cannon," Touch the Clouds said. "I have seen cannon used on my people. Though it sits on a two-wheel wagon, this is no cannon. It is a great repeater."

A repeater?

That could only mean one thing, and Altar hoped he wasn't right. He used one arm to make a cranking motion. "Did a man stand behind it and crank a handle, like this?"

Touch the Clouds nodded once again.

Suddenly, it wasn't the river making Altar shiver.

How'd the graybacks get a hold of a Gatling gun?

He hadn't much thought beyond getting to the damn fort. Not that he was thinking of a frontal assault with four men, but a Gatling gun changed things regardless. Did they have the ammunition for it? Why lug one around if you couldn't feed it cartridges, and it ate them at a prodigious rate?

"Iyéhantu," Touch the Clouds said, bringing Altar's attention back.

"Thank you for your gift of time." Altar bowed his head slightly. "We wish no fight with the Lakota people, but we must recover our women and avenge the death of our friends. I pray no conflict will arise between us."

"See to it you are gone from our lands and no conflict will result."

"I don't know how close we are to the fort and can't say how long it will be until we have our women."

"You will arrive by the setting of the *apawi,*" Touch the Clouds said. "But you will find the lodgepoles tall, and the gate barred against you. The repeating gun overlooks the gate and much of the wall. How is it you intend to free your *winyan* from the *phé tipi*?"

Altar stood silent, the frigid water running between his ice-cold feet. He didn't want to admit to this formidable warrior that he didn't have any idea as to how he'd accomplish his stated goal. It would be considered a weakness in his eyes.

Touch the Clouds's stoic face split in a grin and he chuckled a deep baritone laugh. After a moment, his expression returned to its grave, impenetrable stoniness.

"Touch the Clouds is not surprised that one who would attack five armed men in his underclothes, would not have a plan to attack the great *ča tipi.*"

Altar stood silent still, thinking he must look like a scolded child caught red-handed.

Touch the Clouds continued.

"Much time has passed since Touch the Clouds was a young warrior. But he used to sneak into the *phé tipi* to take food from the *wašíču,* perhaps you can find this way if it hasn't been discovered."

Altar shivered and fought against his teeth chattering.

"Before you reach the *phé tipi* in White Eagle Pass, you will cross a creek with high banks. A bridge was built by the soldiers that still stands. Walk upstream and you will find where the *hé até howáya* and there you should find a path that leads to a covered *tipi* within the *phé* walls. There is a trapdoor you might find useful if it hasn't been barred against you."

Altar stared for a moment. What did he mean by *hé até howáya*? "The father mountain cries?"

"Thank you, Touch the Clouds," he said. "But why do you share this with me?"

"The bones of the *wašíčus* can be scattered, whether you or the *Lakhota* kill them is of no consequence."

Altar suddenly understood. "You, too, are scared of the Gatling gun."

Touch the Clouds's head canted in apparent confusion.

"The great repeater gun you spoke of,"

Altar said. "You are as fearful of it as I am."

"Spotted Elk had said One with a Striped Back was no fool," Touch the Clouds said. "In this he was correct as well. There is also the matter of the *wašíču's* leader. He is a great *tatanka* of a man. He stands as tall and broad as any of the great beasts Touch the Clouds has seen, his beard is dark and long. But he is wicked and mean as any *hoká*. With the repeating gun it would cost the *Lakhota* many *ozuye*."

It was Altar's turn to chuckle. "You would like us to whittle down the spiked *tipi* before you attack."

The tall Indian grinned. "It is as Touch the Clouds has heard the *wašíču* say, 'it could not hurt.' "

Altar bowed his head once again as Touch the Clouds spun his horse around and cantered across the river, plowing through the turbulent current in widening waves, followed by the other warriors in his wake. The squaws' horse splashed through the water as well. As the mount climbed the opposite bank toward the trees, the young woman riding in the rear looked back at him.

He realized he was naked and felt the effects of the extreme cold on his manhood.

The Indian girl smiled, removed a hand

from the waist of the foremost rider, and covered her mouth. She finally looked away as the receding line of Indians disappeared into the forest. She gripped the front woman with both hands again as their horse was urged to keep up.

Despite the freezing temperature, he sensed his skin grow hot with the blood rushing to his face.

Chapter 27
There's going to be plenty of men need killing, ain't gonna be no want for it

"Well, I'll be damned," Shepard said. "Why didn't you say you spoke Indian?"

"Didn't . . . ever . . . come . . . up . . . before."

Altar dressed without talking any further, worried his teeth would chatter louder than his voice. He was surprised Shepard hadn't heard him speaking to the Indian women earlier when he'd set them free, though it had been under his breath.

"What'd that tall son of a bitch say?" Harmon asked.

Altar still didn't reply. He finished buttoning his shirt and then sat on a rock to pull on his boots. His clothes, though damp, had in fact, been warmed by the sun. He stood and retrieved his hat from where it hung on his saddle's pommel and snugged it on his head.

"I thought we was for certain dead," Eppley said. "Starting with you, Mister Altar.

Shucks, talk about getting caught with your pants down."

Altar buckled his gun belt on and finally felt like himself. He took in a deep breath and turned his face to the sun to feel its comforting rays. Regardless, a coldness had settled in his gut, and he knew it was a tough road they'd have to plow. Uncertainty surrounded their chances of freeing those women, of finding his brother, of even surviving. He turned to the men.

"We should be at the fort by sundown," he said.

"That's all you spoke of?" Shepard asked. "Seemed you talked a whole lot longer than it would've taken him to tell you that."

"That's a fact," Harmon said. "What else did that big red bastard say?"

Altar spat. Seemed like every time the diminutive deputy spoke, it stuck in his craw. "Said, them Rebs got a Gatling gun sitting on top of their gate, just waiting for the likes of us or anyone else to come riding up."

"Well, hell!" Shepard ripped his own hat from his head and slapped his thigh. Dust burst out into the air; some twinkled in the light. He turned and kicked at a stone that rattled along the rocky bank to splash into the river.

"What're we gonna do then?" Eppley asked, his sparsely bearded face still drained of color.

Altar pointed down the two-track in the direction of the fort. "We're going to proceed to the fort. Take them women back and maybe kill a few of those outlaws."

"Sure." Harmon sneered, and looked at the sky in apparent disbelief. "Sounds easy enough, Gatling gun be damned, I suppose."

Eppley looked from Harmon to Altar to Shepard, who still faced the river, his back to the group. "You reckon?" Eppley's voice broke.

"Time's wasting." Altar mounted his horse. "Let's ride."

"Well." Harmon peered at Eppley. "Can't say I've a hankering to go charging up to that fort and knock. Seems Eppley here is of a like mind."

Eppley's throat worked as if it were a production for the young man to swallow.

"I told the marshal I'd bring Mister Altar back," Eppley said. "So, I got to ride with him to be true to my word." Eppley's face grew even paler as he spoke.

"If you've a mind to go back," Altar said. "Do it now. Ain't going to speak to your being a coward. I'm aiming to go get those women, just like I promised Merle here. But we're wasting sunlight jawing and all. So, stay or go, up to you. But I'm moving on up this trail." He whistled at Dog, then kneed his horse and pulled the reins. His mount cantered off, up the overgrown two-track with the mule in tow and Dog following along. Shepard trailed, then Eppley after a couple of moments' hesitation. Finally, Harmon kicked back, and his horse trotted off, last in line.

The trail wasn't difficult, though it rose continually, weaving through gorges and past massive stone outcroppings.

Seemed a funny place to put a fort, Altar thought, wondering when he'd get a look at its structure.

It was in a difficult location to reach but wouldn't have been a good logistical position for being resupplied. Perhaps it commanded a good view; it certainly was on high ground. Any enemy force would have a hell of a time reaching them. But whatever the U.S. Army had been thinking was no concern of his. He needed to find that cave, and hoped it led to the trapdoor Touch the Clouds had spoken of.

Altar pushed his mount, always keeping an eye ahead to ensure they didn't happen upon any of the fort outlaws acting as a lookout. Shepard caught up and rode abreast of Altar.

"You're riding harder than before," Shepard said. "What else did the Indian tell you?"

Altar glanced back to make sure the other two were out of earshot.

"He said he was a-waiting for the rest of the *Minneconjou* Lakota nation before they attack the fort."

"And I reckon that attack is somewhat imminent," Shepard said. "On account of your hightailing it down this trail."

" 'Imminent' captures what the man said well enough," Altar said. "His brother Spotted Elk is leading them."

"You know this Spotted Elk?"

"I do."

"I guess he's a mean son of a bitch, too?" Shepard asked.

"Wouldn't be leading the remaining warriors if he wasn't."

"How many warriors constitutes a nation?"

"Damned if I know," Altar said. "But I guarantee it's a good deal more than I'd like to try and wrangle."

"Hell," Shepard said. "I wasn't too keen on tangling with that passel of warriors we just seen, truth be told."

"Agreed."

"Especially with our pants down like yours was." Shepard's chuckle was anything but merry.

They rode on together in silence for several minutes.

"John," Shepard said.

Altar looked over at the former deputy.

Shepard's lips went flat, the lines around his eyes deepened, and his gaze hardened. "What I said before still holds true."

"I figured that."

Neither man spoke for several more seconds.

Then Shepard said, "I'm gonna kill every one of them sons of bitches and any man gets in my way. They gonna pay for what they done to my Bess, and whatever else they done to Elizabeth and Molly."

"I heard you the first time, Merle." Altar turned his head to look at Shepard. "But family is family, and you got your sister and her daughter to think about, just like I got my little brother."

But it was as if Shepard hadn't heard the last part of what he'd said.

"Exactly," Shepard said. "You'd do the same, someone killed your wife."

Altar took a deep breath and let it out,

surprised at how deep not having a wife cut him. But that prospect had been long ago.

"Suppose I would at that." Altar looked back to the trail. "I surmise there's going to be plenty of men need killing, ain't gonna be no want for it, that's for sure."

"Still." Shepard reined his horse to slow. "Don't get in my way, I wouldn't want to hurt — someone I consider a friend."

"That's mighty neighborly of you, but do what you got to do, Merle," Altar said. Then, to himself: "And I'll do likewise."

Chapter 28
This Charlie Munther...
Touch the Clouds is
clearly fearful of him

Altar wondered whether he'd find the creek and bridge before he caught sight of the fort. Certainly, the creek was between them and the fort, but there was a good chance they'd glimpse the fort from a distance.

A little farther down the trail, they'd topped a rise that dipped into a valley, at the bottom of which was the steep-sided creek. A narrow one-lane bridge spanned the gully caused by the running water. Altar had stopped them before they all had made the apex.

It was a natural choke point, and as such, would be the ideal place to post a sentry. He removed his spyglass and scanned the landscape carefully. He stared long and hard, going over the terrain again and again. It was crucial to his plan, such as it was, to remain undiscovered.

It wasn't until he was convinced it was clear that he led his ragtag bunch of cowboys down the slope. The ages of Eppley and Harmon really weighed on him, knowing both men were young and mostly untested. He shook his head. They were more a burden than helpful.

Too late to be thinking like that, he thought.

They skirted the trail and rode along the top of the near side of the creek. Altar recognized they wouldn't be able to remain above the creek for long and he began to look for a way down the side that wouldn't risk breaking a horse's leg.

The water didn't look overly deep, nor swift, but the creek bottom did look rocky and might cause the horses some trouble. He'd assess once they were down there, but he figured it was as good a chance as any that they'd be walking their mounts.

Before the pines choked off this side of the creek completely, Altar found a way to get the horses into the water. It was only a matter of time until they'd be on foot. A lame horse would never do; they only had the six extra and more women than that, and they couldn't plan on stealing any from the fort. As it was, they'd have to obtain extra mounts or a wagon for the women or they'd have to double up.

He stopped, looked over his shoulder. "We're walking. Get them boots off."

"Well, hell," Shepard said.

They pushed on, silent except for the occasional snort of a horse, but even those were few. It was as if the animals were aware of the importance of being quiet. They slogged their way through the water, which had deep pools peppered along the bed.

Where "The father mountain cries in pain"? What the hell did Touch the Clouds mean?

Many times, they stopped to search a part of the bank that Altar or Shepard thought looked promising. For what, Altar wasn't sure. They almost always looked on their left; it would be the bank on the fort side of the creek.

"How's Dog gonna find us?" Shepard asked. "We been walking in this creek for a while."

"He'll find us." Altar smiled. "Don't fret none on account of that critter."

Altar wasn't sure how long it had been when a wide low opening loomed ahead, but it was time enough that most of the feeling had been frozen out of his feet. The mouth of the cave was on their left, with a steady flow of water spilling out to run down and join the creek.

It occurred to Altar that the cave's mouth faintly resembled an eye. Water running from the eye of the father mountain, as if it were crying.

He stopped. It could be.

They watched for several minutes.

Then Altar handed his reins to Shepard, pulled his Remington, and started forward to what he hoped was the cave, an empty one, with no critters. His feet were numb with cold; he could hardly feel the stone beneath the soles of his feet. As best he could, he made sure his footing was good before he stepped. There was little purchase anywhere against the steep incline of what served as a bank, other than the trough the water had carved into the stone through years and years of drainage.

The stone was slippery, and in places green algae made it even worse. He didn't hear anything as he neared the cave opening, except for the running water and the occasional swish of a horse's tail behind him.

He was taken back to his younger days. How many times had he and Bobby explored caves such as this one back in Missouri? Their county was filthy with them. He'd not likely be able to count the number, and he probably couldn't remember but just a fraction of them.

There was no odor emanating from the

cave's mouth when he got close, which brought a sigh of relief from Altar, worried a bear or cougar could be inside. He stepped through the opening and moved forward. A fat snake of unknown species slithered, albeit lethargically, deeper into the darkness. It hadn't been a rattler, so he didn't much care. Shortly, he glimpsed something coppery as the light diminished.

He shuffled over and, in the shadows, saw what he recognized instantly as the remains of a still that had been kicked over. He'd seen enough of them in the army, and some in Missouri as well growing up. What little he could see led him to believe it was old, and had been there for a long time.

A round firepit had been made of stone off to one side. He figured whoever made it had put it close to the mouth of the cave to vent the smoke.

It started to make sense to him. He could well imagine some enterprising trooper slipping down the tunnel and setting up a still to sell the moonshine to his unit. Especially since some of the more remote outposts were run loosely, their commanding officers not having to worry about the draw of a town to work on his troopers' discipline, allowing him to be more relaxed.

There was little sound coming from the

blackness at the back of the space, just the drip of water and gurgle of the rivulet that ran out of the darkness to pour out of the cave's mouth. Altar expected the cave to smell dank, earthy, but he was surprised when he also thought he detected the odor of horses.

He knew he must stink of the animals, even though he'd washed in the river. But he hadn't used any soap on his clothes, and they might still smell like horses. He lifted his shirt and sniffed. Sweat, the odor of his body. Better since he'd washed, but it still wasn't pleasant. There was a little horse scent mixed in with his sweat and the stench of his soiled shirt. But not like what was drifting out of the darkness. He suspected the trapdoor that Touch the Clouds spoke of led into the horse stalls. Smelling the animals was a good sign.

He returned to the cave's mouth and beckoned Eppley over.

"Do you have any of those candles left?" Altar asked.

Eppley nodded.

"Get one lit." Altar holstered his Remington. "Make it quick."

"Yes, sir." Eppley spun on his heel, lost his footing, and practically tumbled into the stream. He righted himself and scrambled, stiff-legged, to his horse to dig into his saddlebag. He pulled out a box and a cinched cloth bag.

He splashed to the bank and opened the sack. He sat the taper on the rock, away from any water. Then he opened his tinderbox and prepared to light it.

"Merle." Altar raised his chin at his horse. "Get my boots, your boots, and your rifle and get on up here."

Shepard grunted an acknowledgment.

"Harmon," Altar said. "You gather the reins and get the horses picketed in them trees." He pointed toward the pines on the side of the bank where the incline was horse friendly, opposite the cave's mouth. "Keep them quiet."

Harmon snorted and looked as if he was about to say something, then didn't.

Maybe that dumbass was getting a little smarter, Altar thought.

It took a minute before Eppley had the candle going with any kind of strength. He brought it over to Altar, cupping his hand around the flame against any breeze that might blow up.

"Here you go, Mister Altar." Eppley handed the candle up the bank.

"Thanks, Dillon," Altar said. "You go and stand watch with Harmon."

"Ain't you gonna take us with you?" Harmon asked as he collected the reins using both hands.

"Just reconnoitering." Altar helped Shepard up the bank with his free hand.

"Mister Altar, all due respect, but ain't that what you said before you killed all them men last night?" Eppley asked.

"Opportunity presented itself, Dillon," Altar said. He got Shepard's attention and pointed to the mouth of the cave. "I want you here. Keep watch, there's a good view, but stay in the cave's entrance as much as you can." Then to the other two with the horses: "You secure those animals and keep your ears open should anyone or any critter try and sneak up on you."

"And what are you fixing to do?" Shepard asked.

"Reconnoiter," Altar said. "Take a look-see at what's back there."

"Seems Dillon's got a point, though," Shepard said. "Considering last time, you took matters into your own hands."

"There's a good deal more than five men up in that fort, Merle," Altar said. "We'll be lucky if any of us walk away from this. It's going to take us all if we're to free them women and get out of here before the Lakota descend on this place and burn it to the ground."

Shepard grabbed Altar's arm. "What'd you say?"

"Touch the Clouds said they were going to set fire to the fort with everyone in it."

"What else he say that you ain't shared?"

Altar saw something more than fear in the eyes of the former deputy, something touching on panic. He'd seen many similar looks in the eyes of men, both young and old, on the eve of battle.

"Said they didn't care who might be within its walls."

"They ain't likely to have any compunction about burning it down with us inside, are they?"

"They ain't."

Shepard's face broke into a grim smirk. "And I thought y'all were friends."

Altar shook his head slowly.

"We respect one another, and freeing the squaws won us a reprieve," Altar said. "But either of us would cut the other's throat without hesitation given the chance. He's a very dangerous man. So is his big brother, Spotted Elk."

"Well," Shepard said. "Ain't that a sharp stick in the eye. Why ain't you worried none?"

"I am worried," Altar said.

"You ain't showing it."

"I'm all knotted up on the inside." Altar rotated the candle to keep the flame even. "There is something, though, that has me a bit more concerned."

"What's that?" Shepard asked.

"The leader of the outlaws. This Charlie Munther," Altar said. "Touch the Clouds is clearly fearful of him."

"Oh," Shepard said. "That could be a problem. Didn't we hear he was a mean bastard?"

"Yep."

"We gonna wait for Dog?"

"Ain't got time," Altar said. "If he's not back, we have to move on. Besides, I don't know how he'd do all closed in like."

The cave was dark, lit by the radius of the flickering yellow candle's light with a thin wispy gray stream of smoke circling up in the thick air. Altar had to duck and in some places crouch to make his way farther into the darkness held at bay by the taper's trembling flame.

All the while he followed the course of the water. At several points he encountered shallow alcoves. In one he found the remains of a long dead trooper face down on the stone, as if someone had pounced on the man's back, yanked his head back, and slit his throat. The decrepit corpse, now more skeleton than cadaver, didn't reveal its final secret, but Altar could well imagine Touch the Clouds killing this man in such a fashion.

His uniform was battered, brown with bloodstains, the soles of his riding boots worn almost through. How many years had he lain thus? Five? Ten?

As Altar worked his way back, he had to dodge around formations that had grown from the floor of the cave, not unlike fangs. He felt a drop of what he thought was water hit him in the head, and when he looked up, he found there were others seemingly growing from the ceiling of the cave as well.

After about fifty feet, he came across a substantial opening leading away from the water, and some small stones looked to have rolled out of the black space. Altar extended the candle into the opening. The passageway, bigger than any other he'd seen to this point, was dry, no water and there was very little moisture. Above all, the candle revealed a light breeze coming from it, like there was a vent of some kind. More rocks were scattered about the floor of the cave, and it was dusty. He stepped into the alcove and decided it was worth a look-see, as he could smell horses wafting from the darkness.

As he rounded a corner, more stone debris littered the floor that rose toward the narrow top of the cave's ceiling. It presented a slope of broken rock and stone. Some pieces small, others hand-sized, and several pieces very large, all piled together with dust and gravel.

There'd been a cave-in at some point in time, he surmised.

Altar saw the little cloud that his boots had kicked up. If they started digging, they wouldn't be able to see on account of the dirty fog they'd create. And without much breeze, it wouldn't settle anytime soon, maybe years.

He stared.

Finally, he made out a darker patch at the top of the piled stone. Was it an opening, or just a recess, ultimately still blocked? He had to know.

He found a ledge up on the wall of the cavity, dripped wax onto the stone, and set the end of the taper into the puddle, waiting for it to make fast.

He carefully stepped where he thought it would disturb the least amount of dust and hold his weight so he wouldn't slide down. Slowly, he ascended the slope of stone. Soon he was hard-pressed to move without raising a shifting cloud of darkness into the air. He could smell the earthy powder in his nose, threatening to make him sneeze.

His legs trembled from the strain as he made his way high enough to see that it wasn't a pocket, but a hole at the very top of the pile. He stretched, placed a hand as delicately as he could on a large stone that looked as if it would hold his weight without moving, and tried to glimpse into the hole.

He couldn't see, but the smell of horses grew in intensity. This was it.

He knew they'd found the passage.

The question was, could they clear enough of the debris in time to make their way through it into the fort? They'd burned plenty of precious time getting here. Did they have enough left to rescue the women? And what about Bobby? He still had to negotiate that briar patch.

Best to get to it, he thought.

He backed down, retrieved the candle, and hurried back to the mouth of the cave. They had four sets of hands between them, none skilled in moving that much rock, not to mention the dust clogging any chance to breathe or see. Didn't Gulliford say he was a prospector? Maybe one of the three men waiting back at the cave's mouth would have similar experience?

None's the luck, he found. But he and Shepard quickly came up with a plan, all the while knowing the hands of time ran faster than they could hope.

They worked as swiftly as they could, all wearing bandanas over their noses and mouths against the particles of minute dirt and ground stone that threatened to choke them. Eppley dammed up the water with what he could haul from the debris pile. Altar and Shepard used tin cups and whatever they could get to hold water to throw on the piled rock and stone to keep the dust from getting too thick. And Harmon, finally his small size good for something, was at the top of the pile digging like some kind of badger, making the hole bigger.

When Harmon got tired, Altar went next, then Shepard and finally Eppley. Altar wanted to make the opening large enough they could get the women back this way, though that wouldn't account for mounts. But his mind was working, thinking of ways he could manage getting horses around from the fort, down to where the cave entrance was. And maybe stranding the outlaws to boot.

It was difficult for Altar to mark the time, being in the cave for so long. But he knew they were burning through it at a prodigious rate. It was now late at night.

He found himself praying that Spotted Elk had been delayed. He'd been in many a battle and hadn't done all that much praying. He couldn't figure why he found himself doing so now. Was their predicament just that hopeless? But hadn't he been in worse situations? Just like the sergeant had reminded him before they left Buzzard Gulch about that fight in the plains. Altar had been in plenty of tight spots.

Or was it because he was about to find his little brother, something he'd been breaking his ass to do for months?

Did he miss Bobby? Sure, he did. Didn't he? But what version of Bobby awaited him? And would he have to fight Merle Shepard? Which, on the face of it, didn't worry Altar, but Shepard was a friend, and he wasn't in the habit of hurting friends.

Any way he looked at it, a very rough road lay before him.

Chapter 29
Quit jawing and move your ass

By the time they'd gotten the opening wide enough, they'd almost burned through Eppley's very last candle, and they were all caked with mud and dust and were blacker than any miner he'd ever seen. They gathered on the other side of the cave-in and began to move through the wider passage that led upwards, sometimes at a steep incline.

The last fifty feet were difficult, almost straight up in a vertical cleft that acted like a chimney rising. Altar climbed with Harmon behind him holding the remains of the candle. The whole time, the odor of the horses and hay grew in intensity.

Even though the cleft still rose, Altar found himself facing boards, on the other side of which he could hear the shuffling of large animals.

And it sounded as if the horses were restless. They could probably smell and hear them. Harmon handed the candle around and Altar could see that they faced a series of boards that probably constituted part of a wall. The wood was weathered and gray.

The three lowest boards were bound together by a curious brace of wood. Then he realized the brace held the planks together so they could be pushed away from the wall, as they were cut on each end an arm's-length wide. He handed the candle back to Harmon, put his palms against the wood, and pushed, gingerly at first and then applying more pressure. It wouldn't budge. Finally, he strained as hard as he could, his back against the stone, but the boards held still, though he could feel them about to give.

He shuffled over and motioned for Harmon to get up next to him as best he could.

He whispered, "Careful, it's about to give, can't make too much noise."

The two men pressed with ever-increasing pressure until the top of the uppermost plank shifted, almost completely coming from under the one above it.

Altar patted Harmon's chest. "Just me."

The makeshift door held against Altar's strength, but just as he was about to call on Harmon to help again, the wood came free. Altar caught the braced planks just before they hit the ground.

Large shadowy shapes milled away from the opening, becoming horses as they walked off without panicking. The space was dark after the candlelit passageway, but his eyes adjusted quickly.

He recognized the powerful smell of a barn, hay, horses, some leather, as things started to focus. Then it occurred to him the horses were roaming free and not closed in stalls. In fact, the whole floor of the barn seemed to be open. Maybe the building was more of a warehouse than a barn, but it clearly was being used for animals now.

Altar lowered the planks to the ground and crawled out of the opening, scraping his back on the wood overhead. He climbed to his feet, staying in a crouch. He picked the boards up and leaned them against the wall.

Reaching back, Altar clasped Harmon's wrist and pulled him through, whispering to him to douse the light. Then he leaned in and whispered to the other two men, "C'mon."

The building was situated longways against the cliffside, and there were doors on either end of the short walls. Some of the animals had wandered out of the door to the left, which led to some kind of paddock in graying darkness that foretold the coming of sunrise.

The door to the right, visible by the lightened darkness around the frame, was closed. Altar hoped it would lead deeper into the fort. He motioned everyone close together.

"Use your knife if ya run into one of them, if you can," he said in a whisper. "Gunfire will wake them all up."

They walked quietly to the closed barn door. Altar pulled the handle and swung the door open enough to see outside.

The lightening shadows revealed a two-story building with no windows or doors directly across from the barn. To the left loomed a thin, low building. Between the two structures, Altar could make out a large open area, probably parade grounds. Vaguely, he made out a timber in the middle of the flat ground, probably a flagpole, and behind that some kind of low building he took to be a barracks. The red glow of dying embers shone some short distance in front of the one door of the barracks, probably a cookfire, he surmised.

As he stared, he started to make out what he thought to be a man lying in front of the fire, like he was asleep or passed out. And another figure sitting on the ground, leaned up against the barracks wall, but whether he slumbered or not Altar couldn't tell.

Where would they be holding the women? Or had the women been given out like slaves and were now amongst the outlaws?

And where was Bobby? Altar needed information, and the only way to garner it would be to get it from someone. Where would the outhouses be, he wondered. Behind the barracks more than likely, if this fort held to any of the others he'd frequented. And what about the Gatling gun on the front gate? Where exactly was that? So many questions.

If the long low building across the parade ground was a barracks, then likely the one to his left was another barracks, behind which, by his reckoning, should be some privies.

He turned and started back across the barn for the open door opposite them.

"C'mon," he whispered. "We're gonna try the other door."

Shepard grabbed his arm. The man's eyes were sunken, and stood out particularly vividly even in the darkness from his mud-covered face. They were bloodshot and hardened almost beyond humanity.

"Why are we wasting time, John?"

"We got to get some intelligence, Merle.

We don't know how many we're up against, or where they got the women," Altar said. "Trust me."

"Sun's gonna be up soon."

"Damn near," Altar said. "Quit jawing and move your ass."

As they walked toward the other side, they passed a hay wagon, its tongue up and leaning back against the front board like a guidon.

Once they'd gone out of the other door, they found they were among horses, twenty or so animals ranging in comparative health from a broken-down nag to good animals, not obviously ill or abused, at least from what he could see in a quick glance.

"Down," Altar said with a hiss.

A tower loomed just on the other side of the paddock. It was tall, giving any lookout a good view in front of the wall, and behind it as well. Its platform was surrounded by three waist-high walls, leaving the only opening facing into the fort.

"Well, hell," Shepard said under his breath. "Anyone up there?"

"Can't rightly tell," Altar said. "Just as well to assume they got someone posted. I know I would."

Several moments passed. Altar couldn't see any men standing in the tower, but his angle wouldn't let him see the entirety of the platform, and the shadows were deep on the far side of the structure.

"Spread out," Altar whispered. "Follow, go slow."

He started for the paddock's fence line underneath the tower in a crouch, his Remington in hand. He could feel more than see the others coming along with him.

"Merle," he whispered, pointing to the long building now to their right. They were barracks, as he'd thought. "Watch that doorway yonder."

Altar stepped through the paddock bars. How did they get up to the tower's top? He didn't see any stairs, at least not on this side. Maybe a ladder? Shepard came to him and knelt.

"You see any jakes?" Altar asked.

"I can smell 'em," Shepard hissed. "Other side of the tower looks like a row of them."

"Wait here while I check out the tower." Altar shuffled off as quietly as he could, his Remington held low against his leg.

Even though he had a knife, he figured he could club someone with the revolver if he wanted to be quiet; his hammer rested on an empty cylinder after all, though he recognized the flaw in his thinking. You couldn't throw a revolver, or if you did it would be downright stupid. He wouldn't have been happy if any of the other men were thinking like he was.

His former squad commander's voice reverberated in his mind: "Do as I say, trooper, not as I do."

How he had hated hearing that, as he sweated in the baking sun, knowing full well there were better ways to do their assigned task. The army beat into its men to follow orders at all costs, and in his case, just beat him. Whipped him, to be more precise. But that hadn't been for anything he'd done as a soldier, not even as an officer, though his flogging had happened at the academy. In fact, they'd ignored a long-standing Presidential order outlawing flogging.

But the academy's commander, a brutal man even by army standards, had justified its use by saying Altar had broken a moral law, one set down by God, not by the army. And just like that, saying Altar had transgressed God's law, he'd been ordered to endure hundreds of slashes, flaying the flesh from his back, hence his Indian name. All on account of a girl, a young woman, the commander's daughter. Altar never professed to be smart; that was something others said about him.

"Do as I say, not as I do." Fine words for

a commanding officer to say to his charges, and yet flaunt his freedom to do otherwise in their presence.

But I'd better stop reminiscing about the past, Altar thought. *Got enough trouble in the here and now.*

A ladder rested against the tower, the topmost rung reaching over the tower's floor by about a yard. Altar holstered his Remington and started up. The wood creaked and felt loose under his feet. Maybe it would've been smarter to send Harmon, he was lighter by far. Up until he got to the top — then who knew what Harmon would do when faced with an outlaw should one be on the platform.

Altar climbed as slowly as he could, considering they were pressed for time.

What if he were to find an outlaw? Would the man be awake? If he were asleep, would Altar be able to cut the man's throat? Certainly, a quiet conversation would be just about impossible with an adversary, let alone asking about his brother without the others at the foot of the tower overhearing.

He remembered Shepard's crazed look as he'd said, "I'm gonna kill every one of them sons of bitches."

Altar liked Shepard, but there was no way he was going to let the man kill Bobby, friend or no.

What to do?

What to do?

What to do?

The next rung emitted a loud creak, startling him.

Up and up he climbed, torn about what he'd do when he arrived at the top of the ladder, which, of course, depended on what he found. As he neared the top, he pushed his hat off to drop onto his back, held by the leather cord. A sound reached his ear as he got closer to the platform. One that gave him at least a little comfort, but nevertheless indicated he'd have to make a choice.

He peeked over the edge and confirmed what he'd been hearing as he ascended.

Someone was indeed there, leaned into a corner of the platform's walls, fast asleep. His snores quiet, yet perceptible. And there was no one else. A rifle lay across the man's lap within easy reach.

"Hsssst." The sound, perhaps quiet, seemed loud and abrasive as it floated up from below.

Altar twisted around to stare down at Shepard, recognizable because of his beard, who looked ready to make the sound again.

Altar cautiously waved one hand to urge the man to be silent. He held out one finger, hopeful Shepard would understand there was only one outlaw, that is if Shepard could even discern the gesture in the darkness.

Carefully, Altar edged onto the platform, not wanting to dislodge the ladder or make any noise. Despite his best efforts, the wooden floor creaked as he put his weight on it.

Altar withdrew his knife from its leather sheath as the outlaw's snoring stopped. The man raised his one hand to his mouth and ran his arm along his lips as he braced the other against the deck of the platform. He coughed quietly, clearing his throat.

"Ain't like you none to relieve me early," the outlaw said, starting to rise.

"Ain't here to relieve you, son." Altar took a couple of quick steps and clapped one hand over the man's mouth, driving his head back against the wooden wall with a deep thunk, while Altar's other hand brought his knife against the man's throat. "Yield or die."

Altar knelt on the man's legs, effectively trapping the rifle underneath his own weight, the trigger assembly directly under his leg.

The outlaw struggled, but his eyes looked dazed and unfocused.

Altar pushed the blade in a fraction until

he could see blood freely spill down the man's neck. The man stopped moving, his confused wide eyes staring into Altar's blackened, mud-covered face.

"I'm gonna ask you some questions," Altar said in a whisper. "Answer quietly and truthfully, and you don't have to die. Yell out and I'll cut your throat. Get it?"

The man nodded emphatically as more blood seeped from the wound.

"Where's the women from Spring Creek?" Altar loosened the palm of his hand over the man's mouth, ready to clamp it tight again should he try and yell.

"Some's in the barracks, couple up in the house," the man said in a hoarse murmur. "And two or three's in the jail, by the main house, the ones got uppity."

"How many women altogether?"

"Don't rightly know," the outlaw said. "Somewheres around ten, twelve."

"You took more than that."

"I didn't take any. I was up here in the fort already. But I was told some died along the way." The man gulped, his eyes growing wider. "I didn't have nuttin' to do with them dying, you gotta believe me, mister."

Altar swallowed and fought the desire to slash this man's throat. The outlaw's focus danced from side to side as if he was looking for someone to save him.

After a moment, Altar felt he'd regained his composure.

"How many of you are there?"

"In the fort?"

"Yep," Altar said.

"Upwards of thirty, I guess," the man said. "But we're expecting more. More's coming behind us."

No, they aren't, Altar thought.

"Where's Bobby Altar?"

The man stared at Altar as if he was crazy. It took a couple of seconds before he said anything.

"Bobby Altar?"

"That's what I said."

"I don't rightly know, why you askin'?"

"Is he here at the fort?"

The man's tongue played across his lips.

"Why you asking about Bobby?"

"Where is he, dammit?" The tension in his hand made the knife tremble. The outlaw's eyes opened even wider.

"Don't know, mister." The man swallowed. "He wasn't with them that brought the women. Maybe he's coming with those coming yet."

Altar worried that maybe he'd missed his brother among the dead outlaws.

Couldn't be, he told himself. *I don't care*

how much he's changed on the inside, I would have recognized my little brother. Where the hell was Bobby?

"Who's in charge?" he finally asked.

"Captain Munther," the man said.

"Where can I find him?"

"He's usually in the house along with his lieutenant last I seen, sometimes he's up to the barracks."

"Where'd this Munther come from?" Altar wanted to know who could frighten Touch the Clouds.

"Kansas Raider, Captain Charlie Munther. Says he rode with Bloody Bill Anderson for a time." The man coughed. "Charlie come to Missouri by way of Louisiana. Right smart fella, but meaner than a snakebit hog. I seen him twist a man's head clean off his shoulders once when we was prisoners up in Camp Douglas."

"What're you all doing up here in Indian country?"

"Ain't gonna be Indian country long," the man said. "Heard they found gold in these mountains. We're the first whites back up this way. Just staking claim. Them Indians gonna have to be moved once the gold strike hits."

That sounded like more trouble for the Lakota, but Altar had more pressing things to worry about.

"I'm gonna tie you up and gag you," Altar said. "I'm a man of my word."

"So's Captain Munther," the man said. "Might as well cut my throat now. Charlie's like to kill me something fierce for failing him on guard duty."

"Well," Altar said. "Maybe something is about to happen to Munther that'll save your ass. Just be quiet."

"Ain't likely," the man said. "Gonna take a whole lot more than you to kill Charlie. You see, he told us he's from the swamps of Louisiana and can't be killed except for magic. Strong magic at that."

"Guess we'll see about that." Altar stood, lifting the rifle up and using the butt of the gun to hammer the man in the head, hopefully knocking him unconscious as opposed to killing him. Then he used strips cut from the man's shirt to gag him, and hog-tied him with his own belt and the shoulder strap from the rifle. He pocketed the shells from the gun, but found nothing else worthwhile in the fellow's pockets.

Altar wiped his blade on the man's gray clothing before sheathing the knife. He'd been tempted to just cut the man's throat, but he was confident the fellow would be out for a while. He hadn't seemed as bad as the others. Plus, he was young, perhaps Bobby's age. Regardless, Touch the Clouds and Spotted Elk would likely take care of the rest.

Altar straightened, and it was only then he saw the tinge of red on the horizon. Dawn.

Shit.

Chapter 30
Put a Cork in it Your Own Self... You Old Wet Hen

Altar hung over the edge of the platform and whispered into the darkness.

"Merle."

A form came up a couple of rungs of the ladder. It was Shepard. Altar handed him the outlaw sentry's rifle. Shepard backed down the ladder.

Altar climbed down and found all eyes upon him. If it hadn't been for the height difference, Eppley and Harmon would've been hard to tell apart with everyone covered in dirt and dust.

Shepard looked up to the top of the tower. "You kill him?"

Altar shrugged, a little disturbed when he realized he didn't really care whether he had or not. "Maybe. Hog-tied him and gagged him after I clubbed him in the head with this rifle."

Altar wiped his hands on his pants and looked skyward. "The sun's coming up. If the Lakota don't come, the outlaws'll be able to see us shortly."

"Well, hell," Shepard said.

"Merle, check the jakes." Altar's whisper was harsh and a little loud. "Wave if you find one occupied."

Shepard walked off toward outhouse row.

"Dillon, watch him and let me know if he waves," Altar said in a lower pitch. He touched Harmon's shoulder. "We're going to that door and see if we hear anything."

The barracks door wasn't more than fifteen strides. Eppley stood at the base of the tower unmoving, and Altar couldn't see Shepard because of the angle of the outhouse row. The morning was silent, except for the breeze and some horse sounds from the paddocks. There was little insect noise.

Altar stepped carefully, trying not to make any sound, or kick a rock, or anything that might rouse someone's curiosity.

His ear to the wood of the door didn't reveal any sound of life on the other side. He gently pushed the door, and it moved inward under his touch and then caught. It was smooth on their side, probably a leather loop or a handle on the inside to be pulled open, he guessed.

A minute later, Eppley and Shepard stood behind him.

"Empty," Shepard whispered.

Altar pulled Shepard up to him and spoke low into his ear. "I'm going to shove this door open. Follow me in. Take Eppley and go the other way. Harmon is with me. Check your side for outlaws and women. If you got to kill anyone, use your knife, and don't let them make a sound. Careful the ladies don't scream; you might have to hold their mouths or something."

Shepard nodded and grabbed Eppley's shirt, pulling him along. Altar situated Harmon behind him. There was just enough light that Altar nodded at each man and saw their acknowledgments. He pulled his knife and waited for the others to do likewise.

He pushed the door open, following it around to prevent it from hitting the wall. He felt Shepard and Eppley shuffle past him and then Harmon was there. The room was wide, with an open door opposite them, and a table in between, a couple of chairs and two benches haphazardly arranged around it. A lantern, its light almost nonexistent, had been placed in the middle of the table; a couple of empty bottles and a deck of playing cards were scattered across the surface.

As Altar's eyes adjusted, he could see a

couple of wall sconces were overburdened with extinguished candles, the wax having dripped down the timber wall. He didn't see anyone other than Shepard and Eppley already moving through the door on their end. Altar tapped Harmon on the chest and started off for the other opening. He leaned in close to Harmon.

"Stay by that door." He pointed to the door opening into the parade grounds. "And watch for anyone coming here. Come get me if you have the time, otherwise you're just gonna have to kill them. Remember — no gun — use your knife."

Harmon didn't acknowledge, but walked around the table and took up a post adjacent to the open door. The small deputy took off his Stetson and peeked out of the opening.

The next room was long, full of bunks up against the wall on either side. Altar couldn't make out whether anyone was in the beds. As much as he didn't want to stroll down the middle of the room, he didn't have a choice. He carefully moved down the open aisle, glancing to either side. Just as he was about to declare the place empty, he came across a bed with someone in it.

He gazed at the lump a moment but couldn't discern much beyond that whoever was in the bed didn't snore. The bedroll was so bundled, he had a hard time telling how big the person was; other than that they weren't huge, he couldn't even tell whether it was a man or woman.

That sure presented a problem, he thought.

He stepped over so the bunk was on his right, his strong side. He didn't want to stare, but he had to find the person's head.

Throughout his life, Altar had felt he could sense someone glaring at him; it gave him a prickly feeling on the back of his neck. And he was hesitant to do the same to someone else just in case they had similar feelings. It had kept Altar alive on more than one occasion.

Finally, he made out a stubble-lined chin protruding from the dark blanket. Not a woman. So, that made him an outlaw.

Altar wondered how safe these men felt. On the trail, Altar usually slept with his pistol handy, sometimes on his stomach with his hand upon it. Could this man be doing the same or were the walls of the compound, and the thirty-odd bandits and the presence of the towers, making him feel safe to where he wouldn't employ those kinds of precautions?

Altar gripped his knife tightly, crouched, and drove his empty hand into the covers to tighten around the man's throat.

The man's eyes shot open. One hand erupted out of the blanket and clawed at Altar's fingers, trying desperately to loosen his grip, while the man's other hand dug deeper under the covers.

It had to be a gun or knife he was searching for, neither of which would be welcome.

Altar drove his blade down, putting as much of his weight behind the knife as he could manage while keeping his feet. The steel cut through a couple of layers of the coarse woven blanket before it was stopped.

The man's eyes bulged out, his mouth open, gasping for breath as he fought. The stink of stale whiskey emitted from his gullet, the foul odor practically gagging Altar as he slashed down with his blade, not sure whether he'd even cut the man.

Their twisting, writhing bodies sent the bunk crashing over, spilling the men onto the floor with an audible boom. Altar fell on top of his adversary, who was still wrapped up in the heavy blanket.

A muffled blast, heavy and deep, left no doubt what the man had been fighting to reach. The discharge felt more like a cannon's concussion than a revolver. Bits of cloth exploded into the air and Altar felt the heat expelled from the barrel scorch his thigh. Still gripping the outlaw's throat, Altar thrust his blade through the man's filthy shirt into his exposed chest. The bony flesh minutely deflected the blade, but Altar felt the steel bite deep past the man's ribs. He pushed until the hilt stopped and then twisted the knife. He grunted with effort and heard an audible crack.

The man's back arched, he croaked something unintelligible with Altar's iron grip fastened to his throat. Blood spewed from the man's mouth and Altar felt the hot droplets splash across his face and neck. The man's limbs stilled, and he finally slumped to his side, unmoving.

Altar rolled the dead man over. A heavy cavalry pistol fell from the blanket to clunk onto the floor. It was ancient. A Colt Dragoon. And huge. He pulled the knife from the man's chest, with some difficulty, as it had got hung up on a rib. Wiping it down on the man's gray pants, Altar saw a familiar butternut yellow strip descended along the leg. Confederate Army pants.

The tack-tack-tack of boots running across the wooden floor foretold Harmon's having left his post. Then more from deeper in the building, Eppley and Shepard hopefully. Altar quickly felt through the dead man's pockets for anything useful. He found nothing. Harmon raced up, paused to swallow, then asked, "Thought you said no shootin'?" His breath came in gasps. Altar didn't think it was from the exertion of running across a couple of rooms. Was the man that anxious?

Altar picked up the cavalry revolver, hefting it in his hand.

Sure made them big back then, he thought.

No need to make reloading any easier than necessary, and he wasn't about to hump that hogleg around. He quickly released the cylinder and tossed it catty-corner from where they were standing.

Eppley, ducking Altar's throw, came up behind Harmon. He towered over the shorter man, whose red hair shone in the night as the cylinder rattled to a stop on the floor.

"Where's Shep?" Altar asked.

"We come across Miss Pearl and one of the outlaws. Sleeping," Eppley said. "Mister Shepard's having a word with 'em."

Altar grabbed Eppley's shoulder. "Where?"

Was it Bobby?

As they started back toward the front, he said to Harmon, "Get back on that door. And for God's sake, put your hat on, your mop's a damn beacon."

He followed Eppley through the middle room into the other side of the barracks, set up like the one they'd just left.

Shepard was hunched over a bunk, talking so low he couldn't be heard over their steps on the wooden floor. A thick woman with mussed hair, wearing a chemise, sobbed quietly off to the wall side of a second bunk that had been pushed up adjacent to the one Shepard was now bent over.

Altar prayed it wasn't Bobby —

"Merle." He pulled Shepard back. The man's face was still blackened, but his eyes were wide, and wild, like he was beyond reason.

Altar looked down.

It wasn't Bobby. *Thank God,* he thought.

The man in the bunk was dead, his naked chest soaked in blood, his eyes expansive as if they had been about to pop from his head, his mouth frozen in a grimace of agony.

Eppley tried to comfort the woman, but she pulled away and gasped, then retched.

Altar checked Shepard's hands. They were empty. The knife was still protruding from the man's chest, among a score of other puncture wounds. A second glance showed the kid couldn't have been much over twenty.

"What happened?" Altar asked.

Shepard's stare was distant and vacant. He lowered his head to look at the dead man, then at the woman, and finally back to Altar.

"Why, Merle?" She wiped her mouth with her hand. "Why?"

Shepard's gaze snapped back to her. His teeth appeared in a smirk beneath his beard and mustache.

"And what about you, Pearl?" Shepard's voice was a hiss. "Sleeping with the likes of him." The last words spoken as if he'd spat.

"He didn't do nothing to you, Merle," she gasped. "You just kept on stabbing him, he didn't do nothing to you."

"Didn't have to do nothing to me," Shepard said, his voice growing toward a roar. "After what they did to my Bess. He had it coming. All of 'em do."

"Merle," Altar said. "Lower your voice."

"But he wasn't with them that was in Spring Creek," the woman said, her voice growing in volume as well. "He was already here when they brung us."

"He's a bastard," Shepard shouted, and glared at Altar. "Like any other son of a bitch who's with them."

I have to find Bobby before Shepard does, Altar thought. *And soon, if that gunshot didn't wake the devil, these two sure are gonna —*

"It wasn't like that, Merle," she said, pleading too late. "The ones that was here wasn't like the others. Not like those animals who brought us, that Munther and his killers."

"Ma'am." Altar held up a hand. "We got a lot of work to do, and not much time. This is gonna have to wait 'til we're all safe."

Pearl's jaw stopped and she went silent. The tears still streamed down her face as she mumbled, "The boy just wanted cuddles." She took her face in her hands and whispered, "Like his mama used to give him."

Altar grabbed Shepard and shook him.

"Can't kill everyone, Merle." Altar shook him again and again, until reason returned to Shepard's eyes. "And we got to find the other women."

Shepard stared at him for a moment, glanced down at his bloody hands, then jerked away from Altar's grasp.

"God dammit!" The voice sounded like it came from across the parade ground. "Shut that bitch up before I come over there and do it myself."

Altar found himself holding his breath.

"Y'all hear me!"

Altar held a finger to his lips.

"Put a cork in it your own self," someone

yelled from the front door. "You old wet hen!"

It was Harmon! What in the hell was that idiot trying to do?

Chapter 31
Should make you dig for them your own self

Altar scrambled toward the front door of the barracks.

"What'd you say!" a loud voice shouted from outside. After a momentary pause, pregnant with expectation, "What'd you say, boy! You son of a bitch."

Altar found Harmon leaning out of the doorjamb about to respond and pulled him back. "You trying to get us killed?"

Harmon's gaze, in his dirt-saturated face, was confused. "Figured it'd help, I reckoned he was expectin' a response, so I give him one."

"We were trying to get in and out without being seen." Or heard, Altar thought as he pushed Harmon away from the door. The deputy tripped over a chair and fell to the floor with a crash.

"You better hightail it, you know what's good for you!" A door slammed hard from across the parade ground. "Let me get my hands on you, boy."

  Altar hazarded a glance out the door and caught sight of a burly man the size and girth of a damn outhouse storming across the parade ground in the brightening morning light.

  The man kicked at a figure lying by the dying fire as he stormed past. He wore a flowing white nightshirt, suspenders holding up trousers, and boots. Matted hair like that of a bison protruded at angles from his head, his face, and from out of his nightshirt's neck hole.

  Altar swallowed. This wasn't likely to be kept quiet. He turned and grabbed the fallen chair and waited. The man's steps sounded heavy, even on the hard-packed earth of the parade ground. His breathing more audible the closer he got.

  There was one bootheel strike on the wooden porch before the door burst open and the man charged through the doorway. He was a massive blur of dark hair with a bearlike snarl and was every bit as enormous as Altar had feared.

  Altar swung the chair as hard as he could manage given the confined space, aiming for the fellow's head. The burly man got an arm partially up to deflect some of the blow, but he was still staggered and fell back against the wall and rolled to the floor. The shards of the chair rattled to the ground inside and out of the barracks.

Altar found he was only holding onto the chair's back, the rest having splintered apart. He raised it over his head and stabbed down with all his weight behind the blow, trying to drive the jagged wooden spindles through the man's eyes into his brain, if he even had one. It was like fighting a grizzly, more savage than human.

The chair back shattered, one jagged shaft gouging a deep furrow across the man's scalp and leaving a matted trail of black hair oozing dark liquid. An enormous hand tried to staunch the flow of streaming blood, while the other sought to grab Altar.

Altar high-stepped over the man's grasp and drove a bootheel into his face. The blow glanced off his cheekbone, and Altar's ankle was seized by what felt like a vice. He was lifted into the air and flipped off to the side as if he were a stuffed toy.

He rolled and got to his feet as the burly man rose like a damn giant. His head, bigger than a bushel basket, seemed to disappear in the darkness of the rafters. A flash of white teeth glinted from the ursine countenance.

A woman's voice shrieked on par with a

steam whistle.

"Kill him!" It was Miss Pearl, who was being pulled back into the other room. "That's Munther, the murdering son of a bitch!"

The large man crouched in a fighting stance, both massive hands held in front of him. Blood pumped freely down his face.

Altar drew his revolver, thumbed the hammer back, and fired.

A deafening click, nothing more.

Munther smiled, his teeth colored red.

"Can't kill me, boy. Not with iron."

And he charged.

Before Altar could pull the hammer back again, Munther wrapped his arms around him and lifted him from the ground again. The man's chest was like an iron plate. The pressure Munther put on Altar's rib cage made it nearly impossible to breathe. His back cracked and his feet dangled above the floor. He felt like a little boy for a second time in just a few short breaths. He prayed his ribs wouldn't splinter and brought his knee up, aiming for Munther's groin, but the huge man had anticipated this and shifted his hips, keeping his privates out of the line of attack.

Munther chuckled. His breath stank of fetid meat.

"They tell you I twisted a man's head clean from his shoulders, boy?" He laughed again, further compressing Altar's chest. "Done it twice, truth be told, started with chickens when I was just a wee lad."

Another chair broke across Munther's broad back.

The big man tossed Altar to the side across the table like a rag doll. Altar fell to the floor, and got to his feet in time to see Munther palm Harmon's face and squeeze. The deputy screeched and went limp.

Munther turned to face Altar. The big man's lips parted in a savage, feral snarl.

"Watch this. I'm going to twist his head clean off."

Altar reached out for a fragment of the shattered chair, grabbed a broken leg, and smashed it against Munther's shin.

The man-mountain howled in pain and let Harmon's limp body drop to the floor.

"I'm gonna kill you first," the giant said, lumbering toward Altar.

Not wanting the man to know about Shepard and Eppley, Altar dove out of the barracks door, rolled to his feet across the porch, and backed into the parade ground, hoping to draw the man out. Altar's hand dropped to his empty holster.

Munther's eyes followed the motion, and

he grinned.

A swooshing sound erupted overhead, ending with several thunks into the roof of the barracks.

Flaming arrows.

"Indians!" The cry, more of a scream, came from the tower by the foremost front gate. "Lots of 'em!"

The crack of a rifle followed. And another. Another wave of burning arrows descended. Shouts from inside the barracks opposite Altar meant all the outlaws were awakened, which was just as well with the Lakota nation on hand.

Munther stepped from under the barracks porch and looked around, wiped the blood from one eye, then spat.

"As white men, seems we have a common foe," Munther said. "After we kill us some redskins, I'm going to look forward to continuing this fight, boy. I sure am." With that, the enormous bear of a man loped off, barking orders at men who were spilling from the barracks door.

Altar ran back inside the barracks and found Harmon still crumpled on the floor in the shadows. He couldn't tell whether the deputy was breathing or not.

"Shepard," Altar called and started for the side where the others should be. "Shepard."

Shepard, who had Miss Pearl wrapped in his arms, her face buried in his chest, was beyond the door, while Eppley peeked from around the jamb.

"Is he dead?" Eppley asked.

"Who?"

"Harmon."

"Can't say as I know," Altar said. "Be quick, see if you can help him."

Eppley quickly stepped to Harmon, then slowly sank to a knee next to the prone deputy, apparently not sure how to proceed.

Altar looked at Shepard. "Touch the Clouds and Spotted Elk are here."

"Shit," Shepard said.

Altar found his revolver as Eppley tried to revive Harmon.

"What happened to that big son of a bitch?" Shepard asked, bringing Miss Pearl into the room.

"Walked off." Altar opened his cylinder breech. The cap had been hit by the hammer. Why hadn't it detonated? "Said we'd finish the fight when he got done with the Indians."

"Why didn't you shoot him?"

"Tried," Altar said. "Misfired."

"He's lucky."

"The bastard told me he couldn't be killed by iron." Altar smirked as he adjusted the cylinder so the next rotation would land on a loaded chamber.

"Hmmm." Shepard stared at him. "I take it you're not a superstitious man?"

"Nope." Altar reluctantly holstered his revolver with only four rounds, but he didn't have the time or the fixings to reload.

"How many times you have a misfire?"

"It happens from time to time," Altar said.

"In a gunfight?"

"This wasn't a gunfight per se."

"Sure would've been handy to put a big old hole through that son of a bitch."

"Ain't gonna argue with you on that score."

Shepard shook his head. "I ain't liking this none."

"Makes two of us," Altar said. "But with these guys fighting the Indians, we got a chance; we need to round up the women and skedaddle."

"Time's a-wasting."

Altar grabbed Eppley and pulled him to his feet. "I got him."

Then to Shepard: "You and Dillon go round up the women from the barracks. I'm taking Harmon to the tunnel, then I'm headed to the jail. Guard said they had women there too. Get them women started down that hole."

Altar saw some of the madness creep into Shepard's stare.

"Get them women, Merle," Altar said. "Save Elizabeth and Molly. The killing can wait."

"C'mon." Shepard pulled Eppley out of the barracks and they started across the parade ground against the background noise of gunshots and war whoops.

Altar half carried Harmon to the barn with Miss Pearl following. They stumbled through the open door and found the trapdoor propped where they'd left it. Altar lowered the deputy down and helped him lean against the wall. The man was dazed and bleeding from his nose, ears, and eyes. The injuries reminded Altar of someone who'd lived through an explosion, which he hadn't seen except for a couple of times in the war.

"I'll be back." Altar touched Harmon's skull and felt an unevenness to the bone. He knelt. Harmon's head lolled back, his mouth hung open, and his eyes rolled up under the lids. Altar shook his head, knowing that couldn't be good.

He turned to Miss Pearl.

"Watch over him, but if someone comes, go hide in the hay 'til we get back."

She nodded as she wiped a sleeve across

her eyes.

Altar ran out of the barn door and came to a stop.

Another man was striding toward the barn, a cavalry pistol held by his side and a saber in the other hand. A porkpie hat held down his curly hair, and he wore an unbuttoned long coat over a collared shirt, and dark trousers.

"Just what in the hell are you doing?" the man called out. "You're running the wrong goddamned way."

Altar thumbed his hammer back as he pulled the Remington, aimed, and fired. His bullet took the man in the face, blowing his hat off. The man's cavalry revolver discharged at the ground, throwing clots of dirt into the air.

Altar ran past the man, sprawled on his back, arms out, dead, blood pooling around his misshapen head.

Altar skipped the main house and ran to the jail, which was on the other side.

The door was ajar. He pushed through and found no one in the first room, just a couple of desks and chairs, and glowing embers in a stone hearth. There was a gun rack on one wall, a double-barreled shotgun resting within its slots. The iron bar normally used to lock the weapons in place was nowhere to be seen. A ring of lockup keys hung from a nail pounded into the mortar of the stone fireplace. As he pulled the keys down, he heard sobs from further into the building. On the other side of the only remaining door, someone's soft voice sung low over the quiet crying.

The door was open and a candle, with barely any wick left, cast a quivering light from a stool that failed to reach every corner of the room. Several cells lined one wall. A woman, her dress lined with wrinkles and stains, nestled a figure on her lap. She sat on a bunk in the middle cell. She was singing a hymn to the prone figure, who continued to sob.

"I'm here to help you. We gotta go." Altar stepped to the cell door and worked one of the keys through the lock's opening. It wouldn't turn. He tried another, then another.

"Not your lucky day," the woman said.

"But it's yours." The third and final key turned.

"Ain't nothing been on account of luck since them bastards came to Spring Creek." The woman stroked the long dark hair of the figure whose head rested on her lap. "Who're you?"

"A friend." Altar swung the door open

with a creak of iron hinges. "Merle Shepard and Dillon Eppley are rounding up the other women. We got to go. Now."

The woman didn't move other than to close her eyes as if she was praying.

"Ma'am, please."

She leaned down and whispered to the figure.

"Molly, dear," she said in a singsong voice. "Seems we're going to be with the other girls; sit up, please."

The arms of the prone woman visibly tightened as her head shook violently and her knees curled up into a ball.

The woman continued to whisper soothing words and sounds. Altar barely heard her say, "This man's a friend of Uncle Merle. He says Dillon Eppley is here too. They've come to save us."

She stroked the girl's hair a couple more times, apparently trying to gentle her way out of Molly's clutching grip. She finally looked up at Altar, her eyes, moist from tears, pleading for intervention.

"She's been like this since —" The woman swallowed. "For a while now."

A coordinated battery of rifle fire split the night. The woman's head jerked toward the door. "What's happening?"

"Indians, ma'am." Altar stepped to her.

"They're attacking. We have to go."

As gently as he could, Altar pried Molly's fingers from around the woman's waist and picked her up. At first the girl fought him, then the pushing changed to a tightening of her arms around his throat, threatening to cut off his air. There were no more sobs coming from her, just the feral hiss of survival. Her strength wasn't comparable to what he'd experienced at the hands of Munther, but she was powerful for her size.

"I'm here to help you," he said hoarsely. The arms finally relaxed enough he could breathe. "Are there any others here with y'all?"

"Not anymore," the woman said.

"Are you Elizabeth?"

"I am."

Altar twisted so his Remington was next to her. "You know how to shoot one of these?"

She stared at the revolver and swallowed. "I'd rather not."

"There's a scattergun next door if that's more to your liking." Altar went through the cell door, careful not to bang Molly's head on the bars.

"I know you're not from Spring Creek, mister." Elizabeth gathered up a wool blanket. "But you sound like one of these

Southern boys."

"From Missouri, ma'am. I was a federal soldier." Altar used his head to point at the shotgun. "You know how to check if it's loaded?"

Elizabeth threw the blanket onto a desk and pulled the shotgun down. It wasn't until he saw her next to the long gun that he realized how short she was. She wasn't much taller than the shotgun's length. When she broke the breech quickly, he knew she was familiar with the weapon.

"Empty," she said.

"Check the desk drawers."

She put the gun on top of the blanket and pulled one drawer out after the next. Finally, from the bottom drawer of the second desk, she brought out a box of shells. With a skip, she returned to the first desk, where she thumbed two shells in place and snapped the breech closed. She quickly undid the two top buttons of her dress and dumped a handful of shells inside, jiggled, and added two more.

She looked up, caught Altar's stare, and smiled. "Ain't you ever seen a woman conceal nothing before?"

He just shook his head.

She balled up the blanket, grabbed the shotgun. and followed him out the door.

Far up ahead, Eppley led a couple of women into the barn. Several more were running across the smoky parade grounds, and one was at the door to the barracks.

No Shepard.

The roof of the barracks they'd been in earlier was now ablaze, black smoke curling high into the brightening morning. The other barracks was untouched, as it was shielded from the wall by another building. But that building was consumed in flames that danced high into the morning air.

As if in answer to Altar's look, a staccato series of cracks erupted from the tower, shooting periodic flashes horizontally outward from the fort. Billowing sulfuric smoke was blown back by the breeze.

The Gatling gun — it had to be wreaking its havoc upon the Lakota.

Where the hell was Bobby in all this chaos, Altar wondered as he carried Molly toward the barn. Elizabeth was somewhere behind them.

Eppley knelt next to Harmon as Altar came up carrying Molly.

"Dillon," he said. "Take Molly."

Eppley looked up, confusion in his stare. Then he rose, needing a hand on the ground to push off as if he was injured. Harmon looked much the same as when Altar had left him, and that wasn't good.

As Altar handed over Molly, who reminded him of one of his little sisters, Eppley grimaced.

"You hurt?" Altar asked.

"A little." Eppley hefted Molly, who clasped him tight. The deputy's grimace deepened.

"Where?"

"My back." Eppley half turned. "Think it was an arrow, but it just cut me, thank God."

There was a slash across Eppley's shoulder blade that had indeed sliced through his blackened shirt, but it wasn't bleeding much, due in large part to the dust and dirt clogging the laceration.

"Good thing you didn't catch fire," Altar said.

But Eppley was murmuring to Molly in low comforting tones, though the stress underlying his voice betrayed his true anxiety.

Another woman stumbled into the barn, followed by a cloud of smoke.

Altar grabbed her. "Where's Shepard?"

"Still searching for Elizabeth and Molly." She coughed. "Said he wouldn't leave without them."

Altar turned to Elizabeth. "Help Dillon

get people started into the tunnel and see if you can tell who's not here," he said. "I'm going to get Merle."

He held out his hands for the shotgun. She handed it over.

"Them shells ain't gonna do you no good in that tunnel," he said, again holding his empty hand out. "And I might need them."

She smiled.

"Should make you dig for them your own self." Elizabeth reached into her cleavage and came out with four shells, which she placed in his hand. He didn't wait for her to search for any more, and turned and ran from the barn.

Chapter 32
. . . some people say Munther killed him . . .

The parade ground was filled with a swirling diaphanous vapor in which vague manlike gray figures toiled on the far side of Altar's field of vision, which had been greatly reduced. The smoke burned his eyes and fouled his throat. He coughed, but ran on, each breath torturing his lungs.

When he was almost upon the untouched barracks, Shepard came out, his revolver in his hand. His head worked back and forth before he started across the parade ground, seemingly for the main house.

Altar cupped his empty hand next to his mouth. "Merle!"

Shepard took a couple more steps, then stopped, glancing toward him with eyes so red Altar couldn't make out the irises.

"I can't find Elizabeth and Molly!" Shepard's voice was reduced to a croak, caught in his dry throat.

"I got 'em. They're by the tunnel." Altar

grabbed the man's shoulder, shaking him. "They need you. Molly especially. Go!"

Shepard's eyes widened.

Altar pushed the man toward the barn. But Shepard caught his wrist.

"Where're you going?" It hurt to hear Shepard speak, his voice was so parched.

"I got to find Bobby."

"Leave him," Shepard cried. "Let him fall with his ilk."

Altar caught Shepard's shirt and knotted it in his fist. "I kept my promise to you. I got one more to keep."

"It'll be your death."

"Maybe. Go save what's left of your family," Altar said. "Let me do the same. Gimme two shots before you close the trapdoor, so I know you're safe."

Shepard started to say something, but Altar shook his head.

"Go," he said and pushed Shepard toward the barn. Then he turned and ran for the barracks he'd just vacated, whose roof was yet unfired. As he got closer, he saw there were men on top of the barracks, throwing buckets of water where arrows or embers sought purchase. They'd knocked down any blaze to this point, but the roof smoldered as if it was about to burst into flames.

Altar ran across the porch and through

the door. The first room was just like the one across the parade ground, lit by a couple of lanterns suspended from hooks on the wall. A man struggled with someone half lying on the table.

"I gotta get that bullet out, and whatever fabric's in the wound." The doctor wore a coat that looked black in the lantern light.

"Hell with that, Doc! Let me up. Indians gonna kill us all if we don't stop them."

The two men continued to struggle. Neither man was Bobby.

What am I going to do? Altar asked himself.

He needed answers — a plan.

Holding the shotgun one-handed, Altar pulled his Remington, held it by the cylinder, and clouted the injured man in the head with the handle. Dazed, the man fell back on the table and fought no more.

"There you go, Doc." Altar holstered his revolver. "Seeing as how you're plumb outta chloroform."

The doctor didn't say anything, but started to cut away at the man's clothing, trying to examine the wound underneath.

"You seen Bobby Altar?"

"Bobby Altar?" The doctor cut away the sleeve from the arm and started to probe the eviscerated flesh. "No, not since Douglas."

"Not since when? Didn't he come up here with you?"

"Not with me, he didn't," the doc said, never taking his eyes off his surgery. "I was among the first to get here to the fort. Best talk to Munther."

Another man banged through the door to the barracks. He was short and fat and carried a couple of bone saws in one hand and a pistol in the other. A dusty derby hat sat askew on his head; the tendrils of a mustache drooped beneath his chin. Worn-out suspenders struggled, in combination with a belt, to keep his pants up despite the effort his belly made to push them down.

"If'n you don't believe me," the doctor said over his shoulder, "ask Scooter here."

"What's that, Doc?" Scooter said, jamming the revolver under his belt.

"He's looking for Bob Altar."

The newcomer stood just to the side and behind the doctor, holding the saws. He stole a glance at Altar, his right eye off-kilter.

"Hospital's about burnt to the ground," Scooter said. "But I was able to get these 'uns." He held out the two saws to the doctor.

"Can't say I need 'em just yet," the doc said. "Just hang on to them for me."

Scooter looked at Altar. "Why's you looking for Bob?"

"He's my brother."

Scooter's left eye studied Altar. The other drifted toward the wall.

"You that federal brother of his he was always talking about?"

"One and the same."

Scooter swallowed and glanced at the doctor in his walleyed way.

"What'd you tell him?" Scooter asked the doctor.

"That Bob's not here and he should talk to Munther."

"Yep, that'd be best." Scooter swallowed again. "You tell him about his leg?"

"What're you talking about?" Altar growled and took a half step forward without even realizing it. "Was Bobby wounded?"

Scooter took a step back.

"I had to take his leg off above the knee." The doctor looked at Altar. "Both the tibia and fibula were shattered by a musket ball, and got rolled on by his horse over in Jackson County, Missouri, the Battle of Westport."

"He can't much ride a horse no more," Scooter said.

"If he ain't here, what do you think happened to him?" Altar asked.

"Can't say," Scooter said. "Some people say Munther killed him, twisted his head clean off his shoulders."

"I told you time and again, Scooter." The doctor turned his attention back to the unconscious man on the table. "It's a physical impossibility. Can't be done. Don't give no life to that nonsense."

"People seen him," Scooter said. "At least, seen him do it up in Camp Douglas."

The doctor shook his head as he continued to probe the wound.

"They say Munther can't be killed, except by magic," Scooter went on, as if in defiance of the doctor's protestations.

The doctor turned around, his hands bloody past his wrists. Splotches of blood stained his shirt under the coat.

"Scooter!" He pointed a scalpel at the walleyed man. "Enough of that malarkey." The doctor looked to Altar. "Regardless, Bob's not here and has never set foot in this fort. I'm sorry, but we got no idea where he might be." He turned back to his work at hand.

Scooter swallowed.

Altar couldn't help but wonder if the man's anxiety brought on all of his swallowing, or was it due to something else, like a physical condition or mental one. A lot of people were affected by the war in any number of ways.

"The way I hear it told," Scooter said, "was after they joined that Mormon wagon train that Bob and Munther got into it." Scooter looked at the doctor's back. "And Munther killed him night before the . . . Indians attacked."

"Quit telling them lies and get me some thread and a needle, Scooter," the doctor said without looking up.

Scooter patted his pockets, then frantically looked around.

Altar turned and walked back into the brightening morning and the last battle of Fort Merritt.

Apparently, the one man who knew about Bobby was this Munther. So, either Altar had to take the dubious word of Scooter or continue his search on his own. One thing was clear: He had to find Munther and make him talk.

He glanced around at the escalating chaos — fires everywhere, arrows raining down, gunshots, and the screams of the wounded and dying men and beasts.

Easier said than done, Altar thought, looking around for the giant of a man.

A bellowing voice that he recognized came

from over by the front gate tower. Altar went that way.

Munther, still wearing his bloody nightshirt with suspenders holding up his trousers, was at the base of the tower shouting up at the soldiers on the platform.

"Get ready to bucket me down cartridges!" The voice projected everywhere, it was so powerful. "Plenty of them. I'm going to bring up the other gun."

Munther turned and hurried off behind the barracks.

Other gun? Another Gatling? Altar wondered, but he thought not. He followed, vowing to find out what happened to his brother or die trying.

There was a row of outhouses, and Munther swept past them and headed toward a stable with its double doors standing open. A gate to a paddock in front of the stable was also ajar but there were no animals to be seen through the nebulous meandering smoke. Altar thought he could hear wild snorts and whinnies coming from within the structure.

They must be smelling the smoke, he thought. *That and all the gunfire.*

Munther went straight into the stable and disappeared in the shadows.

What was in there besides horses? He'd

said something about a gun.

Altar knew this was his only chance to get the answer he needed — to find out about Bobby. Plus the Lakotas' attack was intensifying. He had to work fast.

He hesitated a moment, then cocked the scattergun's hammers back and followed, slipping through the door as quietly as possible.

This stable was larger and much longer than the barn they'd crawled into from the tunnel. But it had stalls, many of which were occupied by scared horses. It resembled the stable at the United States Military Academy at West Point, but on a smaller scale.

It was in the shadow of that very stable, on a parade ground of a much grander scale than Fort Merritt's, that Altar had been whipped half to death.

Altar crept along the left side of the aisle next to the stalls, the shotgun in his hands ready to fire. A couple of lanterns suspended from hooks along the open corridor cast light on the hay-strewn dirt floor and threw shadows into the horse pens.

Munther's bellowing could be heard deeper in the building. When Altar encountered an empty stall, he'd step into the shadows and strain his ears trying to hear anything else from further within. In this way, he slowly progressed through the stable.

When he got to the end, there was an open space with a door leading out into the parade ground from the side of the building. Two men were walking away from attaching a team of horses to a flatbed freight wagon. Munther, there too, swiveled something that looked at first like a two-wheeled cart around.

Only it wasn't.

It was another Gatling gun.

The big man suddenly froze, as if sensing Altar's stare. Then he looked back and grinned. "Well, I'll be goddamned." Munther shook his head. "Thought you was smart enough to run — you're one dumb son of a bitch."

He stood and dropped the tongue of the gun's cart. Then he whistled at the two men walking from the wagon and pointed at Altar.

"Kill me that boy!"

Chapter 33
Where's Bobby,
you son of a bitch

The two men looked surprised, but both went for revolvers stuck in their waistbands.

Altar fired one shotgun barrel from his hip, instantly dropping the man on the left. He shifted his aim to the second man and pulled the other trigger. There was a pop, and a puff of smoke rose from the shotgun's firing chamber.

Another damn misfire.

Altar dove to his right, into an empty horse stall. Splinters flew from the nearby post as the shot's reverberation rolled over him. He broke the breech, flipped the two shells out, and quickly fished another two from his pocket. These he jammed into the firing chambers and closed the breech as he looked for the shooter. The man who'd been shot moaned and cursed, and could be heard moving on the ground not far away. Altar saw nothing of the other shooter.

"How bad ya hit?" a voice asked, from a

couple of stalls down.

"Bird shot is all, Gus." The answering voice was laced with agony. "If it'd been buckshot, I'd be dead for sure."

Altar got a bead on the injured man, recognizing that his voice came more or less from the area where he'd seen the guy go down. Altar leaned out, his finger already squeezing one trigger. He swung his aim to the prone figure and fired. He hadn't noticed the lesser recoil before, but this time, the scattergun bucked hard in his hand, and the figure was driven down into the dirt floor.

The man didn't make another sound.

Not bird shot in this, Altar thought.

He rolled back into the stall just as the other man stood and fired over the side of it, blowing a chunk of wood from the gate where Altar had just been standing. Altar fired the second barrel. The buckshot caught the man under his jaw and exploded upward. He fell straight down, like he'd been mule-kicked.

Altar heard a tinny click unlike anything he'd heard before.

"Guess I gotta do it myself," Munther said as a queer metallic ratcheting sound began.

The first rounds came through the horse stall's divider at about waist height. Splinters whipped past Altar as the boom echoed in his head. He dropped to the ground and flattened out as more bullets pierced the wood. Cascading slivers of kindling rained down on him as another concussion split his ears. Yet another projectile bore through the stall's barrier, followed by another and another. His ears rang with the deafening roar of the Gatling gun. Soon the air was filled with sawdust and the stall was covered in what looked like serrated pieces of snow, the barn filling with the acrid smoke from the burnt powder, mixing in with that of the fires.

Altar couldn't hear himself think as blast after blast after blast tore up the stall, but at least the rounds were going over his head. He was grateful the gun was on wheels and was so close. Munther would have to pick up the cart tongue while continuing to rotate the crank handle to get the weapon to shoot low enough to hit him.

But when would the damn thing run out of bullets?

Altar rolled onto his back and reloaded the shotgun with his last two shells, concentrating on keeping low. He couldn't tell whether the two cartridges were buckshot or not, nor even if they'd fire when struck by the firing pin.

He rolled back to his belly and tried to peer through the billowing gray haze and the bullet-ridden wall. And still the flames shot horizontally from the Gatling gun as its bullets blew through whatever was in their way, blowing shards of wood everywhere.

Suddenly it was quiet except for the metallic ratcheting noise that slowed to a stop.

"God dammit," Munther said. "Gus? Denny?"

Altar saw the wispy tendrils swirl as a large figure moved through them.

Munther must've run out of bullets. Was he coming for Altar or to the two shooters Altar had killed?

"Son of a bitch!" Munther growled like an animal. "Them two you killed was good boys."

Altar pulled the stock into his shoulder best he could, aimed the shotgun through the shattered stall a couple of inches off the dirt toward where he estimated the big man had stopped, and pulled the triggers. The force of both barrels going off at the same time punched the stock back violently into his shoulder at an odd angle. He felt something give as pain radiated down his right arm and across his chest.

He heard a howl of agony and felt, more than saw, something heavy hit the ground.

"You bastard!" Munther bellowed. "I'm going to enjoy killing you with my bare hands!"

Altar stood and grasped the shotgun by the smoking hot barrels. When a huge form charged through the stall's opening, Altar swung the butt around with every ounce of strength he could muster, striking Munther across his chest, and throat.

The big man fell to the side but clutched the shotgun and pulled it from Altar's grasp as easily as if he'd taken a peppermint stick from a child.

Munther tossed the shotgun through the air to rattle around another stall.

A horse cried and kicked the wall with a resounding thud, which resulted in several more horses kicking their stalls, all the while making bloodcurdling shrieks unlike anything Altar had ever heard come from a horse's throat.

Munther advanced.

Altar pulled his Remington and fanned the hammer, holding his trigger back, firing four rounds into Munther's chest. The man staggered backward a couple of steps, then stopped. After a second he grinned, not even breathing hard.

"I told you, boy," Munther said. "Iron can't hurt me."

He lunged at Altar.

Altar ducked and scrambled out of the way, bobbing under the man's outstretched arms. Munther's lower legs were bloody, and his boots had shot holes peppered in their leather, a couple of which leaked blood.

Munther's arm swung back and caught Altar across the chest.

It felt like he'd been rammed by a bull.

The breath was driven from his lungs as he stumbled backward. Pain radiated across his chest from Munther's backhanded blow, and his shoulder ached from the scattergun's double-barreled kick. Altar tried to suck in air even as he pulled his blade, watching Munther storm out of the wrecked stall, the acrid smoke parting in billowing waves.

He was like a bear in a goddamned nightshirt. All the horses, maybe a dozen, were going crazy in their stalls from the gunfire and smoke.

Altar couldn't help but wonder how this man was even standing, let alone fighting and not bleeding from four holes in his torso.

Altar sidestepped and stabbed into

Munther's gut. The blade thrust twisted aside, and Altar nearly lost his grip with the abrupt stoppage as his hand numbed.

"When're you gonna learn, boy?" Munther grabbed a handful of Altar's hair and lifted him onto his toes. "You can't hurt me." Munther's head craned back, then shot forward.

Altar sliced at the giant's wrist holding his hair and twisted his face against the granite-solid grip.

Munther's forehead blasted Altar's cheekbone as the blade sliced into something soft. What light there was winked out momentarily as hot blood sprayed across Altar's face, whether his own or Munther's, he was unsure. His hair was released and he fell back, reeling but managing to keep his feet under him.

"Well, I'll be damned." Munther leaned over, holding his wrist, blood oozing from between his fingers. "You done scratched me, boy."

Altar crouched as best he could, holding the knife in front of him.

Munther whipped a handful of dirt and straw into Altar's face. He tried to block it with his arm but had to shake his head to see. In the next instant Munther picked something else off the ground and took a long stride. Altar caught a glimpse of the giant of a man swinging a broken board. Altar whirled but still caught the brunt of the blow on his right arm as the wood broke in two. The knife fell from his numb hand.

He punched with his left fist, but the angle was bad, and the blow bounced off Munther's jaw as if thrown by a child. Altar skipped back to stay out of reach, his lungs fighting for air, as he worked the fingers on his right hand, trying to get some feeling back. His cheekbone felt broken, and warm blood trickled down his face, which was swelling tighter by the second. Would it impinge on his sight?

Munther threw the remaining piece of board at Altar, who sidestepped and let the wood sail past.

"I've had about enough of you, boy. Time to quit playing and end this."

Munther strode forward, trapping Altar in the stall. As Munther drew closer, Altar stepped forward, faked a punch, and kicked at the man's groin, but his assailant shifted with animalistic grace. Altar's booted foot bounced off Munther's thigh. The ursine man shoved Altar with both hands, sending him crashing into the heavy planks of the back wall.

Munther punched a sledgehammer-sized

fist into Altar's gut, doubling him over. Then Munther grabbed Altar's head and flung him, face first, into the boards again. Altar pawed at the wood to keep from falling only to have Munther drive two fists down on his back. Altar's knees buckled and he dropped.

He rolled as Munther's booted foot glanced off his shoulder. Altar whipped a handful of straw at Munther and stood, but he couldn't straighten all the way up.

Munther laughed as he circled. Altar's heavy breathing sucked in the horse-scented, dusty air as he continued to work some feeling back into his right hand. His ears throbbed in time with his bursting heart; the screams of horses and cracks of rifles fought against the ringing in his head brought on by the Gatling gun's synchronized concussive blasts. The swirling smoke had dissipated into a light gray fog mixed in with the fumes from the burning buildings.

The horrors of his previous wartime battles revisited him, and he wondered, *how long until the Lakota overrun the gate?*

Did Shepard and the women get out?

He'd never heard what should have been the signal shots from Merle, but how could he expect to discern them from all the other shooting?

"Time to put an end to this, as pleasurable as it's been." Again, Munther started toward Altar. "I got me some redskins to kill."

Altar pushed off the wall and charged at the giant of a man. At the last second he shifted to the right and ducked under the big man's outstretched arms, just as Bobby used to do to him when they fought behind the barn. Munther's hammer fist still caught Altar over a kidney. He winced and stumbled backward into the aisle but managed to keep his feet.

His fingers grazed the floor and he felt something. A board. Grabbing it with both hands, he rotated back to face Munther.

The big man had turned and was following him.

Altar's blood-crusted face split into a grin.

"Quit dancing, boy," Munther said. "I'm going to shove that board up your ass."

Altar swung the piece of wood as he stepped into Munther, trying to split the outlaw's head open. But the big man caught the board in his hand and jerked it out of Altar's grasp. A jagged bunch of wood splinters lacerated Altar's palm. Munther punched him in the face, the blow colliding with his already swollen cheekbone.

Altar stumbled back, shaking his head to

get rid of the cotton between his ears.

"You ain't shit, boy," Munther said. "It's time for you to die."

Altar didn't respond, just took deep breath after deep breath. The grayness in his vision and thoughts lessened as he swiped at the splinters, dislodging as many as he could.

Munther stepped up and backhanded Altar, who rolled with the blow, but stumbled and fell into a stall atop a pile of hay.

The gray, acrid smoke parted as the giant of a man stormed into the horse pen.

As Altar scrambled to meet the giant's charge, his hand encountered a thick wooden dowel worn smooth from use. He wrapped his fingers around it and picked up a heavy cast-iron pitchfork. He brought it up and thrust it at Munther as he charged into him. Not having time to spin the haft, Altar drove the prongs curved-side down. The points struck Munther's stomach and were blunted by something solid as they plunged into sinew and flesh.

Munther's enormous weight propelled him forward as Altar rammed the tines in deeper.

The giant's mouth formed a silent "O," his squalid breath ragged as he tried to back away from Altar in halting uneven steps.

"You dirty bastard," the big man muttered

through teeth clenched tight.

Altar yanked the pitchfork free with some difficulty, rotated the gore-wet tines to point upward, and rammed it back into Munther's belly, only to have the prongs unbelievably turned away again by the man's gut.

Altar stepped back, breathing hard.

His adversary stood there, hunched over, blood welling up from his groin and thighs. Something wasn't right. There was something under Munther's nightshirt, something with a squared bottom.

Munther smiled through the pain. "You're a son of a bitch."

"I reckon so," Altar said. "Where's Bobby Altar?"

"Bobby Altar." Munther's head cocked. "Bobby Altar. What in the goddamned hell you want with that one-legged yellowbelly son of a bitch?"

"He's my brother."

Munther grimaced and laughed. He spat.

"Well, I'll be goddamned." Munther put his hands on his knees and vomited. "Another goddamned, pain in my ass Altar. Son of a bitch." He spat again and again.

"Where's he at?"

Munther stood to his full height and straightened something under his nightshirt.

"Goddamned uncomfortable." Munther

continued to adjust whatever it was under his shirt.

"Where's my brother?"

"Boy," Munther said, his face contorted from the pain. "I ain't gonna tell you nuttin' about that no good, back-turning son of a bitch."

"Tell me and I won't kill you."

"You'll let them redskins do your dirty work, will you? Let them kill me slow-like. Roast my chestnuts over a fire or some such." Munther shook his head. "Goddamn, boy. I'm afraid to look down my pants, I think you skewered my pecker."

"I want to find my brother," Altar said. "Did you kill him?"

Munther tried to laugh, which turned into croaks, and he shifted his weight to a different stance. "Damn pain's gettin' bad."

"Tell me where Bobby is," Altar said. "I'll make it fast."

"Well, I ain't telling you shit." Munther spat a blood clot. "I'm taking that to my grave, boy. Do what you're gonna do, but you'd better hurry, them Indians seem a mite riled."

Altar took a deep breath. Abruptly, he realized the gate tower's Gatling gun was silent.

He walked around Munther, who flinched

as Altar passed him. The first man from the wagon was dead with his revolver lying in the dirt next to his body where the aisle spilled into the open space. Altar crouched to pick the gun up.

Munther charged, bellowing a deep, moist war cry.

Altar stood and brought the pitchfork up. He caught the tines just under the bottom of whatever was under Munther's shirt and thrust. The giant's body crashed into him, but still he forced the pitchfork forward. The prongs bit and sank deep, driven even farther as the great weight knocked Altar backward. The haft of the pitchfork banged into the dirt floor. Munther's body balanced for a second before he pitched to the side and lay still.

Altar knelt by the enormous head. Munther's eyes fluttered. Altar dug under the big man's nightshirt and exposed a stiff layered leather plate, connected by thongs to another on his back.

"Where's Bobby, you son of a bitch?"

Munther's lips curled back in what looked like a grin, exposing reddened teeth, frothing bubbles between the gaps.

"I killed him," Munther said, his twitching countenance displaying a bloody rictus. "Twisted his head clean oooo . . ." A tremor ran through Munther and his eyes were no longer focused, but vacant and clouding.

Altar knew he was dead.

Chapter 34
The doctor's vacant stare told him everything he needed to know

Altar staggered backward until he bumped against the side wall of the horse pen. He settled his weight against the planks and breathed for a moment, his lungs working like a bellows. But the smoke-filled air was anything but refreshing; it burned his lungs with every breath. Somehow, he was alive. And the figure lying on the ground a few feet away, was dead.

And so, according to Munther, was Bobby.

Bobby, what the hell happened to you? he thought.

The sound of war whoops grew louder and snapped his attention back to the present.

The Lakota were in the fort.

He glanced out the open stable door and saw a man running for the back of the fort, only to be trampled by a mounted Lakota warrior. Two other Indians rode up and jumped off their horses and started to stab and hack at the man on the ground.

Altar had to get out of here.

Now.

But how? Getting back to the tunnel was out of the question; the building was on fire. Glancing around desperately, he suddenly had an idea. It was risky, but what choice did he have?

He retrieved his Remington from the ground and holstered the empty revolver. His knife was nearby; he sheathed it and then picked up the dead man's Colt army revolver, unfired to Altar's knowledge, and stuck it in his belt. He didn't have time to find the other firearm.

He ran to the nearest stall. A wild-eyed horse was inside, terror evident in its anxious prancing. It wasn't saddled and he didn't have the time or inclination to do so. He opened the gate and shooed the animal out. The next occupied stall he found was the same. He let that animal out too. He let a dozen horses out of their pens altogether, waving them away with his hat, and ran for the flatbed freight wagon with its hitched team. If he managed to negotiate his way out of this hideous dream, they could use it to transport whatever women didn't have mounts.

As he was double-checking the hitch — it

wouldn't do for the team to cut loose in the middle of his flight — a Lakota warrior wearing a bloodstained leather tunic festooned with tufts of human hair ran into the stable. The man held an axe. He looked around, then saw Altar.

The warrior let loose with a throat-rending scream and charged, raising his axe overhead.

Altar, hat still in one hand, stepped away from the hitched team and drew the pistol in his belt. He cocked the hammer, leveled the Colt, and fired. His aim was off; the bullet only knocked the Indian down and sent his axe tumbling into the shadows. The shot didn't kill him, though it didn't look like he was going to fight anytime soon.

Altar jammed the Colt back in his waistband, crushed his hat onto his head, and started toward the wagon. He was just swarming up the side when powerful hands grabbed him and pulled him back. He stumbled and fell. The Lakota warrior stood there in a crouch and drew his knife from the belt around his tunic.

No time to draw the Colt, cock its hammer, and fire. Altar scrambled to his feet and pulled his own knife from its scabbard.

They circled one another, feinting thrusts and cuts, looking for an opening. Altar didn't see any blood at first from the shot he'd fired, and was beginning to think he'd missed the Lakota altogether, when he saw a stain spreading from high up on the man's chest. It was on the side without the knife.

Which was the warrior's strong hand?

Was the Indian fighting with his weak hand?

Altar definitely was fighting a wounded man, a distinct advantage. Were there others of which he was unaware? He stepped toward the warrior, pressing the man. The Lakota stepped back, bumped into a horse, and slashed awkwardly at Altar's face, missing by a handsbreadth.

Altar lunged at the Indian and thrust savagely at the man's stomach. The Lakota sidestepped and clamped down on Altar's knife arm with the wound-side arm. Altar was surprised at the strength of the clench even as the warrior's hot blood flowed onto his shirt, hand, and face.

The Indian stabbed down, the sheen of his knife's blade dulled by the swirling clouds of smoke. Altar wrenched his arm back, his blade cutting into the Indian's armpit. The Lakota's aim faltered, and Altar was able to knock the blade aside with his empty hand. He followed with an elbow to the warrior's chin.

Both men staggered but kept their feet, knocking into milling horses. Somehow, the warrior was in front of Altar, facing away from him.

Altar stepped closer and plunged his knife into the man's back at kidney height. The Lakota warrior arched backward and screamed. Altar withdrew his blade and cut the man's throat. The Indian's shriek drowned in a rush of blood.

Altar sheathed his knife. He pushed through the horses to the wagon and climbed up. He jumped onto the spring seat, unwrapped the reins from the brake lever, and yelled: "Hiya!"

He swallowed, trying to soothe his aching throat. "Hiya!"

He snapped the reins, and the horses lurched forward. Other horses who had been milling about panicked and ran ahead of the team. He cracked the reins again, as hard as he could, and screamed. The hitched horses gathered speed, driving several other horses in front of the wagon. They bounded out of the stable, mounts scattering across the parade ground like leaves in a gale.

"Hiya!"

He snapped the reins again as the team broke into a gallop. The view that came into focus was from a hazy, smoke-filled nightmare. Several pockets of white men, who he wanted to assume were outlaws, were trying to rally and fight the Indian warriors, while others fled, pursued by the Lakota bellowing their courage-shredding war cries. The whole scene was muddied by swirling gray-black clouds of smoke against a backdrop of belching flames, the heat from which consumed whatever they touched.

The wagon bounced and rattled across the parade ground, with the herd of riderless horses leading the way. Crouching low, Altar drove the team between two mounted Indian warriors, wishing he had a free hand to shoot one of them. But it took both hands, a rein in each, to steer the team as he tried to keep his butt on the undulating wooden seat of the wagon.

Just as he was lining up his escape from the fort, he saw a hatless Scooter run from the porch of the barracks where he and the doctor had been doing surgery. Scooter didn't make five steps before he was ridden down by a mounted warrior whose axe descended in a swooping arc to cleave the short fat man's head nearly in two.

The doctor stopped dead in his tracks, staring at Scooter's body as it convulsed in the parade ground dirt, geysering blood in the air. The warrior wheeled his mount around and kicked his heels into the horse's ribs, bawling his war cry and swinging his axe in circles over his head.

Altar reined the team around and drove them toward the doctor's side even as he told himself it was stupid to intercede. He screamed something unintelligible to get the Indian's attention.

The left-hand horse clipped the Indian's mount at shoulder height. The lighter plains pony nosed into the ground, throwing the warrior off. The man crashed to the earth and lay still. His axe careened end over end and thunked into the parade ground's flagpole.

"Doc!" Altar was sure his throat was bleeding inside; it was so dry and lacerated from screaming and shouting. "Get on!"

The doctor stared as if he'd never seen a friend killed in front of him.

"God dammit, Doc!" Altar roared, bringing the wagon to a dirt-rending stop. "Let's go!"

The man looked up. Then reality broke into his dazed expression, and he ran toward the wagon. The doctor scrambled up and over the sideboard, and Altar whipped his team with the reins. He wheeled the animals around in as tight a circle as he could hold, while two Indians he'd ridden through kicked their mounts toward them.

"Take the pistol in my belt!" Altar yelled.

The doctor reached for Altar's Remington.

"No!" Altar leaned back to expose the handle of the army Colt tucked in his waistband. "This one!"

The doctor yanked the revolver free and looked at the weapon as if he didn't know what to do with it.

Altar flayed the mount's backs with the reins. "Don't you know how to shoot?"

The doctor's vacant stare told Altar everything he needed to know.

Altar transferred both reins to his left hand. He snatched the revolver from the doctor's grasp and cocked the hammer back. He pushed the doctor flat onto the bed of the wagon, took aim at the nearest warrior, and fired.

The pursuing horse and man crumpled to the ground in a heap of limbs. The second warrior's horse couldn't jump the tangle of flesh and bone and fell, spilling its rider across the parade ground.

The gate of the fort had been torn down, the broken sections lying across the opening, the long wooden poles smoldering. The fire had nearly consumed the lumber. The team balked at first, but Altar snapped the reins and yelled, his throat burning from the fumes. The wagon bounced and shook as the wheels thankfully rolled over the torched remains of the gate.

And then they were out of the fort, trundling across an expanse of grass and rock. Altar tried to make out the road leading away from the burning structure and steered the wagon onto a rutted trail. He drove the horses hard, through pockets of Indians on the two-track that served as the path. It was like running a tomahawk-filled gauntlet.

The wagon hadn't gone much beyond rifle range of the fort's walls when a row of mounted Indians barred the way.

There had to be at least fifteen, all armed with rifles. The two men in the center were both extremely tall, their legs hanging low, moccasin-clad feet nearly touching the ground.

I hope it's Touch the Clouds, Altar thought. *Or his father, Chief Lone Horn or his brother, Spotted Elk. We're goners if it's anyone else.*

Chapter 35
I Ain't Got Time
to Die Just Yet

Altar reined in the horses, nearly falling backward as they fought the bits in their mouths. They came to a stop within easy shot of the mounted warriors. Wanting to be recognized, he took his hat from his head.

"Stay low," Altar said to the doctor, who was on his belly.

One of the tall Indians rode forward through the haze of smoke.

Altar recognized Touch the Clouds. The Lakota veered to Altar's weak side, away from his holstered Remington.

"One with a Striped Back," Touch the Clouds said in Lakota. "Where are your *winyan*?"

Altar coughed. He was still fighting the horses, who apparently wanted to get as far away from the fire as they could.

"They hopefully left by the tunnel," he replied, in the Indian's own tongue. "Touch the Clouds spoke the truth. The way through the *hé até howáya* is still there."

The tall Indian clearly saw the doctor on the bed of the wagon, but his expression didn't reveal his thoughts.

"It is good," he said. "Touch the Clouds was concerned it might have been sealed by falling stone in time's passing."

"We had to clear some rock," Altar said. "But we made it through because of your insight."

Altar paused, waiting for Touch the Clouds to speak again, but he didn't.

"Their leader was a bear of a man, as Touch the Clouds had said, and I have killed him." A fresh cough wracked Altar. "You will find his body in the stable."

The Indian's stoic face softened.

"This *tatanka* of a man was said to have been a great *ozuye*. He would have taken many *Lahkota ozuye* to the *wanagi makoce*. Instead, this *tatanka* will burn where he fell. By besting him, One with a Striped Back has proven again that he is a great *ozuye* too. You may go in peace."

Then Touch the Clouds nodded at the doctor. "This man. He may not leave. He too shall be consumed within the *phé tipi.*"

Altar glanced at the doctor, then turned back to Touch the Clouds. "I need him."

"Why would a great *ozuye* such as One with a Striped Back need such a man?"

"He is a medicine man of our people," Altar said. "And we have a wounded man who needs assistance."

"Who is hurt?"

"Harmon," Altar said, realizing as he spoke that Touch the Clouds would have no idea who he meant. "The short man with the bright red hair."

Touch the Clouds broke into a grin. "The *Lahkota* have a saying. The *zintkála* with the brightest feathers has the shortest *čhé.*"

Altar smiled. "I wish I'd said that."

"What'd he say?" the doctor asked.

"Take your *winyan* and this false medicine man and leave our lands," Touch the Clouds said. "I can promise no more than two sleeps before we are hard on your trail."

"Touch the Clouds is good to One with a Striped Back." Altar gathered the reins in one hand. "I will take my women and leave."

"See that you do." Touch the Clouds nodded. "Otherwise, your scalp shall ride on my lance."

And if they find gold, Altar thought, *you will either be killed or forced to move yet again, even farther from your ancestral lands.*

Touch the Clouds twisted to look behind

him and waved at the band of warriors blocking the two-track. The line split in the middle, forming a corridor along the sides of the path.

Altar snapped the reins and clucked at the horses. They started forward, fighting the bits like they wanted to run. Passing through the mounted warriors was harrowing for the doctor, who cowered on the wagon's bed. Each warrior was clad in a leather tunic, most splashed with blood and gore. Several of the warriors had human hair fastened to the front sight of their rifles.

The two ruts worn into the earth curved, following the slope down the rise. After more than half an hour of jolting over the grooves, Altar came to a split in the path.

He looked over his shoulder to get a fix on the fort. A towering column of boiling, black smoke churned in the morning light from the plateau where the fort had stood, making it easy to locate. He chose the left fork, figuring it led to the bridge over the creek that headed to the cave. Not that the wagon could traverse the bank, much less the creek.

Altar's eyelids felt heavy, his hands shook, and it was all he could do to keep sitting up to drive the team. Exhaustion descended on him like a blanket of moist sod, threatening to force him to collapse.

When was the last time he'd slept?

The wagon topped a rise and the narrow bridge spread out below, spanning the creek, which looked much the same as it had from the opposite ridge yesterday. He snapped the reins and continued down the two-track. After they crossed the bridge, he turned the team off the path and rolled toward the woods. He figured to try and conceal the wagon amongst the trees, while he and the doc walked upstream to find Shepard and the others.

He hoped Harmon was still alive, and this surprised him a little. Then he figured it shouldn't. After all, Harmon did break that chair over Munther's back. *If that didn't save me, it went a long way towards giving me enough time to marshal my forces.*

Plus, Harmon's present condition was a direct result of those efforts. He'd spent a lot of time disliking Harmon and not trusting him, but in the end, when it counted, the man had come through. He deserved whatever chance the doctor might give him.

Altar scanned the terrain up ahead, searching for a sign of Shepard and the others, but there was nothing. Had they made it?

Lord, he thought. *Please let them be alive.* They had to have made it. If not, all this would be for nothing. Bobby dead, Shepard and the others too . . .

The thought of returning all the way to Missouri just to tell his mother Bobby was gone made his stomach sink. He couldn't imagine having to pass through Spring Creek and deliver the news of everyone's death and then going on to tell his mother about Bobby. He'd given her his word he'd bring him back.

What about that damn fellow, Gulliford? Altar snorted in disgust as he thought of the weak-kneed marshal. Would Gulliford even let him pass through the town without locking him up again? Maybe, he'd have to bypass Spring Creek. But how could he do that? The bad news would have to be delivered to the families. It was only right.

Despair took hold of his thoughts, and his soul. He needed to get up that creek and hopefully find Shepard and the others. He had to. It was the only way to put these miserable reflections to rest, once and for all.

Altar steered the horses toward the forest.

"Where are you going?" The doctor's voice sounded brittle as it rose an octave.

Altar startled. He'd forgotten about the man.

"We're looking for some friends of mine,"

Altar said.

"Out here?" the doc asked. "Were they waiting for you?"

"No."

"But don't we need to get out of here before them Indians come looking for us?"

"We're not going without my friends," Altar said.

"If it's all the same," the doctor said, "I'd just as soon get the hell outta these parts."

The wagon rolled to a stop next to the tree line. Altar turned to look at the doctor.

"Those Indians wanted to let you burn in the fort, on account of Munther and those other Johnny Rebs you were with."

"But I was just as much a prisoner as those poor women. When I saw what kind of men they were, I wanted to leave, but Munther wouldn't let me. He kept me alive only because of my medical training."

Altar leaned out from the wagon and spat. "Just the same, you're only alive because I saved you and convinced Touch the Clouds you were needed to save one of my friends. So, let's quit jawing, go find them, and get the hell out of here."

The doctor looked down and nodded.

Altar hopped off the wagon and tied the reins to a tree branch. He didn't have any tools besides his knife with which to cut branches down to pile around the wagon. He'd just have to take the chance no one was coming that would take it.

"C'mon." Altar motioned for the doctor to get down.

"I can't make it. I need to stay right here. I won't try and leave."

Altar drew the army Colt. "Me and you are headed up that creek on foot one way or the other, Doc. You can go peaceably, or not, it's up to you. But you're a-going."

The doctor took one look at Altar's expression and then jumped down and started limping toward the creek.

The smoke wasn't visible, but its ubiquitous odor hung in the air. Altar and the doctor both coughed as they splashed up the stream. The doctor moaned after Altar told him to take off his boots and wade barefoot. Altar removed his boots as well and the water engulfed his feet with a searing cold that quickly shifted to almost complete numbness. Though all thoughts of sleep fled his mind for the moment.

Altar didn't think he'd missed the cave. But there was still no sign of the others, and he was beginning to worry about why they hadn't encountered them already. Where the hell were they? The thoughts of the arduous climb up the slanted shaft to gain access to the fort hung in his mind. It had taken a lot out of him. How could a bunch of women and two men carrying a wounded man hope to have made it?

Damn, he thought. *They're dead.*

Ten women and two men carrying a third, incapacitated one trying to negotiate a fifty foot, near-vertical stone passageway . . . How difficult would that be, especially in total or near total darkness? And the smoke from the burning fort — would the chimney channel it downward, like with the scent of the horses? If so, how could they avoid being overcome by the fumes? No, he told himself. The smoke would be vented upward. It had to be. Right? *If not, they'll all have suffocated from the vapors.*

When he and the doc got there, should he venture in? Of course he would, though he might have to tie up the good doctor to keep him from running. But what if Harmon or someone else was in the cave and hurt, and needed the doctor?

We got to get there first, he thought.

He and the others had traversed the creek to the cave not even a day ago, yet he couldn't remember how long it had taken them. What he knew for certain was that his feet were about frozen off, though for now the cold water was keeping him awake.

He kept the doctor in front of him. The man had stopped complaining and seemed resigned to following Altar's directions, at least until he wasn't. How Altar wished for Dog.

Where was that damn cave? Could he have missed it? No, the horses were tied there. But what if they were gone too? What if some Indians had found them? Too many damn questions. He knew he had to stop doubting himself.

I just have to believe, he thought. *I just have to believe.*

They stopped, and Altar scooped a couple of handfuls of water to smooth his parched throat. He'd been hacking up black gunk in his coughing fits, spotted with blood. He spat, and the doctor watched the black phlegm swirl away in the current. Then the doctor coughed and spat. What he produced from his lungs was clearer, leaning to gray.

"You were exposed to the smoke worse than me," the doctor said. "Your expectorant resembles what you might expect a miner to produce. You should be good after a time."

Altar looked at the man. "Thanks, I ain't got time to die just yet."

"There's a whole bunch of people back at the fort who might've said that very thing yesterday."

Altar looked away, upstream, then back at the doctor.

"And just what in the hell were you all thinking," Altar said, "coming up here? You're a long way from the South."

The doctor shook his head. "Not everyone was a Southerner." His accent betraying that he was in fact from the South. "We had some blue-bellies, and even a Choctaw or two."

"Why'd you come up here?"

"I guess you could say for the gold," the doc said, looking at the sky. "But some just wanted to get away from the humiliation we suffered as an army. Others, well, others wanted to keep fighting, but there wasn't any future in that."

"I told you I was looking for my brother." Altar took his hat off and sprinkled water inside. "I tracked the group he was in from Missouri. Clay County, to be exact. But they ended up a pack of murdering outlaws, about which I'm a mite confused, as I know Bobby wasn't that kind of man."

"No, he wasn't," the doctor said. "Most weren't."

They started back upstream. Altar's hopes grew fainter with every step they took without finding Shepard and the others.

"Most of us met at Camp Douglas, the prison camp." The doctor waded in front, his wake swirling away in the current. "A couple of the Union guards told someone that gold had been found up here in the mountains, and that led to a whole lot of speculating. Many of us got released, and instead of returning to the South, we headed north. But the bad men, Munther and his like, were held back for crimes committed in the camp. We didn't expect them to follow us when or if they got released, but they did."

"I don't see Bobby being in that kind of group."

"He wasn't," the doc said. "But he'd had trouble with his amputation, the conditions being so god-awful. He got out about the same time as Munther, apparently. Bob had always said he wasn't welcome back in Missouri and wanted to make another home. He'd been a part of the planning committee from the start."

"Shh." Altar held a finger to his lips.

The doctor mouthed, "What?"

Altar tapped his ear. The sound grew louder. Something was running toward them through the water.

From around the bend, Dog charged through the creek, splashes of water rising on either side of the damp beast. His tongue was out, and Altar swore the animal was smiling.

He grinned as well. "Hey, boy. Ain't you a sight for sore eyes."

The doctor looked from the dog to Altar and back again.

"You know that animal?" His voice rose somewhat.

"Sure do."

Chapter 36
She recoiled from his outstretched hand and wouldn't look him in the eye

Altar crouched and took Dog into his arms, getting soaked in the process. He rubbed the animal's head, neck, and back, while Dog licked him and shook his tail so hard it splashed the doctor, who had to step back to avoid getting drenched.

It took several minutes to get Dog calmed down so they could start back upstream.

It wasn't long after they rounded the bend themselves that Altar spied the cave mouth. It looked the same as when he'd been there yesterday. There were no signs of the horses, but he didn't know exactly where Harmon had picketed the animals. He hoped now that Harmon had done a good job.

Altar climbed from the creek and tenderfooted it into the cave mouth. The doctor followed him. Dog stayed in the creek, then jumped out on the opposite bank where he shook himself off.

Altar strained his ears and was rewarded

with the sound of voices. They were faint, but they were there. He turned to look at the doctor.

"Seems we might get out of this predicament yet."

It took the better part of an hour to get everyone from the cave. Harmon was still alive but seemed worse off. Shepard and Eppley put him down on the lip of the cave's mouth, before wiping the sweat and grime from their faces in what seemed a coordinated movement.

"Doc," Altar said. "Can you check this fella out? He's the one saved your life."

The doctor looked at Altar, then at Harmon. He knelt next to the prone man and began his examination. Eppley bent over and explained what had happened.

Shepard looked at the doctor from the corner of his eye. "Who's that? He one of them?"

"No," Altar said. "A doctor. He was a prisoner, too."

Shepard eyed the man with suspicion and then nodded.

Altar sighed, thinking of his brother, and of his mother, and his sisters. "Let's find them horses." He started down the bank. "And get them saddled. We got no time to spare."

Shepard grabbed his arm. "You find out about your brother?"

"Way I hear it, he was killed."

"Best you talk to that long-haired girl over there." Shepard pointed at a young woman sitting by herself, away from the other women, on the opposite bank holding a hand out for Dog to sniff. She wore a dark blue dress and had straight brown hair. "Her name's Flora and she's a Mormon."

Altar looked at Shepard. "What'd she say?"

"Best she tell ya." Shepard stepped over and grabbed Eppley's shoulder. "Let's go fetch them horses."

The two of them splashed across the creek. Altar followed, watching the young woman pet Dog. She couldn't have been much older than fifteen, definitely not over eighteen. As he neared, she looked at him and when their eyes met, he could've sworn she was much, much older.

"Howdy, ma'am."

Dog didn't pay him any attention as she scratched the beast under the chin. She didn't say anything, just stared at Altar, almost through him as if he wasn't in front of her. Her expression reminded him of men in the war with their vacant, dead stares, usually following a battle or some other kind of trauma.

He lowered himself into a crouch, waiting for her eyes to focus. Finally, he spoke again.

"You're Flora?" he asked. When he got no response, he reached over and rubbed the top of Dog's massive head. The animal ignored him, but she cocked her head and looked at him, as if seeing him for the first time.

"Hello," she said, so softly he wasn't sure he heard her. She didn't say anything further but folded her hands in her lap. Dog's head shifted and the glare the canine gave him seemed to rebuke Altar for interrupting the attention the dog had been getting from the young woman.

"My name's John."

She recoiled from his outstretched hand and wouldn't look him in the eye, just at his nose or something in the middle of his face — a smudge of dirt or blood, maybe.

"Shepard told me I should speak to you about my brother," he said.

"Your brother?"

"Bobby Altar."

She cast her eyes downward, and her mouth, which until now had been neither a smile nor frown, sank as well.

"Can you tell me what happened to him?"

She shook her head.

Altar pressed on. "I was told he'd been killed."

She shook her head again and her gaze rose to meet his, her eyes shifting across his face as if she were searching for an answer to a question she'd not asked.

Altar was conscious of pushing too hard, but he desperately wanted to learn about Bobby.

"Flora, about my brother . . ."

Her eyes widened and focused on him.

"Bobby?" she said. "You know him?"

"I was told Munther killed him."

She shrank from the mention of the monster's name.

"Who told you that?" Her voice was meek and so quiet, Altar had to fully concentrate on her lips as if watching her speak would help him hear.

"He did, before I killed him."

She shook her head violently, hair swishing back and forth so vigorously that it sounded like a horse's tail swatting at flies. "He lied."

"About Bobby?" Altar asked.

"He lied."

"Please." He paused and collected himself. He was anxious to know, but her fragility told him he'd have to go easy. "Tell me what happened?"

Her head stopped moving, her hair settled, and she swallowed.

"The night before . . ."

He waited for her to continue and when she didn't, he said, "Yes?"

"He rode away."

"The night before? Before what? The massacre?"

She nodded, shallow and quick.

When she didn't say or do anything more, he said, "Who'd he leave with?"

"No one."

This wasn't making a whole lot of sense. He took a deep breath and continued.

"So, he rode off, by himself, the night before . . . ?" Altar paused. "Before the attack? Where was he headed?"

Her hands rose to cover her face and she sobbed.

Altar pushed his dirty hat back on his head and looked up into the sky as if he'd find divine guidance. There was none, only blue sky with traces of gray and black smoke drifting away on a mild breeze.

Dog whined and laid his big head in Flora's lap, apparently sensing her sorrow.

"What happened?" Altar asked.

The crying slowed and she wiped at her nose. Altar wished he had a handkerchief to give her, but his was in his saddlebag. She dabbed the tears from her eyes with her fingers.

"Bobby and Munther fought," she said. "And Bobby had to leave after."

"Why'd they fight?"

She lowered her face into her hands once more, and the weeping began again with her hair obscuring her countenance. Altar looked away from the raw emotion. He could only imagine what this girl had been through. She'd lost everyone she'd ever known and who knew what savage horrors she'd suffered at the hands of the outlaws. When he averted his gaze, he saw that many of the other women were staring at him, most with open hostility. After a few moments, Flora's sobs subsided. She wiped at her eyes again, then gathered her dress hem, brought it to her nose, and dabbed.

"I was supposed to go with him," she said. "When Munther found out, they fought. He beat Bobby something fierce, I thought he was dead."

"But you said he left." Altar's stomach rolled over and he tasted bile at the back of his throat, imagining the brutality Munther had inflicted on his brother.

"They just rolled his body in a ditch along

the trail and left him there." She cried quietly.

Altar didn't say anything.

She continued, "I tried to go to him, but they just laughed and hit me and hit me and hit me . . . Finally, I got thrown in a wagon with some of the other women." She wiped her nose, this time with the sleeve of her dress, apparently caught up in the tale too much to care about appearances. For a fleeting moment she looked her age or even younger.

"Next morning," she said in a whisper. "Before . . . before the killing started. I saw that his body wasn't there anymore. And after . . ." Her breath caught in her throat. "I heard Munther yelling about Bobby being gone. One of the men — I think he was called Smith — said he hadn't been able to find Bobby's body and there was a wagon missing."

"Where'd Bobby go?"

She shook her head, tears rolling down her cheeks. "I don't know."

Altar sat back on his haunches. "Where were the two of you planning on going?"

She sniffed. "He mentioned San Francisco." She wiped her nose again. "He even said maybe back to Chicago. He thought being in a city would be easier for a man with only the one leg."

Altar pulled his hat back down, shading his face from the sun.

She shaded her eyes as well with her hand. "Are you going to look for him?"

"I am," he said. "I promised our mother I'd bring him back."

She drew her arm across her mouth.

"He'll not go," she said. "Not back to Missouri."

"I'll talk to him." Altar stood. "But we have to get out of these mountains first."

She grabbed his hand. He looked down into her wide, wet brown eyes.

"Take me with you," she said. "I beg you. If you love your brother. Bring me with you."

"The trail's no place for a young woman."

She laughed, but it was a cold, caustic sound that had nothing to do with mirth. "Funny you should think me a 'young woman' after . . . after that." She looked away from him.

He stared at her for a few moments. Finally, he touched the brim of his hat with his fingers, nodded, and walked off.

He hadn't taken ten steps when he caught sight of Shepard talking to Elizabeth. She was shaking her head vigorously. Eppley stood behind the two, his face turned away as if he was trying to give them privacy.

Weren't they supposed to be getting the horses saddled?

Then it occurred to him that Merle was telling her about the death of her son, Conner. He had to look away. Just as he had been given renewed hope about finding his brother, this mother was being told of the death of her oldest child.

Chapter 37

... A Tough Looking Son of a Bitch with a Smooth Handled Revolver

Sometime later a hodgepodge of riders stopped at a crossroads, miles out of Spring Creek. Altar and Shepard, who were in the lead, turned their horses to face back at the others coming behind.

"Whoa!" Shepard shouted and lifted his arm, fist closed, into the air. The sporadic line of horsewomen and the wagon slowed and stopped under the branches of a large maple tree that extended over the road.

Altar laughed. "You're getting good at that army shit, Merle."

"More like regular cowboy shit, if you ask me," Shepard said.

The wagon, drawn by two horses, continued forward until it came abreast of them. The wagon bed was filled with women who didn't have a mount, plus the doctor and Harmon. Dog was lying in the bed too, had been for a couple of days. The huge beast had taken to Molly, Shepard's niece, and she to him. They weren't often apart.

Eppley set the brake on the flatbed and hopped down.

"Gotta stretch my legs," he said. "That and empty my bladder. This damn thing's about to rattle my teeth from my head and shake my kidneys from out of my back. Gimme a horse any day."

Shepard laughed. Altar grinned.

The doctor stood in the back of the wagon and stretched his arms up high. Then he reached down and helped Harmon to his feet. The short man was unsteady and leaned down to use the wagon's side for support. Altar rode over and offered his hand to the deputy, who took it and leaned heavily on it to lower himself to the ground. He was bootless and his head was wrapped in bandages, strips shorn from the women's skirts, to the extent his hat would no longer fit and his red hair was covered.

"Thank ye." Harmon gripped the side of the wagon once again and stood awkwardly as he was wont to do.

Altar lent a hand to each of the ladies as they dropped to the ground as well and finally to the doctor. Whose name, he'd since found out, was Horace Platt.

The very last person to take his hand was Elizabeth. She'd been crying on and off for the entire trip back, and her red-rimmed eyes hadn't healed yet. Altar couldn't blame her. He'd liked Conner and recognized the world was worse off without him.

How many boys, just like Conner, had the country lost in the war, he wondered. How many mothers would never again know the touch of their son's arms wrapped around their necks?

"I've been meaning to thank you," Elizabeth said finally, letting go of his hand. "Merle told me all you done for us." The small woman sat at the open rear of the wagon, her short legs dangling off the edge.

"My pleasure," Altar said. "But to be truthful and all, I feel like I owe you an apology."

"What on earth for?"

"In my mind, I can think of a hundred ways I could've kept that low-down, no —"

Her finger pressed against his mouth.

"John Altar," she said in her strictest tone. He'd heard her use it occasionally on their trip back, especially with Molly and Dog. "I'll hear none of that talk."

"But it's —"

"Ah, ah," she said. "What'd I just say?"

He felt the merest tug of a smile on his lips. He liked talking to the woman, but had little occasion to do so, mostly on account of he'd avoided her, ranging around their little wagon train, ensuring nothing would encroach on their safety.

But now they were going to part company, and he had no idea for how long. In fact, if he were completely honest with himself, there was a good chance he'd never step foot in Spring Creek again. But he didn't have to share that with her, though he thought he could see it in her eyes.

She reached over, grabbed his arm, and pulled. He leaned from his saddle, and she stretched out and kissed him. A tear swelled and fell from one of her eyes. Before she could wipe it away, he thumbed it from her face. He brought that thumb to his mouth and kissed it.

"John Altar." She dabbed at the other eye as she stood. "If I ever hear that you're within a hundred miles of this place and you don't stop by to see me, I'll tan your hide like you'd never believe."

"Yes, ma'am." He touched the front brim of his hat and smiled. He liked when she used his Christian name.

She turned and stepped over to sit again with Molly and Dog, her back to him. Though he thought he detected a sneak peek his way when she fluffed her hair.

He reined his horse around and rode away

from the wagon. Wouldn't be fair to Elizabeth for him to linger. It was time to go.

A small rider, smaller even than Harmon, leading the mule with empty panniers, cantered up and stopped. It was the Mormon girl, Flora Claywell, dressed in the deputy's extra clothes, which were baggy and ill-fitting on her frame. The boots looked several sizes too big, and the black Stetson sat very low on her forehead to where she was often pushing the brim out of the way so she could see. The only time the hat didn't set so low was when she piled her long brown hair up under it. That propped the beat-up Stetson more or less where it belonged.

She wore the deputy's gun belt, though it was woefully large and had to be tied around her thin waist. She'd tied the holster to her thigh to keep the revolver from banging against her leg as she rode, and secured the firearm with twisted leather bands. She could have passed for a kid playing dress-up if it wasn't for her eyes. Those brown irised orbs stared out from a face that seemed to belong to someone of a wholly different time and age. More like what you'd see from an ancient Indian woman forced onto a reservation, not a seventeen-year-old girl.

"Tie the mule to the back of the wagon,

Flora," Altar said.

She nodded and reined her horse over to the rear of the flatbed freight wagon and secured the pack animal to a ring bolt on one of the planks.

Altar rode up and looked at Shepard. "You sure you're good with this?"

"Yep," Shepard said. "Don't worry none about Gulliford, he'll buy that you was killed in the gunfight and burnt up in the fire at the fort."

Altar couldn't help but glance around at the thirteen other souls who could blow the story up. "Plenty of people here to say otherwise."

"And each and every one of those people owes you their life," Shepard said. "You're all good. I'll get those panniers filled and I'll bring them and this ornery mule back out to you at Elizabeth's place."

"Thought you said her place burned to the ground?"

"They had a barn out back that didn't burn too bad," Shepard said. "Good portion of the roof was still standing, and most of three walls last time I was out that way. It'll make a good place to camp for a day or two. Just wish I was going with y'all, is all."

"You got family to take care of, Merle."

The former deputy sighed and nodded.

"Reckon so, seems like I should repay you somehow, though. My Elizabeth and Molly wouldn't be on this earth if it wasn't for what you done."

"What we done?" Altar smiled. "Truth is, I was looking for Bobby and they just happened to fall in line with that search."

"So you say." Shepard snorted and grinned.

"You going back to being a deputy?"

"Can't rightly say," Shepard said. "Don't know if I'd like to work for Gulliford again, though he's not a bad man. Not to say he'd take me."

Shepard laughed.

"Be a fool not to," Altar said. "Seems you'd make a right better marshal."

Shepard wiped his eyes.

Altar ignored the tears. They'd appeared quite often, especially after Shepard told Elizabeth about Conner's death, though he had left out the specifics.

"Take this here fork." Shepard pointed down the road to the left, back into the mountains. "Elizabeth's place'll be a couple of hours' walk, half that on horseback. But you better pull that hat down low on your head in case you come across anyone that seen you before."

"Ain't nobody gonna be looking at me,

when I got Flora riding next door." Altar nodded at the young woman. "Even dressed like she is, she's a right beautiful lass."

"After what these folks endured . . ." Shepard trailed off and spat. "I'd be surprised they'll see anything other than a tough looking son of a bitch with a smooth handled revolver, riding with a girl no bigger than a kid."

Altar agreed but didn't want to give any thought to what he'd become. People saw a gunfighter, a killer. And at this point, he didn't have much to argue against that reckoning. He needed to find Bobby and get their asses, including Flora's, back to Missouri.

Altar whistled for Dog. The beast's head rose from the wagon bed as Dog looked at him, and then lowered to rest in Molly's lap. She commenced to rubbing the beast's ears.

"Well, I'll be damned," Shepard said. "Looks like Dog's gonna stay awhile yet."

"Does appear that way," Altar said. "He can catch up if he's a mind to."

Altar and Flora waited for the gathering to remount and ride off. He believed what Shepard said about no one being interested in telling Gulliford about his being alive, but he figured it was better to leave everyone guessing which way they'd gone.

After the group was well out of sight, he and Flora reined their horses around to face down the left fork.

"Ready?" he asked.

She nodded, holding the brim of her hat up to see. "Sure am."

"Then let's get going."

Altar clucked and gave his mount a nudge with his knees, and they started from under the shade of the maple tree, down the trail toward Elizabeth's three-sided barn.

ACKNOWLEDGMENTS

I would be remiss if I didn't acknowledge those who have been an enormous help in bringing this story to fruition. First and foremost, Michael A. Black has been a staunch friend for years, and without his support I would not be the writer I am today. He was in my ear urging me to finish this book from day one. I want to thank my children, Tom, Joe and Emma, for always being there for their mother and me. Cathy Siciliano has also been a great help and has been encouraging me to write. Thank you, Cathy. Of course, Marshaé Harvey's patience and willingness to visit various states has been a great comfort. A person couldn't ask for a better companion, let alone beautiful sidekick. And, of course, I can't forget my sister, Julianne, who's always willing to lend a hand and has been a comfort in so many different ways. Thanks Boo. I also would like to give a hearty thanks to Diane

Piron-Gelman of Word Nerd Editorial Services, and Tiffany Schofield of Thorndike Press for your roles in bringing *Stand for the Dead* to print.

ABOUT THE AUTHOR

David Case is a graduate of Northwestern University's Graduate School's writing program. He served for over 31 years with the Chicago Police Department and is currently working in the well-balanced community of Bridgeview. Dave's first novel, *Out of Cabrini,* a modern-day thriller, was published by Five Star and was well received. He's excited to bring a western to print, having watched and been a fan of westerns since he was knee-high to a grasshopper. He's authored many short stories and articles as well and currently lives in the Chicago suburb of Palos Heights.

The employees of Thorndike Press hope you have enjoyed this Large Print book. All our Thorndike Large Print titles are designed for easy reading, and all our books are made to last. Other Thorndike Press Large Print books are available at your library, through selected bookstores, or directly from us.

For information about titles, please call:
(800) 223-1244

or visit our website at:
gale.com/thorndike